D0823285

PRAISE FO
EXPLOSI

TWISTED WEB

"I devoured [Grace's] books during a rainy week off and became so hooked . . . an enormous amount of fun."

—*The Detroit Free Press*

"Nolan Kilkenny crackles with intellectual and physical skills and takes the reader on a fast-paced journey. . . . the proverbial page-turner, a great read for that long flight or those sun-filled hours on the beach."

—*The Polar Times*

"*Twisted Web* displays Grace's mastery of action and technology. . . . If you like techno-thrillers that move at breakneck speed . . . no one concocts them better than Tom Grace."

—*Michigan Today*

"[An] action-packed adventure . . . [A] rock-'em sock-'em tale."

—*The Livonia Observer*

QUANTUM WEB

"[An] exciting techno-thriller. . . . Grace has created a moving portrait of America's technological prowess . . . nicely textured adventure."

—*Publishers Weekly*

"Tom Grace's second high-tech thriller again offers international intrigue, believable technical wizardry, relatively complex characters, and plenty of suspense. Fans of Tom Clancy and Clive Cussler won't be disappointed."

—*Library Journal*

"Technical and cerebral . . . it heralds the emergence of a new kind of modern-day hero."

—*The San Diego Union-Tribune*

"The book defies you not to turn the next page as the mystery unravels at breakneck speed."

—*Kalamazoo Express Weekly* (MI)

SPYDER WEB

"Absorbing, carefully plotted, beautifully executed. . . . A rich tale that makes for a fun read."

—Clive Cussler

"A nerve-rattling, fascinating good ride. Espionage will never be the same."

—Allan Folsom, author of *Day of Confession*

"Grace fuses brawny action-hero derring-do with brainy computer hacking."

—*Publishers Weekly*

"A new kind of thriller for the next millennium; one Ian Fleming would have envied for his James Bond in the new world of cutthroat competition in industrial espionage."

—William Stevenson, author of *A Man Called Intrepid*

"Very entertaining. . . . This thriller has a lot to offer—international intrigue, realistic characters, lots of technical wizardry."

—*Library Journal*

"Spirited. . . . The finale, taking place in the depths of the murky Thames, offers an exciting close."

—*Kirkus Reviews*

"A high-suspense international cyber-thriller . . . a fast-paced, information-age drama."

—*The Ann Arbor News* (MI)

"Computer aficionados will find *Spyder Web* a fascinating novel, and lovers of suspense will have more than enough action and intrigue here to satisfy their deepest needs."

—*I Love a Mystery*

"A Tom Clancy–style tale about computers, industrial espionage, and a rugged, old-fashioned hero named Nolan Kilkenny."

—*Traverse City Record-Eagle* (MI)

"Thrill-packed. . . . It doesn't matter whether you're computer literate, because there are plenty of thrills from the human side of the story."

—*Abilene Reporter-News* (TX)

"A winner. . . . *Spyder Web* is one of those rare thrillers that combines authentic detail, vivid characters, an intriguing premise, and a rocket-fast story line."

—Joseph Finder, author of *The Zero Hour*

Also by Tom Grace

Spyder Web
Quantum Web
Twisted Web

TOM GRACE

BIRD of PREY

POCKET STAR BOOKS
NEW YORK LONDON TORONTO SYDNEY

The sale of this book without its cover is unauthorized. If you purchased this book without a cover, you should be aware that it was reported to the publisher as "unsold and destroyed." Neither the author nor the publisher has received payment for the sale of this "stripped book."

This book is a work of fiction. Names, characters, places and incidents are products of the author's imagination or are used fictitiously. Any resemblance to actual events or locales or persons living or dead is entirely coincidental.

An *Original* Publication of POCKET BOOKS

A Pocket Star Book published by
POCKET BOOKS, a division of Simon & Schuster, Inc.
1230 Avenue of the Americas, New York, NY 10020

Copyright © 2004 by The Kilkenny Group, L.L.C.

All rights reserved, including the right to reproduce this book or portions thereof in any form whatsoever. For information address Pocket Books, 1230 Avenue of the Americas, New York, NY 10020

ISBN: 0-7434-5786-2

First Pocket Books printing March 2004

10 9 8 7 6 5 4 3 2

POCKET STAR BOOKS and colophon are registered trademarks of Simon & Schuster, Inc.

Cover design by Lisa Litwack
Cover photo © Peter H. Sprosty / Photonica

Manufactured in the United States of America

For information regarding special discounts for bulk purchases, please contact Simon & Schuster Special Sales at 1-800-456-6798 or business@simonandschuster.com.

To my father, Tom Grace,
who let me watch men walk on the moon
and encouraged my imagination

Acknowledgments

What if . . . ?

Each of my novels was born out of my asking a *what if* question that sets the stage for the story. Of course, once the action begins to unfold, the dam bursts and the questions flow fast and furiously. In searching for answers, I have encountered many knowledgeable and patient people who have helped me along the way and have earned my thanks.

To Capt. Robert Johnston, USN Retired, a friend and fellow Michigan man, for his input on life aboard a modern naval vessel.

To Capt. John S. Heffron, USN, for his help in understanding the navy's newest submarine, the USS *Virginia.*

To Simon Clapham for sharing his knowledge of commercial satellite insurance and the marketplace that is Lloyd's of London.

To Steve Fuzessry of Ocean Works and Lt. Michael Thornton, USN, for giving me a sense of what it's like to explore inner space in a Hardsuit.

To Nathan Jacobson for his help in Russia and the use of one of his repatriated Red Army War Hogs.

To several people involved with space operations who,

for various reasons, wished to remain unnamed but whose help was invaluable.

To Judge Daniel Ryan and Dr. David Gorski, two old friends who come to my aid in matters of law and medicine.

To Geppetto's Workshop for Enth, a data mining wonder without equal.

To my editor, Mitchell Ivers, for his insightful comments and wise counsel. I couldn't ask for a better partner in crime.

To Louise Burke, Hillary Schupf, Lisa Keim, Barry Porter, Steve Fallert, Paolo Pepe, Melissa Gramstad, Josh Martino, and the rest of the Pocket Books family for everything they do to make my books a reality.

To Esther Margolis for her thoughtful critiques of the early drafts, the benefit of her vast publishing wisdom, and her unflagging support of my literary career.

To my five children, who remind me every day how important it is to do the things you enjoy.

To my wife, Kathy, the love of my life, for believing in a man who spends his days dreaming up adventures.

BIRD of PREY

1

Jiaquan, People's Republic of China
June 8, 12:10 PM

Four . . .

Li Ch'ien swore he would remain calm, but the angry giant beneath him had awakened and nothing in his ten years as a fighter pilot in the People's Liberation Army Air Force had prepared him for the controlled release of so much power.

Three . . .

Li occupied the center seat of the *Shenzhou-7* spacecraft with Captains Shi and Yung at his sides. He was the senior man aboard and commander of the mission, but his rank and the honor of leading China's third manned flight into space did little to stanch the flow of adrenaline that was pumping into his bloodstream by the liter.

Two . . .

The three *yuhangyuans*—space travelers—sat facing upward toward their destination, their bodies cocooned in bulky, multilayered spacesuits. Puddles of sweat were already forming at the back of Li's head and along his spine and he hoped the moisture wouldn't affect the medical sensors adhered to his body. The muscles of his face ached, his jaw tightly clenched to prevent his teeth from shattering. The vibration from the main engines was that intense.

Despite Li's confidence in the proven reliability of the Chinese spacecraft, the destruction of the U.S. shuttle *Columbia* just sixteen months earlier flashed briefly among the thoughts racing through his mind. Wary of the bad luck it might bring, Li began humming a song from his childhood in an attempt to banish the recent disaster from his mind.

Until they reached orbit, the *yuhangyuans* were merely passengers, a position despised by any man who truly considered himself a pilot.

What was that phrase? Li thought, trying to recall the euphemism employed by the first American astronauts: *Spam in a can.*

One . . .

Li held his breath, excitement heightening his senses. Beneath him, over one million pounds of thrust thundered from the eight YF-20B engines clustered around the base of the rocket. In China's relentless drive to place men in orbit, the towering Chang Zheng-2F rocket had proved to be as reliable as America's legendary Saturn V.

Following the successful flight of the unmanned spacecraft *Shenzhou-3,* President Jiang Zemin bestowed a more poetic name on the vehicle that bore his nation's hopes and ambitions: Shenjian, *Divine Arrow.* The rocket had fulfilled its promise the previous October when it placed China's first man into orbit aboard *Shenzhou-5.*

Like an archer's fingers straining at a taut bowstring, the restraining bolts securing the rocket to the pad released and the *Divine Arrow* beneath Li and his comrades leaped toward the heavens.

Skye Aerospace, Long Beach, California
June 7, 9:11 PM

"The Chinese launch is confirmed, just made it inside the midday window," Owen Moug announced as he cradled the phone.

C. J. Skye nodded, but kept her eyes on the cinema display of her Power Mac G5. The launch of *Shenzhou-7* had originated in Gansu Province, far inside China's desert interior, from a place whose name translates into English as Liquor Springs. The window was an opening in the halo of debris—both natural and man-made—that populated the lower orbital arena surrounding the planet. Launching without a clear window was as risky as merging onto a freeway blindfolded.

Skye studied the image displayed on the screen before her, a graphical depiction of the Earth as seen from space looking down at the northern Pacific. Leaning back, she watched as two arcing lines flew over the rendered globe. The first line, in yellow, sprang from a point in central China and sped on a southwesterly course. It had already passed over Taiwan—doubtless as much a political statement as a requirement of physics—and was fast approaching the Philippines. A dot at the leading end marked the current location of *Shenzhou-7*.

Another dot, a bright red one at the end of the second line, marked the position of an object already in orbit, circling the Earth's poles. Skye estimated her satellite was about one thousand miles west of San Francisco, racing due south. She mentally extrapolated the two paths and predicted the Chinese spacecraft would be in range somewhere over French Polynesia.

From behind her desk, Skye sat pensively watching the monitor. The desk was the largest piece of furniture in her office, a massive assemblage of hand-carved wood that had belonged to her father, and to his father before him. She called the desk the "Titanic," not only for its size, but as a reminder of the devastation her playboy father had wrought during the years he sat behind it as the captain of Skye Industries.

Skye's grandfather—the first C. J. Skye—started out as a young man with a small tool-and-die company. Over the course of five decades, he built a global corporation with interests in shipping, aviation, aerospace, energy, mining, defense, and electronics and amassed one of the world's great fortunes. At its zenith, the sheer size and reach of Skye Industries drew a mixture of fear and envy from competitors and a disproportionate share of antitrust interest from the federal government. The founder of the Skye dynasty had often joked that were it not for him, at least a third of the corporate attorneys in America would starve.

The son turned out to be pale echo of his illustrious father. When Charlie Skye finally took his place behind the imposing desk, he had inherited a vibrant corporate empire that he knew little about and cared for even less. Rumor had it that Charlie had enjoyed the pleasures of many women atop his father's island of mahogany, including the starlet second wife who bore C.J. It was even possible that she had been conceived on its inlaid surface—Charlie Skye had drunkenly hinted as much on more than one occasion. Beyond the rumors, C.J. knew for a fact that for twenty years her father systematically looted Skye Industries, and when the authorities finally came for him,

Charlie Skye ate a bullet at his desk rather than face prison.

"Having second thoughts?" Moug asked. He stood beside the desk, studying both the monitor and his employer.

"About what?"

"This time, there's three men up there."

Skye glanced over at her vice president of Defensive Systems. "And you're wondering if I might not be *man* enough for the job?"

"I never said that, C.J."

"That's the kind of crap I've been getting all my life."

"And you use it to your full advantage," Moug countered.

Like those of many other captains of industry, C. J. Skye's office carried the trappings of both personal and professional glory. Models of Skye satellites and launchers were displayed with photographs of rockets thundering heavenward and politicians currying favor with the industrialist. In a place of honor stood Moug's favorite part of the collection, a model of *Stormy Skye,* the racing yacht that had reclaimed the America's Cup from Switzerland.

The ship had the sleek lines of a thoroughbred, an object sculpted to fly through wind and water. Skye not only had financed the winning entry, but had captained the ship through one of the closest and most fiercely fought series of races ever held. What made the victory by this underdog historic was that *Stormy Skye* had won with an all-woman crew.

A hint of a smile formed on Skye's face. Moug was right; she'd used every advantage in her arsenal to build a profitable enterprise from the one small piece of her grandfather's empire that she'd been able to salvage after the fall. The rest of Skye Industries' corporate carcass had been butchered and sold off piecemeal to satisfy creditors and shareholders after the true extent of Good Time Charlie's financial chicanery came to light.

"If the Chinese want to play in the big leagues and take lucrative payloads away from me," Skye said, "then they'll have to learn to accept defeat as well as victory in their great leap forward."

"My thoughts exactly," Moug concurred.

In Orbit

Though shown in red on the monitor in Skye's office, the killer satellite, now several hundred miles north of the equator, was actually black. The angular planes and matte finish of its composite hull exemplified the latest advances in stealth technology. Its shape had purpose—the spacecraft was a weapon, a long slender spear tip of chiseled obsidian in space.

A computer onboard the black satellite continuously analyzed the rising arc of *Shenzhou-7*'s fiery ascent toward the heavens. It compared the real-time data to a mathematical profile it held in memory, looking for the perfect time to strike.

Aboard Shenzhou-7

Li could barely move his limbs as three g's of acceleration pressed him against the back of his seat. The separation of the escape tower—which fortunately went unused—the four strap-on boosters, and the rocket's first stage all transpired without incident. And as the second stage continued to push them higher toward space, those first discarded remnants rained down on sparsely populated regions of Inner Mongolia and Shaaxi Province.

Through the porthole, Li watched as the clear blue sky faded into blackness and the brightest of the stars became visible. Then the thunder stopped. Nearly five minutes after igniting, the second-stage engine exhausted the last of its hypergolic fuel and shut down. Li's ears rang in the silence.

"Go for second-stage separation," a voice announced over Li's headset, the first he had heard in almost ten minutes.

Back in China, mission controllers prepared to jettison the last of the rocket that had hurtled them into space.

Long Beach, California

Skye's attention was now fixed on the lower right corner of her monitor, where a clock counted off the elapsed time from launch. It read T plus nine minutes, twelve seconds.

"Are you familiar with the legend of Wan Hu?" Skye asked.

Moug thought for a moment. "Can't say I am."

Skye didn't respond, her attention fixed on the monitor.

In Orbit

As it tracked *Shenzhou-7*, Skye's killer satellite detected a sudden loss of acceleration. Its onboard computer compared this change to the mathematical profile stored in its memory by Skye herself, and in a millisecond found the match. This event triggered a cascade of commands from the computer, instructions reflecting a change in posture from target acquisition to attack.

A cluster of spinning gyros fine-tuned the killer satellite's orientation relative to its prey. Near the middle of the long slender craft, tiny clouds of deuterium, helium, and nitrogen trifluoride swirled together inside a mirrored cylindrical chamber, combining into fluorine gas. With the addition of hydrogen, the gaseous brew ignited, and the controlled burn released a flood of energized photons.

The chamber, an optical resonator, amplified the barrage of particles and, like the barrel of a rifle, channeled them into a single beam of coherent light. The beam then pulsed through a complex optical assembly in the pointed end of the craft, where it was enlarged and focused on a target over a thousand miles distant.

Like a child with a magnifying glass, the spacecraft's optics condensed the full power of the laser into a silver-dollar-sized circle on the surface of *Shenzhou-7*. The spacecraft's thin aluminum skin vaporized instantly and the beam stabbed into the vital innards of the service module.

The spherical tank containing the crew's oxygen supply ruptured when pierced by the intense beam of light, its cryogenically liquefied contents immediately phase-changed into an excited gaseous state exerting a pressure thousands of times greater than the tank could bear. Metallic shards from the tank ripped through the fragile craft's guidance and propulsion systems, setting off a series of secondary blasts that coincided with the firing of the explosive bolts to release the rocket's second stage.

The explosions rocked the crew of *Shenzhou-7* violently,

plunging them into darkness, their ship powerless and spinning wildly out of control. Instinctively, Li and his men attempted to switch over to emergency systems, so familiar with their craft they could perform those tasks by memory, but there was nothing to be done.

Shenzhou-7 had been dealt a mortal blow by a weapon that hurled lightning from the heavens: *Zeus-1*.

Archipelago de Juan Fernandez, Chile

Seated in an old chair out in front of his weathered home, Salvador Delmar took a long pull on a bottle of rum and smacked his lips. The night was cool and clear, but still very pleasant considering the impending arrival of winter at this latitude.

Looking up, his eyes roamed aimlessly across the vivid field of stars. A fisherman, Delmar had spent much of his life in solitude, lost in his thoughts. The southern sky was full of familiar constellations, patterns of light in the darkness that told stories or served as guides to himself and his ancestors.

Delmar spotted the faint streak light and, thinking it an artifact of a stray bit of moisture in his eye brought on by the cold, blinked to clear it away. The streak remained and grew brighter, expanding into several fiery lines against the starry background. Shooting stars.

Delmar shuddered at the sight of the luminous streaks, almost recoiling in his chair. Until recently, he had been like most people who thrilled at the sight of celestial fireworks. Then, on a cool night in March 2001, he had the misfortune of being too close when chunks of falling star crashed into the sea.

To this day, the memories still haunt Salvador Delmar's dreams.

Long Beach, California

As *Shenzhou-7* fell to Earth, Skye walked over to her office minibar and retrieved a mineral water from the small refrigerator.

"You want one?" she asked.

"I'm fine," Moug replied.

Skye drank straight from the plastic bottle—pragmatism was one of the things Moug admired most about her. She was tall for a woman, able to look the six-foot Moug right in the eye, and solidly built. Her idea of a power suit was a white cotton shirt, twill pants, and a pair of Top Siders. Skye's shoulder-length brown hair, now heavily flecked with gray, fell into the hands of her personal hairdresser only for the occasional trim. Makeup, if used at all, appeared sparingly. The same went for jewelry, no doubt because of an aversion to her mother's taste for extravagant baubles. Skye's favorite pieces were a pair of simple diamond stud earrings and a diamond pendant. Both had been gifts from her grandparents. Despite being a child of affluence, C. J. Skye had cultivated a strong work ethic and a taste for simplicity.

"So what about this Wan Hu?" Moug asked.

"According to legend, he was a sixth-century Chinese poet and inventor who dreamed of touching the heavens. Using the highest technology of his day, Wan attached forty-seven rockets to a chair and strapped himself in for the ride."

"Did he make it?"

Skye smiled. "On launch, Wan, the chair, and the rockets disappeared in a burst of fire and smoke, and were never seen again."

Moug glanced down at Skye's monitor. The yellow line denoting the path of *Shenzhou-7* stopped over the eastern Pacific. "Looks like Wan Hu is getting some company."

"They shouldn't have undercut my bid on the Asian satellite radio project. Now, if the Chinese react as I expect, their space program will be stalled for a few years while they try to determine what went wrong."

"Leaving our field with one less competitor. On a similar note, I got word today that one of ZetaComm's new satellites is going up in two months."

"Who's handling the launch?"

"NASA," Moug replied. "It's going up on the shuttle *Liberty.*"

2

Cape Canaveral, Florida
August 1

This is the moment I've worked for my whole life.

Kelsey Newton stepped out of the Operations and Checkout Building and glanced up at the night sky. It was black and featureless. During the preflight weather briefing, she and the rest of the crew of *Liberty* had learned that a high-pressure system had swept the skies and the prospects for tonight's shuttle launch were excellent. A halo of bright light enveloped the space center, obscuring the stars she knew were there.

Despite the heavy orange flight suit, Kelsey moved purposefully. Press photographers bathed the seven astronauts in bright lights and pulsing flashes as they strode to the Astrovan, each member of the shuttle crew smiling and waving, proud that their moment had finally come. In the throng, Kelsey caught a glimpse of camera crews from her home state of Michigan and, like a nervous bride coming down the aisle, she hoped she wouldn't stumble. This was her first mission and she strove to maintain a professional demeanor, but at this moment she found it impossible to suppress the broad smile on her face.

As a young girl, Kelsey had cheered when Sally Ride became the first American woman in space and vowed that she, too, would make the journey. At an age when the only stars her girlfriends dreamed about were in rock bands, she immersed herself in math and science. Physics was the key to her dreams, not Duran Duran. In addition to training her mind, she followed a disciplined regimen of running and swimming to train her body. As a senior at the University of Michigan, Kelsey had led the women's swim team to a Big Ten championship and earned All-American honors. Every activity she embraced was in some way a part of her long-term goal.

A doctorate and research grants followed as Kelsey pursued a career in experimental physics. Her work in ultrafast optics led to the creation of a light-based computer processor—an invention that brought her notoriety, patents, and a potentially lucrative stream of royalty income. Along the way, she developed many ties with NASA, assisting other physicists with experimental payloads. She officially joined the astronaut corps as a mission specialist for the International Space Station in 1999, eagerly awaiting her turn to travel into space.

Her opportunity came when construction on the ISS was finally complete and plans for more aggressive scientific missions to the station began to move forward. Kelsey and one of her experiments, a detector array specifically designed for the station, were assigned to shuttle mission STS-173. Kelsey's moment had finally arrived.

This shuttle mission had three primary objectives: the deployment of a communications satellite, the installation of Kelsey's array, and an exchange of crew at the ISS. Kelsey and two of her *Liberty* crewmates were the first half of a six-woman crew that would live and work on the station for the next five months—the rest following in early September. While the selection of an all-female crew had not been planned, the world media latched on to the possibility of such an arrangement as crew assignments from the United States, European, Russian, and Japanese space agencies evolved. After the fervor of the America's Cup win by an all-woman crew, NASA could not overlook the public-relations potential of six highly trained, intelligent women from around the world ascending quite literally to the high point of their profession and made the selections official.

Liberty's crew of seven was composed of two groups: those returning to Earth with the orbiter in fourteen days and those staying aboard the ISS for the rest of the year. And on more than one occasion during the course of preparation for their mission, members of the first group offered to swap places with those in the second.

Liberty's permanent crew consisted of Commander Dick Lundy, Pilot Stoshi "Tosh" Yamaga, and Mission Specialists Caroline Evans and Pete Washabaugh. *Liberty*'s commander was a lanky, balding, fifty-five-year-old Air Force officer from Iowa with three previous shuttle missions under his belt. Tosh—a cocky, Asian-American naval aviator with graying black hair and the combat credentials to back up his swagger—saw this mission, his second behind the controls of a shuttle, as further proof of his aeronautical prowess. Caroline Evans and Pete Washabaugh came to the astronaut corps as civilian aerospace engineers and between them had completed twelve space walks. At five-four and a hundred pounds soaking wet, Caroline was the most petite of NASA's currently active astronauts. Pete presented an equal challenge to NASA's outfitters: His six-four frame required the largest space suit in the agency's inventory. Fitting problems aside, both had proven equally adept at extravehicular activities in space.

As for the group bound for the ISS, Kelsey, at thirty-five, was the youngest of the crew assigned to STS-173 and the mission's only rookie. The other two women—Molly Peck and Valentina Shishkov—had five previous trips into space between them.

Based on seniority, Molly was named commander of the five-month expedition. A flaming red-haired fisherman's daughter from the west of Ireland, she was the first ISS commander drawn from the European astronaut corps, further enhancing her standing as the pride of Galway.

Valentina was a forty-four-year-old gymnast-turned-biochemist and a veteran of launches from both the Baikonur Cosmodrome in Kazakhstan and the Kennedy Space Center. She smiled knowingly at Kelsey as the Astrovan approached pad 39A, her dark-brown eyes glistening with the shared excitement, fondly remembering her first journey into space.

The ride out to launchpad 39A took just fifteen minutes, but anticipation slowed the time to a crawl. During their days of quarantine at the Cape, a nervous excitement had permeated the crew. Now, as the reality of the moment hit them, that adrenaline-induced mood dissipated like a morning fog. They were now just a few hours from space.

Launchpad technicians helped Kelsey and her crewmates step out of the van. There, the astronauts paused to gaze at the shuttle towering over them—an action shared throughout history by brave voyagers and the vessels that carried them far from home.

Banks of powerful work lights bathed the shuttle in a halo of cool white—an artificial sun under which dozens of men and women labored. The external fuel tank rumbled and fumed like an expectant volcano as over a half-million gallons of cryogenically liquefied propellants boiled inside.

"Looks like you've done a heck of a job getting her ready," Lundy said to the launchpad manager. "Thanks."

The manager nodded. "Have a good flight, Commander. They're waiting for you upstairs."

The astronauts rode the elevator up to Level 195 and followed the steel-grate catwalk into the sterile white room. There, several technicians clad from head to toe in lint-free suits guided the astronauts through the hatch and seated them inside the orbiter. *Liberty*'s four permanent crewmembers were seated on the flight deck, with the ISS-bound astronauts strapped in below on the middeck.

After helping Kelsey into her padded seat, the technicians secured her restraints and tied her into *Liberty*'s comm system. Air-to-ground voice checks filled her ears—calm, professional, and reassuring. Kelsey gave the techs a thumbs-up and they departed, closing the hatch behind them. Launch was now less than two-and-a-half hours away.

Kelsey tried to relax, but she knew what was coming and the primal part of her being was preparing for flight or fight. And never far from her thoughts were the tragic losses of *Columbia* and, just sixteen months afterward, *Shenzhou-7*. The two disasters, so closely spaced in time, had erased the casual hubris fostered by so many years of successful manned spaceflight.

In the confines of the helmet, Kelsey could hear the blood pounding in her ears. She closed her eyes and began taking long, controlled breaths. Slowly, her body released some of the anxiety, taking the edge off. Kelsey had sacrificed a lot to be in this seat and wished right now to simply enjoy the moment. Her pursuit of this lifelong dream, coupled with the demands of her work as a physicist, had left very little room for family or a social life. This situation troubled her parents, who hoped to be grandparents while they were still young enough to enjoy the little ones, but they also understood what being an astronaut meant to their daughter. At this moment, she knew they were in the visitors' gallery proudly awaiting the launch.

Then she thought of Nolan, and knew that somewhere he was watching, too. No matter how often they were separated, or by what distance, their connection to each other, which had begun when they were children growing up on the same block in Ann Arbor, was never entirely broken.

Nolan Kilkenny had traded paradise for an inferno. After an arduous flight from Hawaii, he'd followed the Beeline Expressway due east toward the Cape. The air-conditioner in his rental car had struggled the entire way with the summer heat and humidity, and as traffic choked the roads near the Kennedy Space Center, it was near expiring. Sensing the futility of inching across Merritt Island, Kilkenny sought the advice of a Florida state trooper and headed south to Cocoa Beach.

He reached Jetty Park early in the afternoon with a small but steadily growing crowd. By sunset, the park was full and a prelaunch beach party was in full swing. One nearby group seemed intent on proving they indeed knew a CD's worth of Jimmy Buffet songs by heart. Kilkenny kept to himself, patiently gazing at the island on the north side of the Banana River, his thoughts on Kelsey and the adventure on which she was about to embark.

Near where he sat, a young child moved tentatively across the beach toward the river's edge. He watched as she stood with her toes just inches from the cool dark water, uncertain if she dared to take one more step. She bent and scooped up a handful of sand, some of the granules slipping through her pudgy fingers, then tossed the rest at the water. The constant breeze blew much of what she'd thrown back in her face, the coarse grains blinding her. Nolan was on his feet just as the first wail sounded from her trembling lips.

"There, there, it'll be all right," he said in a soft, reassuring tone. "It's just a little sand, that's all."

He carefully brushed the sand from her face and slowly, the girl reopened her big brown eyes.

"Tamara!" a woman called out, "What's wrong, baby?"

Nolan looked over and saw a woman, well into her last trimester, rising from a beach blanket.

"Is that your mommy?" he asked.

The girl turned toward the voice, tears still dribbling down her cheeks, and pointed at the woman. Nolan scooped her up in one arm and met the concerned mother halfway.

"I think she'll be okay," Nolan said to the concerned mother. "Just got some sand in her eyes."

The girl stretched her arms out and wrapped them around her mother's neck. With the safe return of her child, the woman's expression softened.

"That was very kind of you."

"No problem. I have a little experience with this kind of thing."

"You have children?"

"Not yet, but sand in the eyes was an occupational hazard for me a few years back. I used to dive for the navy."

"Tamara, can you thank the nice man for helping you?"

"Fank woo," the girl whispered, a thumb planted in her mouth and most of her face nestled against her mother's shoulder.

Nolan smiled and returned to his spot. If NASA hadn't called, he and Kelsey might be sitting on a beach somewhere, perhaps contemplating a new life growing inside her. A small part of his brain still selfishly resented that call because it put what he saw as the next and most important stage of their lives on hold. He loved Kelsey and was ready to be a husband and a father. Single-mindedly, they had both pursued their professional goals and achieved a level of satisfaction and status that now gave them the freedom to make choices about their future together.

Twelve months down, Nolan thought as he watched the horizon, *only five more to go.*

At T minus nine, the launch entered the final built-in hold. The back-room controllers had completed all the system checks and it was now time to determine the go/no go status of the launch. The buzz of the nearly three hundred voices in the firing room faded into a restrained quiet in anticipation of NASA Test Director Hal Atwood's final poll.

"STM?" Atwood began.

"Support Test is go."

"OTC?"

"Orbiter Test is go."

"TBC?"

"Tank Booster Test is go."

Atwood polled the eleven test contractors and each replied in the affirmative.

"Houston, are you a go?" Atwood called out to Fred Jesup at the Johnson Space Center.

"Mission Control is go," the flight director replied.

Atwood nodded to the people in the firing room. "*Liberty,* you are a go. From all of us at the Cape, good luck and Godspeed."

"Launch Control, this is *Liberty,*" Lundy's voice boomed clear over the speaker. "Thanks for everything. It's a beautiful night to fly."

Nolan's cell phone pulsed with the opening bass line of "Brand New Cadillac" by The Clash. He answered before the clip recycled.

"Kilkenny."

"Did you get there?" a woman asked, her voice smooth and self-assured.

"What do you think?"

"If you're half as smart as you pretend to be," Roxanne Tao replied, "you're somewhere near that shuttle."

"I'm about as close to the space center as someone without a guest pass can get."

"Good boy. This is Kelsey's big day and you owe it both to her and to yourself to be there."

"I can't argue with you about that."

"If you did, you'd lose."

"Probably," Nolan admitted. "Hey, thanks again for helping me patch things up with Kelsey."

"You two would have figured out things on your own, all I did was speed the process up a little. If you hadn't been so pigheaded in the first place, my little intervention would have been completely unnecessary."

"True."

"And on the positive side, you did learn some very important things about wedding planning."

"Namely to keep my nose out of it."

"Exactly. The rules of etiquette clearly state that the groom is an invited guest. To suggest that a girl toss aside a lifetime's worth of dreams and simply run off and elope, for *convenience?* It just isn't done."

"Why do I get the feeling that I'll be hearing about this for the rest of my life?"

"Because you will. And if there's any justice in the world, this story will be handed down among your descendants, passed from generation to generation as an object lesson about the appropriate place for men in a relationship."

"A morality tale of failure and redemption?"

"Exactly. Are you nervous?"

"Why? Because the love of my life and future mother of my children is strapped to a rocket capable of releasing as much energy as a small tactical nuke?"

"Something like that. I'm not superstitious, so I don't believe bad things come in threes. Kelsey will be fine."

"I know."

At two minutes to liftoff, Kelsey locked her visor down and switched on her oxygen supply. The walkway on which the crew had boarded *Liberty* had already pulled away and, one by one, the shuttle's ties to Earth were being severed. The spacecraft shuddered as the main engines gimbaled into position.

At T minus fifty seconds, *Liberty* switched over to internal power.

Listening to the seconds being counted down, Kelsey suddenly became aware of her own heart pounding inside her chest. As her senses heightened, time dilated. She remembered feeling the same mix of fear and excitement crawling up the first hills on the roller coasters at Cedar Point. The training simulations had taught her what to expect, but had never made her feel this way.

At T minus thirty seconds, *Liberty*'s onboard computer took control of the launch.

At T minus sixteen seconds, three hundred thousand gallons of water flooded into the space beneath the launchpad to dampen the roar of the shuttle's engines.

At T minus six seconds, *Liberty*'s three main engines fired off in succession. The shuttle bucked, straining against the eight bolts that held it to the Earth. Billowing clouds of smoke and steam roiled out from beneath the launchpad.

Kelsey gripped her armrest tightly as the engines thundered beneath her, counting down the last few seconds.

At T minus zero, the twin solid rocket boosters ignited. As *Liberty*'s main engines reached 100 percent thrust, the restraining bolts detonated and the shuttle lifted off.

Kelsey gritted her teeth and held on. The energy released by the engines shook the spacecraft violently, the vibration so intense she could barely hear communications through her headset. As the shuttle cleared the launchpad, it performed a combined pitch/yaw/roll maneuver that aimed the craft on a broad high arc across the Atlantic. Kelsey felt the rollout but, with three g's pressing her back against the seat, she had no sense that *Liberty* was now flying inverted. Her limbs were so heavy she found them difficult to move.

Barely a half-minute into the flight, with the aerodynamic pressure bearing down on the shuttle racing toward Max Q, Lundy announced he was throttling back the main engines to 85 percent. The shuttle slowed just enough to keep the stresses bearing down on the spacecraft from exceeding the safety limit. Thirty seconds later, Kelsey heard Lundy's voice again.

"Control, this is *Liberty*. Throttling up."

"Roger, *Liberty*. Throttle up."

The beach party in Jetty Park had paused as launch time neared. As they did at New Year's, many of the revelers were counting down the final seconds. Nolan slid the phone back into his pocket and stood silently near the water's edge, staring at a faint glow of artificial lights far behind the silhouetted mangrove forest on the opposite shore.

The shuttle rose like a false dawn, the fire plume beneath it glowing white-hot against the night sky, impossible to miss. The people on the beach cheered and clapped as *Liberty* ascended. Nolan smiled, silently sharing their enthusiasm.

As the shuttle rolled into its eastward arc, it surprised him to discover that, at a distance of only a few miles, he couldn't hear the roar of those immense engines. He could easily distinguish the four main components of the shuttle and had assumed that any explosive force powerful enough to hurl the equivalent of a thirteen-story building into orbit should make a proportional amount of noise.

Thirty seconds after *Liberty* appeared above the mangroves, the thunder of the launch hit the beach. Panicked flights of birds bolted from the trees and Nolan quickly realized that he was distant enough to see the launch well before he heard it.

His eyes followed the line of smoke and fire across the night sky until, at last, he lost it in the stars. With the show complete, the other spectators began drifting back to their cars, another workday to face in the morning.

Nolan understood the dangers Kelsey faced, working in a dangerous environment, where equipment failure can quickly lead to death. In his days as a Navy SEAL, he had spent a lot of time in the confined space of submarines, and had swum from the ocean depths onto many hostile shores.

At least no one up in space is trying to kill you, Nolan thought. He remained on the beach, watching the heavens.

3

Liberty
August 3

Kelsey floated near the ceiling of the flight deck, her fingers wrapped around a handhold to prevent her from drifting as she gazed out the overhead windows. The orbiter was flying inverted over the Earth, but the illusion of zero gravity rendered the distinction between up and down irrelevant. The physicist part of her brain reminded her that it was Earth's gravity that held the shuttle in orbit and that its effect at this altitude was almost 90 percent of what she normally experienced every day of her life.

In terms of scale, she realized, she really hadn't traveled all that far. If the Earth were the size of a basketball, then *Liberty* would be a tiny speck skimming less than a quarter-inch above the surface. What kept the shuttle from falling back to Earth or careening out into space was a delicate balance of speed and gravity. At 17,500 miles per hour, *Liberty* was falling around the Earth, rather than into it. As a consequence, Kelsey and her fellow astronauts were continuously experiencing the instant of weightlessness one briefly feels when bouncing on a trampoline.

Kelsey stared, transfixed by the iridescent blues of the

Pacific Ocean. Twenty minutes earlier, she had seen the Godavari and the Ganges River flash briefly in the sunlight, like veins of silver etched into the landmass of the Indian subcontinent. It was midday on the world beneath her, but already her sense of connection to an earthly time and place was gone. Since arriving in space, Kelsey had witnessed four dazzling sunrises—an event that, from *Liberty's* point of view, occurred every ninety minutes.

Like everyone else onboard, Kelsey had shed her helmet and spacesuit as soon as they reached orbit. She wore shorts, a T-shirt, and padded socks—standard NASA issue for this work environment. Her long mane of straight blond hair was tied back in a French braid to keep it under control. Molly and Valentina floated beside her at the observation windows, staring wide-eyed at the planet below.

"What do you think of the view, ladies?" Lundy asked as he floated up through an interdeck access hatch onto the flight deck, followed by Tosh.

"It's still the most exquisite thing I've ever seen," Molly answered in a soft Irish brogue, not taking her eyes from the window. "Simply breathtaking."

"Da," Valentina added, transfixed. "Magnificent."

"There's Hawaii," Kelsey said. She then thought of Nolan, who was working on a project there.

"Seeing the world like this is definitely one of the perks of this job," Lundy concurred. "This is my fifth trip up and I still ain't bored with it. 'Course you'll log a bunch more hours in orbit than I got by the time your stint is over. When you return, let me know if you ever got tired of looking down on us."

"I can't imagine that ever happening," Kelsey replied.

Molly checked her watch and was surprised at how quickly the time had passed at the window. "I presume you're here to roll the orbiter over for the EVA?"

Lundy nodded. This EVA—extravehicular activity, NASA-speak for a space walk—was the first of two planned for this mission. The first was to launch the communications satellite, the second to install the array at the ISS.

"All good things," Molly sighed. "Sister Valentina, we'd best pop down and give our crewmates a hand with the EMUs."

"Yes, Mother Superior."

With two fingers, Valentina gently pushed off from the ceiling, twisted in midair and effortlessly glided through the access hatch. Molly followed her down, though with considerably less aplomb.

"Looks like Val's got her space-legs back quickly," Tosh commented.

"I don't think on my best day in space that I ever made moving around look that easy. That lady has a real knack for microgravity." Lundy turned to Kelsey. "How are you feeling?"

"Better. The first twelve hours were a little rough."

"Usually are. Say, what was that *Mother Superior* thing all about?"

Kelsey smiled. "Inside joke. During our preparation for ISS, Molly was really putting us through our paces and the other girls and I nicknamed her Mother Superior. As it turns out, Molly has a pretty good sense of humor, so she ran with it."

"So now all the rest of you are . . ."

"Sisters of the Most Holy Celestial Convent," Kelsey offered reverently.

"I guess that's better than being called the Vestal Virgins," Tosh said.

"This group of women? I don't think so."

"Things are going to be cramped on middeck for a little bit, so it'd probably be best you stay up here with us. And you might want to grab hold of something when we fire the thrusters."

"Thanks," Kelsey replied.

Tosh and Lundy returned to their seats and ran through a systems check before to rolling the orbiter over.

"Houston, this is *Liberty,*" Lundy said. "We're ready to perform a one-eighty-degree roll."

"Roger that, *Liberty,*" Fred Jesup replied from the Johnson Space Center. "You are good for roll."

Tosh gripped the joystick in front of him and gently tilted it to the left. In response to the command, several of the small thrusters placed around *Liberty*'s exterior briefly fired and the orbiter began a roll to the left. Through the forward flight deck windows, Kelsey watched the Earth and stars spin around the shuttle's nose.

Lundy and Tosh watched the instrument panel as graphic displays updated *Liberty*'s orientation relative to the Earth. As the roll neared 180 degrees, Tosh tipped the joystick right, firing a reverse thrust to halt the roll.

"Damn, I'm good," Tosh said.

"Must be all them video games you played as a kid," Lundy replied. "Houston, this is *Liberty.* We're proceeding with EVA, over."

"Roger that, *Liberty.* Good Luck with EVA."

"Can you hear me okay?" Pete asked.

"Five-by-five," Caroline replied.

"Both y'all are coming through fine up here." Lundy's voice sounded clear inside their helmets. "Ready to take a stroll?"

Molly and Valentina took a final look over the seals and fittings on the extravehicular mobility units (EMUs) donned by Pete and Caroline, then gave the spacewalkers a thumbs-up.

"Ladies first," Pete offered.

Caroline pulled herself through the access hatch—a circular opening with a flat bottom, like a letter D lying on its back—and into the shuttle's internal airlock. She then stepped through the outer hatch into a short tunnel that led to an external airlock mounted in the forward section of the payload bay. As she entered the cylindrical chamber, she saw two more hatches—one directly in front of her, the other at the top of the cylinder. The first provided access to the payload bay; the second allowed *Liberty* to dock with the ISS. Caroline pulled herself upright. Pete followed her into the exterior airlock and closed the hatch behind him.

"We've got a good seal," Molly said. "Going for decompression."

"We're ready when you are," Pete replied.

Though it was muffled by their helmets, the two spacewalkers heard the whoosh of air escaping from the chamber, venting directly into space.

"Airlock is depressurized," Molly announced, peering though the four-inch-diameter hatch window. "You two can proceed."

Caroline grabbed the lever for the outer hatch and carefully turned it counterclockwise 440 degrees. Once the latches retracted, she gave the door a firm tug, pulling it back a few inches to break the seals. In this position, the door easily spun out of the way on its articulated hinges and the spacewalkers stepped through the opening.

The large payload bay doors stood open, radiating excess heat from *Liberty* into space. Above them, the blackness was flecked with trillions of stars. Caroline and Pete stood in a dark shadow cast by the aft wall of the crew compartment, but the rest of the payload bay was bathed in harsh sunlight. They quickly lowered the gold-plated visors down over their clear polycarbonate helmets—in space, sunlight was literally blinding.

"Lovely day for a spacewalk, eh, Pete?" Caroline asked.

"Yeah, too bad we have to work, but somebody's paying through the nose to have us push that satellite into orbit."

"Then let's give 'em their money's worth."

Directly in front of the two spacewalkers stood the collapsed framework of the *Zwicky-Wolff* Dark Matter Array that they were hauling to the ISS. The folded structure of the array looked like an overgrown spiny anemone.

Using handholds attached to the sides of the payload bay, Caroline and Pete maneuvered past *Zwicky-Wolff*, legs floating freely behind them. Their movements came as second nature, the result of hundreds of hours spent underwater in the huge pool at the Johnson Space Center simulating this EVA. While water provided a buoyant form of weightlessness similar to that experienced in space, it also resisted their movements and dragged on the bulky EMUs. Moving in space was far easier. Both breathed normally, their heart rates calm and steady.

The communications satellite they were to deploy occupied the rear half of the payload bay. It consisted of two rectangular segments: a squat propulsion unit mated to a long electronics package. Compared with the engineering elegance of the array, the satellite looked like a pair of shoeboxes covered in crinkled foil.

The spacewalkers lowered themselves onto the bay on opposite sides of the satellite and began surveying the $250-million craft, still locked in its protective cradle. Three antennae, one large and two small dishes, were folded tightly against the upper segment and a pair of ten-foot-square folded solar wings flanked the base.

"Any sign of damage?" Caroline asked as she inspected the downlink antennae.

"Nothing looks like it rattled off on this side. The solar panels look good."

Pete slipped his feet into restraints mounted on the payload bay deck. Several other sets of footholds were placed throughout the bay, each sited for a specific task to be performed during this mission. As he unthreaded a bolt on one of the mounting brackets, Pete felt the torque from the power tool run up his arm and through his entire body, attempting to wrest his feet from the deck. Without the footholds, the bolt would stay where it was and he'd be spinning around the tool. Bolt by bolt, he worked down the twenty-foot length of the satellite.

As the spacewalkers worked, Kelsey followed their progress through the aft station windows. Tosh gripped the hand controller for the Remote Manipulator System (RMS) and activated *Liberty*'s robotic arm. From its stowed position along the port side of the payload bay, he rotated the arm up from its fixed base ninety degrees, then checked the elbow and wrist joints through their full range of motion.

"I'm clear on this side," Pete announced as he stowed his power tool.

"It's almost like we know what we're doing," Caroline answered, keeping the pace. "Tosh, we're ready to move the satellite."

"I'm on it," Tosh replied.

Tosh carefully maneuvered the Canadian-built arm, alternating between remote views taken from the arm-mounted cameras and eyeballing it through the window. He eased the end of the arm down and grasped a mounting point near the center of the satellite.

"How's it look?" Tosh asked.

"You got a good grip," Pete reported.

"I'm going to lift the bird a little bit. Spot me."

Kelsey and Lundy watched as Tosh slowly pulled back on the joystick. The robotic arm responded imperceptibly at first, bending at the elbow then lifting the five-ton satellite up from its cradle. Tosh felt no resistance feeding back through the arm to the joystick—no snags.

Pete crouched to inspect the gap between the satellite and the cradle. "You're a good three inches up. All clear."

Tosh turned to Kelsey and Lundy, a devilish smile on his face. "Watch this."

The spidery robotic arm moved like an extension of the pilot's body. Tosh hoisted the satellite high above the open bay and, in a bold display of aerial gymnastics, twirled it on the end of the arm like a drum major's baton, rotating as it rose fluidly upward. When he completed the complex maneuver, the robotic arm held the satellite perfectly vertical and centered just two inches above the Stabilized Payload Deployment System (SPDS).

"Whoa! You nailed it, buddy," Pete said excitedly. "A bull's-eye over the turntable."

"I am *so* good," Tosh declared.

"You are *so* lucky you didn't hit anything," Lundy countered. "At your pay grade, it'd take about a thousand years to work that satellite off."

"*Liberty*, this is Houston, over," Fred Jesup's voice crackled businesslike over the speaker.

"Go ahead, Houston," Lundy replied.

"Most of the folks down here were quite impressed with that little dipsy-doodle maneuver."

"Thank you, thank you," Tosh said smugly.

"Unfortunately," Jesup continued, "that does not include the kind folks from ZetaComm. I believe one of their engineers deposited a unit of masonry in his shorts when he saw his bird do that little Cirque Du Soleil impression. If y'all don't mind, let's try and keep the rest of this mission by the book."

"We copy you, Houston."

"We appreciate that, *Liberty*. Houston out."

"Big Brother is watching," Lundy admonished his pilot. "Consider yourself warned."

Tosh nodded and turned his attention back to the RMS, his bravado perceptibly deflated. Outside, Caroline and Pete guided him through the last few inches, gently setting the satellite's engine nozzle on the center of the circular turntable.

The spacewalkers fastened themselves into another set of foot restraints and began performing a series of activation procedures. More than a piece of cargo, the satellite was as much a self-contained spacecraft as *Liberty*. Caroline tackled the guidance and propulsion systems while Pete dealt with power, computers, and communications. They took each step patiently and ran cleanly through their checklist in forty minutes.

"We have a heartbeat," Pete announced as he set the breakers and switched on the battery power.

"Gyros spinning up," Caroline said. "She's ready to fly."

On the flight deck, Lundy switched on his microphone. "Houston, this is *Liberty.*"

"Go ahead, *Liberty,*" Jesup answered.

"We're about ready to launch the bird. Is ZetaComm ready to take delivery?"

"That's affirmative, *Liberty.* They are in contact with their satellite. You are clear to launch."

Tosh punched in the commands to activate the SPDS. The turntable rotated the satellite slowly at first, building speed with each revolution. When the turntable reached the desired rate of spin, the pilot hit the launch button.

The turntable popped up from the base like a slow-motion jack-in-the-box and pushed the satellite off into space. No blast from an engine—just a quiet nudge in the right direction. The communications satellite sailed upward from *Liberty* following a line that ran straight through its center of gravity.

"Quite a thing to see, huh?" Lundy asked as he and Kelsey followed the spiraling departure through the upper observation windows.

"Pure Newtonian physics," Kelsey replied, "of the Sir Isaac variety, of course."

"Yep. Spinning the satellite before sending her up is the equivalent of firing a bullet down a rifled barrel."

"Or a pitcher throwing fastballs," Tosh added as he joined them. "A rotating projectile flies straighter."

The three astronauts continued to watch as the satellite quietly spiraled away into the darkness.

Long Beach, California

The dot soaring over the graphic depiction of the Earth's surface on Skye's display split in two. The original dot—*Liberty*—continued on its previous trajectory, while the second slowly fell back as it reached for higher orbit. Skye checked her watch.

"They on schedule?" Moug asked.

Skye nodded. "NASA does pride itself on punctuality, which makes it all the easier."

"By this time next week, you'll have added ZetaComm to our list of valued customers. Lucky for them bandwidth was available on our constellation at only a modest premium."

"Luck," Skye said, fixing her gaze on him, "is just the ability to take advantage of opportunities that present themselves."

4

Chantilly, Virginia

Colonel Benjamin Kowalkowski, director of Space Operations for the National Reconnaissance Office, stood on the balcony outside his glass-enclosed office, an expectant look in his lined and weathered face as he gazed down on the space operations center. In the large room spread out before him, dozens of people sat behind rows of multiscreen computer workstations. They were the eyes and ears of the United States of America; the shepherds of the nation's spy satellites.

The air in the cavernous room felt dry and cool and it carried a slightly metallic taste—an artifact of intense filtration. The room was finished in metal, plastic, and glass—all in grays or black, sterile and artificial. Concealed luminaires provided a dim, indirect glow over the room; an ergonomic effort to minimize glare on the large flat-screen monitors. As befitted the shadowy purpose of Kowalkowski's command, it was hidden far from the light of day, deep beneath the NRO's sprawling Virginia campus.

Kowalkowski studied the large wall monitor. It displayed a flattened map of the Earth and the orbital tracks of all the reconnaissance satellites managed from this room.

Spacecraft bearing the names *Keyhole, Vortex, Jumpseat, Magnum, Triplet,* and *Lacrosse* soared high over the Earth, watching and listening to the world below. The silver-haired director of Space Operations searched the map, looking at the new track that signaled the arrival of the first in a new generation of radar imaging satellites: *Oculus.*

Deployed by *Liberty* less than an hour ago over the west coast of Africa, *Oculus* was currently 180 miles above the Coral Sea, its track heading diagonally across the Pacific Ocean toward Hawaii. Kowalkowski descended from his aerie and headed directly to the workstation occupied by Nicola Rooney.

"Talk to me," Kowalkowski demanded as he peered over Rooney's shoulder at the LCD displays.

Rooney didn't flinch. She'd worked for Kowalkowski for six years and knew exactly how he behaved during the *initial deployment of a strategic technical asset*—bureaucratese for the launch of a spy satellite. Her normally even-keeled boss became a nervous father awaiting the birth of a child.

"We are at plus forty-three minutes from separation with *Liberty,*" Rooney said precisely, her eyes never leaving the monitors. "All onboard systems are operational. So far, so good."

"Then we're two minutes to boost phase," Kowalkowski said.

Rooney nodded. "*Liberty* will soon be far enough away to safely fire the engine."

In Orbit

As it neared the six-hundred-mile apogee of its polar orbit, *Zeus-1* watched and waited. *Liberty* had already passed beneath the sleek black craft, racing toward the terminator between day and night on Earth, and the distance between the orbiter and the satellite that had spiraled out of its payload bay had quickly grown into miles.

Zeus-1 now ignored *Liberty,* its lethal intent focused solely on the satellite hurtling into higher orbit.

Chantilly, Virginia

"Initiating boost sequence," Rooney said calmly.

Rooney's command traveled from her workstation through the NRO network to a collection of dishes mounted atop the agency's huge office buildings. A millisecond later, the short string of binary code reached *Oculus.*

In Orbit

A blue-white tongue of flame erupted from the bell-shaped nozzle on *Oculus*'s tail, the icy liquefied fuels blending there in an explosive reaction. The short burst of thrust coupled with a minor adjustment in orientation aligned the spy satellite for an elliptical orbit that would allow it to pass over any point on Earth once every two days.

A two-inch-diameter spot of red light appeared on the crinkled layer of foil covering the satellite's propulsion unit. The metallic skin flashed incandescent, then disappeared altogether in a puff of silver-gray vapor.

The spherical aluminum tank containing *Oculus*'s supply of liquefied oxygen offered equally poor resistance to the focused power of *Zeus-1*'s laser. The cryogenic fuel inside reacted violently when the icy, sluggish molecules were suddenly sent boiling by five megawatts of energy. Rippling shock waves of concussive power burst through the weakest points on the tank's surface, the laser's silver-dollar-sized entry and exit wounds.

Dozens of tiny aluminum shards tore through the foil shielding, flying into space. A few pieces of the shrapnel tore into the bus segment, damaging portions of the craft's electronics. Others punctured the other fuel tank containing liquid oxygen. In gaseous form the two fuels mixed and ignited. *Oculus* reeled with the explosion, tumbling into an uncontrolled spin from an attack that had lasted barely a second.

Chantilly, Virginia

"Signal lost?" Rooney said, questioning the message on her screen.

"Problem?" Kowalkowski asked.

"I don't know. Boost phase initiated perfectly." Rooney typed furiously as she spoke, trying to reestablish contact with *Oculus*. "Telemetry was good, then nothing."

Kowalkowski studied the large wall monitor, a sick feeling tightening in his gut and he picked up the phone.

Dahlgren, Virginia

Tim Heshel had just stepped into his office with a fresh cup of coffee when the multiline phone on his desk began to purr. "Naval Space Command, NAVSPASUR Office, Commander Heshel speaking."

"Hey, Tim, it's Ben Kowalkowski at NRO."

"Kow, what can I do for you?"

"I need you to quietly take a look at something."

Heshel closed his office door and sat behind his desk. "Shoot."

"The shuttle launched a new satellite today, but it went silent during the boost phase."

"Why are you guys interested in a commercial bird?" Heshel asked.

"It's one of ours," Kowalkowski replied, "and that bit of information is *not* for public consumption."

"Got it."

"Last track should put our satellite about five minutes west of Hawaii. She's about half the size of *Hubble.*"

Heshel cradled the phone against his shoulder and turned to his dual-screen workstation. "How high?"

"Just under two hundred nautical."

"Hang on, I'm checking the Fence."

The Fence was an invisible wall of energy traversing the United States from Southern California to the Georgia coast. Produced by a string of six 217-megahertz continuous-wave, multistate radar installations, it reached fifteen-thousand nautical miles into space and could track an object as far east as Africa and as far west as Hawaii. Computers at the navy's facility in Dahlgren used signals generated by the Fence to calculate the position of every object in orbit larger than two inches.

"I have a projection of your bird's orbit," Heshel reported. "It should be approximately twenty degrees north latitude, one-seventy west longitude, right on the western edge of the Fence."

"That sounds about right," Kowalkowski said.

"Whoa."

As the dot at the end of the projected orbit hit the

Fence, it fragmented and was quickly covered by a clutter of overlapping identification numbers.

"What?" Kowalkowski asked.

"Looks like your bird is fragged."

Heshel zeroed in on the cluttered image. The Fence had resolved twenty distinct objects in immediate proximity to the new satellite.

"There's one big piece and a lot of little stuff up there," Heshel said. He switched to the second monitor and quickly brought up a flat map view of the world with the new satellite's orbit superimposed. "I'm going to run a quick collision check and see if I can't model your bird."

"Collision?" Kowalkowski questioned angrily. "I thought you guys cleared the launch window."

"We did," Heshel replied, his eyes carefully studying the information on his displays. "All right. Tatnall Station in Georgia caught *Liberty* releasing your bird about an hour ago. Then there's a forty-minute gap before we reacquired your satellite over Hawaii. I interpolated the orbit in between and cross-referenced it against everything that's up there and came up empty. The window *was* clear, so if it was a collision that took out your bird, either it was with something too small for us to track or you caught a chunk of incoming from further out. Both are trillion-to-one shots."

The display of real-time data from the Fence on the screen to Heshel's right was replaced with a crude three-dimensional animation of a long, indistinct mass spinning end over end. Also visible were several smaller objects speeding away from the larger one. Heshel ran the animation in reverse and watched the cloud of fragments shrink back into the damaged satellite.

"That's interesting."

"What?" Kowalkowski asked.

Heshel stepped the animation forward slowly. And then he saw it—a pair of distinct conical eruptions from the base of the satellite.

"Kow, from here it looks like the back end of your satellite exploded."

In the Tracking Center outside Heshel's office, Lieutenant Alana Taggert glanced up from her workstation at Heshel's office. The door was closed. She selected the most recent additions to Space Command's catalog of orbiting objects—*Liberty* and the ZetaComm satellite.

Since deploying the satellite, *Liberty* had moved on and was now making adjustments in its orbit in preparation for a rendezvous with the ISS. Taggert always enjoyed tracking the shuttle in orbit; it was one of the few dynamic objects in a halo of satellites and space junk that was otherwise as predictable as the phases of the moon.

Switching to the ZetaComm satellite, she was surprised to find it below two hundred miles in altitude. After safely separating from the shuttle, the satellite's booster should have pushed into a much higher orbit by now. Zooming in, she saw the same field of debris Heshel was studying.

On her way home from work, Taggert stopped in at a convenience store/gas station and topped off the tank of her VW Beetle. Even though she had a cell phone in her purse, she followed the rules that had been laid out for her and slipped a few coins into the slot and dialed a long string of digits.

"Yeah?" Owen Moug answered.

Taggert recognized the flat tenor voice immediately. She knew little about the man who possessed it other than his name and his interest in communications satellites. That was the entirety of their relationship—she told him things and he paid her for the information. Strictly business. What he did with the information mattered little to her, but she suspected it involved the stock market. When a company lost a half-billion-dollar satellite, its share price was bound to take a hit.

"I have some news you might be interested in. Zeta-Comm's new satellite failed to make orbit."

"Thank you," Moug said, then he hung up.

Taggert cradled the handset and walked back to her car, trying to decide what she would do with the five-thousand-dollar check that her part-time consulting firm would soon receive for services rendered.

5

USS **Virginia**
August 4

Lieutenant Commander Jeff Paulson went aft of the control room and peered through the open door of the captain's quarters. "Captain?"

Commander Scott Johnston held a finger up at his executive officer and quickly finished rereading the paragraph he'd been struggling with for the past few minutes.

A career submariner, Johnston had spent much of the past seventeen years cruising beneath the waves. It was in recognition of his skills and the excellence with which he performed his duties that the navy offered him the honor of taking command of the *Virginia.* A variant of the *Seawolf,* she was the first in a new class of submarines, one that extended the stealth and lethality of a fast-attack boat from deep water into the shallows close to shore.

"It's goddamn science fiction," Johnston muttered, shaking his head as he looked up at the man standing in the doorway of his cabin. "Yeah, Jeff."

"We're nearing the center of the box," Paulson reported. "How do you want to proceed?"

"Maintain present depth and slow her down to five

knots. Run a broad, circular sweep. I want to loiter here for a while, nice and quiet, see if there's anybody in the neighborhood. How's the sonar?"

"Still giving us fits. I don't know what our two guests are doing, but the system's so degraded right now that cavitation's about the only hope we have of catching another sub out here."

Johnston snorted a laugh. "No way *Nevada*'s CO is going to drop his drawers like that. I was Mike Granskog's XO before I got my first command—tricky sonofabitch *knows* how to hide a boomer."

"Maybe that new gear'll help us find him."

"On that, I'm a Missouri man—*show me.*" Johnston rapped a knuckle on his briefing booklet. "You've read this. What's your take on acoustic daylighting?"

"Looks like some new kind of passive sonar."

"Echolocation and holographic imaging? Next thing you know, somebody'll talk the navy into trying to communicate with goddamn dolphins."

"I just wonder why they offered up *Virginia* as a guinea pig. I mean, this boat's so new the paint's still wet."

"Officially, we got tagged for this experiment because of our integrated electronics systems. We're the most advanced boat in the fleet, ergo the easiest to graft a new technology onto."

"Unofficially?"

"One of our two guests down below is a former SEAL."

"Got to be the redhead," Paulson surmised. "The guy with the ponytail is definitely a life-time civilian."

Johnston nodded. "The ex-SEAL's former CO now has flag rank and a hard-on for this project."

"And since *Virginia* was built for spec ops, I get the picture. Got to love that Beltway back scratching. Any chance this thing might actually work?"

"How the hell should I know?" Johnston answered with a shrug. "I'm just a dumb sub driver."

Paulson cracked a faint smile at the self-deprecating remark. He'd read the commander's official one-page navy bio when he was first assigned to serve under him and knew Johnston had graduated with the highest honors from both the Academy and the University of Florida. As further testament to the commander's acumen and ability, the navy rumor mill had Johnston up for promotion to captain before his next posting and pegged him as an odds-on favorite to achieve flag rank.

"Captain in Control," the duty officer announced.

Johnston went directly to the large console centered in the aft end of the control room to check the latest plot. The quartermaster of the watch, seated behind the navigator's console, calmly went about his duties as the captain looked over his shoulder at the high-definition flat-screen display.

An icon representing the submarine appeared in the center of a dark-blue image, its position constantly updated by a continuous stream of data from the helm, sensory, and propulsion systems. A dashed line trailed behind the icon, defining the path that the submarine had taken since beginning its sweep of the area.

"Zoom out, Nav," Johnston ordered. "I want to see the whole box."

"Aye, sir," the navigator answered as he manipulated the display.

The submarine icon shrank down into a white dot as

the image panned back to reveal the gray, dotted outline—a hundred-square-mile expanse of ocean southwest of Hawaii. The navy had designated the area surrounding *Virginia* for a submarine training exercise. The fact that none of the participants in this exercise had been forewarned of *Virginia*'s presence in the area was, in Johnston's thinking, immaterial.

Johnston studied the display. Hidden somewhere in the deep waters surrounding his boat were three submarines of the Pacific Fleet—the boomer *Nevada* and the attack boats *Cheyenne* and *Pasadena*. The 560-foot-long *Nevada*, with her arsenal of twenty-four nuclear missiles, would attempt to avoid detection during the exercise, while the smaller and faster attack boats tried to sniff her out. Soviet submariners had played hide-and-seek with their American counterparts for decades, but the USSR's cash-strapped successor didn't have the rubles required to maintain the once-formidable fleet at sea. Other nations—China in particular—were forging ahead with plans to launch blue-water submarine fleets, and it was with them in mind that the U.S. Navy strove to keep its forces sharp.

"Sonar," Johnston called out. "Anything?"

"Nada, Captain. Of course, they'd have to be banging pots and pans against the hull for me to hear 'em."

"That bad?"

"It comes and goes," the sonar man admitted. "It just seems like every time I think I have something, my screens go blank."

"Keep at it," Johnston replied. "XO, I'm heading down to have a chat with our guests. Continue the search pattern."

"Aye, aye, sir," Paulson replied.

* * *

"C'mon, baby, you can do it. I know you can," Grin said in a low soft voice.

Seated behind a makeshift console in the center of *Virginia*'s torpedo room, Bill "Grin" Grinelli urged his computer to synch-up the submarine's acoustic sensor array. The center row of the weapons room had been reconfigured at Pearl Harbor to provide workspace and quarters for him and Nolan Kilkenny during their time onboard. Racks of Mk-48 ADCAP torpedoes stood on either side of the open space, a fact the computer systems expert and avowed pacifist found somewhat unnerving.

Nearby, Kilkenny lay prone on the deck, his arms deep inside the base of a holographic display. The tall cylindrical device consisted of two projection units clad in gray plastic panels set above and below an empty imaging chamber wrapped in clear acrylic.

Grin's laptop display filled with scrolling columns of hexadecimal characters, the disgorged contents of his computer's random access memory.

"Damn!" Grin cursed.

"Screen of death?" Kilkenny asked without looking away from the connection he was working on.

"Puked all over me again. You know, it would've been nice if I'd had a couple months to craft a truly fine piece code for this job instead of cobbling something together on the fly."

"Well, it's your own damn fault."

"How do you figure that?" Grin asked.

"Dawson was so intrigued with our demo that he was ready to go to bat for us with the navy to fund a full-blown system."

"That's what we were shooting for, wasn't it?"

"Yes, but then you went and told him that it was possible to tie what we had into an existing sonar array."

"I told him it was *theoretically* possible."

"And that was like handing the admiral a blank check." Kilkenny bundled the last set of fiber-optic cables with a zip tie and reattached the two missing base panels. "The fish tank is all back together again."

"Good, then you can give me a hand with this interface. I think the ship's network knows I'm not navy."

"It's a boat."

"What?"

"In the navy, surface vessels are ships and submarines are boats."

"Pardon my breach of nautical etiquette. Will you kindly get over here and help me find a way to tap into this *boat's* network?"

"Gladly."

Kilkenny took a seat beside Grin at the workstation and brought up the schematics for the submarine's sensor array on his laptop. Like the rest of the crew, they wore the blue, one-piece coveralls known as poopy suits and the footwear of their choice, as long as the soles were made of rubber. Kilkenny opted for a pair of Oakley Assault Shoes while Grin, ever the individualist, donned his most vibrant pair of yellow-and-black-checkered canvas high-tops.

With his clean-shaven face and close-cropped red hair, Kilkenny easily blended in with the sailors serving aboard the *Virginia*. Grin, in contrast, received looks ranging from envy to disgust for his blatant nonconformity. If the wiry computer genius's graying ponytail and pointed goatee weren't enough to draw the ire of career navy men, the tattoo of an impish elf seated on a crescent moon scattering pixie dust that he sported on his forearm was. After all, real men had eagles or hula girls inked onto their bodies, not whimsical sprites.

Kilkenny turned his head when he heard the hatch to the torpedo room open and, as Johnston entered the compartment, reflexively snapped to attention. Grin, deeply engrossed in the data streaming across his display, was oblivious to the captain's arrival.

"Carry on," Johnston ordered, pulling the hatch closed behind him. "You know, as a civilian, you're not required to do that."

"It's the environment, sir. Old habits die hard," Kilkenny replied. "What can we do for you?"

"I just wanted to see what you two are doing down here," Johnston said in a tone all commanding officers use when they want a no-shit situation report.

"The last of our equipment is up and running, but the tie-in to the sub's network is giving us some trouble. This experiment was thrown together at the last minute, so we're sort of winging it."

"I understand," Johnston replied, the muscles in his jaw tightening, "but I've got a problem in the control room and I'd really appreciate it if you could get my sonar back up and running. At present, we'd be hard-pressed to detect a whale mating against our hull."

"I think we can accommodate your request," Grin said as his screen filled with an orderly flow of data.

"You got a clear feed?" Kilkenny asked.

"Third time was the charm with that little hack you

whipped up, my man." Grin flipped his hand over his shoulder and Kilkenny slapped it. "I'm going to slip that little bit of code into my personal collection."

"What the hell are you two yapping about?" Johnston asked.

"As you already know, *Virginia*'s network wasn't designed to accommodate what we're doing," Kilkenny explained. "Our initial attempts at tapping in did nothing but chew up the data feed."

"I got that much from my sonar man."

"And the tech manuals we were given on your systems are—like most computer documentation—worthless," Grin added.

"So what did you guys do to fix the problem?"

"We improvised," Grin replied, his fingers rapidly tapping at his keyboard. "Despite the fact that my colleague now spends most of his time playing venture capitalist, Nolan can still think like a hacker when he has to."

"I wrote a couple of small programs to manage the feed. Your guy upstairs has priority, of course, but now"—Kilkenny paused to study a new window of information on the screen—"it looks like we can tap in and get the same real-time data."

Grin stroked his goatee as he studied a flow schematic of *Virginia*'s shipwide network. All the pathways were drawn in a brilliant green. "Yes siree, I think we're ready to give it a try. Gentlemen, if you will kindly direct your attention to the holographic display at center stage."

As Grin's fingers danced across his keyboard, the acrylic-enclosed imaging chamber flickered with cool light. Then a ghostlike three-dimensional projection of the

Virginia appeared in the center of the cylindrical void, her multibladed screw turning at five knots, the long tendrils of her towed array trailing behind.

"The image looks pretty clear, good detail," Kilkenny said as he slowly moved around the chamber.

Johnston stood with his nose almost touching the clear plastic. "I saw something like this at the Electric Boat shipyard—a CAD simulation."

"This is no simulation, Commander," Kilkenny replied. "This *is* what the *Virginia* looks like right in the here and now."

"Let there be light," Grin announced with a broad, satisfied smile on his face. "Acoustic daylight, that is. No more shall you sail in darkness beneath the waves."

"I still don't get it," Johnston said. "How can sonar pulses be converted into something you can see?"

"Dolphins do it," Kilkenny replied matter-of-factly. "With echolocation, they can acoustically *see* everything in the water around them. And if it's a biologic, they can also detect what's inside."

"But submarines aren't dolphins," Johnston countered.

"True, and admittedly dolphins are a lot better at this than we are, but they had a big head start. Think of it like this," Kilkenny explained. "Your eyes react to light waves reflected off objects around you. They transform that information into electrical signals that a specialized portion of your brain processes into a mental image. Dolphins do the same thing, but with sound waves. It's all a matter of pairing a highly sensitive receiver with a very powerful computer. Dolphins have a melon. In our brains, it's the visual cortex."

"And now your submarine," Grin said, pointing at the

gray cube clamped to the deck, humming softly, "has a small but exceptionally powerful supercomputer."

Johnston studied the image of his submarine carefully. Except for the color, it looked just like the *Virginia*. As he watched, the rudder turned slightly.

"Why isn't it turning?" Johnston asked.

"It is, but so is your boat. This image is based on all the sound energy in the water striking *Virginia*'s sensors. That's what tells us the boat's orientation. Bow to stern," Kilkenny motioned down the centerline of the torpedo room, "is on this axis. No matter what *Virginia* is doing—pitch, yaw, or roll—as long as the imaging chamber is bolted down and the gyros are working, our image of this sub will be exactly in line with the real thing."

Grin fingered a couple of keystrokes. "Maybe this'll help."

The submarine shrank to half its previous size. Three axial lines then extended from the center of the sub, defining the Cartesian planes. The lines, all equal in length, became radii for three metered rings that surrounded the image of the submarine.

"The ring on the x-y plane defines true north," Kilkenny explained.

Johnston watched the x-y ring slowly spin in concert with the submarine's turn. "And the other two describe true vertical and horizontal."

"That's correct. As far as our computer is concerned, this sub is the center of the universe."

A grayish flicker appeared at the edge of the imaging chamber, then just as quickly disappeared.

"What was that?" Johnston asked.

"Can't say. Grin, could you zoom us out a bit?"

"My pleasure."

The holographic representation of the *Virginia* was now down to just a few inches in length. Near the top of the holographic image, the surface of the ocean roiled with swells.

"You're now looking at a cylinder of ocean about a mile across," Grin announced.

Johnston scanned the model carefully. "And there's our contact. Looks like a pod of whales off our starboard."

"Would you like a closer look?" Grin asked.

Before Johnston could reply, the submarine slid out of view and images of five Pacific gray whales filled the hologram chamber. Mouths open, they were straining plankton from the sea.

"This is amazing," Johnston declared, transfixed by the cetaceans. "It's like—"

"Like someone turned a light on outside," Kilkenny offered. "Seeing in the dark is the whole idea behind this project. And if you like our whales, you'll love our submarines."

6

Houston, Texas
August 6

"Sorry I'm late," Fred Jesup apologized as he entered the conference room.

He was the last to arrive, despite the fact that this hastily scheduled meeting was being held at the Johnson Space Center because his presence was required. As flight director, he could not travel to Washington during a shuttle mission. Jesup looked a bit disheveled with his shirttails bunching up around his ample waist and a thick folder stuffed with loose papers wedged in his armpit.

The two people waiting for him sat at one end of the long rectangular conference table. Jesup had met with Linda Ryerson a handful of times since her appointment to NASA's top job three years ago. She was a bureaucrat, but one with a scientific background and an appreciation for the agency's mission. The tenacity she'd shown in dealing with congressional budget committees had earned his respect and quelled any rumors within the agency that she was hired to bolster the current administration's standing among African-American women.

"Linda," Jesup said with a nod, then he extended his free hand across the table to the man in the dark-blue suit.

Ben Kowalkowski introduced himself as he gripped Jesup's hand firmly. He gave it two brisk pumps, then released. Jesup set his folder on the table and took a seat.

"Glad you could make it, Fred," Ryerson began. "Sorry about the short notice. I hope we didn't catch you at a bad time."

"Actually, three of our astronauts are prepping for a spacewalk." Jesup combed his thinning gray hair back with his fingers. "We're deploying *Zwicky-Wolff* in a few hours."

"That's *Liberty*'s other payload," Ryerson explained for Kowalkowski's benefit. "Fred, before this goes any further I have to tell you that some of what you're about to hear is classified. You've been cleared for this because a situation has developed and you now have a need to know."

"I understand," Jesup replied.

"Good. Now, the purpose of this meeting is to discuss the satellite we launched from *Liberty* two days ago. There's been a problem."

"The launch was clean, as was the handoff to ZetaComm."

"Yes," Kowalkowski said, "the problem with our satellite occurred after the handoff."

"So you're with ZetaComm?"

"No."

Jesup gave Ryerson a *what-gives* look.

"*Colonel* Kowalkowski is with the NRO," Ryerson said, pronouncing the acronym en-ar-ow.

"Are you telling me that what we put up was a spy satellite?"

Ryerson nodded.

"Why wasn't I in the loop?"

"Security," Ryerson replied matter-of-factly. "You were told what you needed to know to launch a communications satellite."

"But *that* bird wasn't a comm sat."

"Yes it was," Kowalkowski interjected. "A very specialized communications satellite."

"Cute," Jesup replied, not the least bit amused by the colonel's semantics. "Look, I know what the NRO does and I'm all for it. Hell, we've flown DOD payloads before. What was so different about this one?"

"There were other considerations," Ryerson said.

"Such as?"

"We didn't want anyone to know that we were putting this satellite up," Kowalkowski explained, "and Vandenberg launches are monitored pretty closely. They watch our rockets and we watch theirs."

Kowalkowski didn't need to elaborate on who *they* were. Since the early days of the space race, studying launches had been a reliable means of gauging a nation's technical capabilities. Several nations were now in the game, and orbital launches were impossible to hide. A lot could be learned about the purpose of a launch by studying the payload shroud and watching where a rocket went.

"So by calling this one a commercial payload," Jesup speculated, "you hid your bird in plain sight."

"That's correct."

"Much as I wish it were otherwise," Ryerson said.

"With our quick return to space following the loss of *Columbia,* shuttle operations have once again become routine in the eyes of the media. The cable news channels are the only ones that carry our launches and landings live anymore, and then only if it's a slow news day. This situation provided an opportunity for the Department of Defense."

"ZetaComm in on this?"

Kowalkowski nodded. "They built our satellite."

"And this constellation of theirs we're putting up?"

"Most of the launches are legitimate," Ryerson answered.

"Our fleet is getting pretty long in the tooth," Kowalkowski explained. "A few of our satellites are almost five years past their design service life. The world's changed in the past few years and we need more and better capabilities."

Placated, Jesup held up his hand. "You're preaching to the choir. What's wrong with your satellite and how can I help?"

"Our best guess is that one of the fuels tanks exploded when we went into boost phase, stranding our satellite in a useless orbit. We lost it at that time, but eventually reestablished contact. Onboard diagnostics show the propulsion unit is totally out of commission, as are the solar arrays. The rest appears undamaged."

"Thus worth salvaging," Jesup concluded. "What's your bird's altitude?"

"Between one-eighty and two hundred nautical miles." Kowalkowski opened a metal briefcase and retrieved a CD-ROM. "Here's a projection of its orbital path for the next ten days."

Jesup placed the disk in his overstuffed folder. "I'll have my team work up a recovery plan. We'll grab your bird on the way back from ISS."

"Great," Kowalkowski said, "because a billion dollars is still a lot of money to lose, even to the NRO."

"Speaking of budgets, how do you want to handle this PR-wise? Shaggin' a broken bird always looks good on TV."

Kowalkowski grimaced slightly. "I'd prefer you kept our satellite out of the media's eye as much as possible. Couldn't you just black out that part of the mission?"

Both Jesup and Ryerson shook their heads.

"That would actually call *more* attention to the retrieval," Ryerson replied.

"If we don't try to hide it, the press'll think everything is status quo." Jesup paused. "Here's a thought: We announce that the comm sat we launched failed to make desired orbit and that we're going to bring it back it for another try. Nothing too elaborate, just a short, run-of-the-mill press release. Now, when it comes time to actually grab the bird, *Liberty*'s comm system goes on the fritz and that part of the mission doesn't get recorded."

"And that wouldn't make the press suspicious?"

"Nope. Little stuff happens all the time. By the time Lundy finishes troubleshooting the problem with our engineers, your bird will be safely stowed in the payload bay. We will have to bring *Liberty*'s crew and a couple of my engineers in on this to pull this off."

"All right, but just the players you need," Kowalkowski agreed. "I *don't* want the people you're ferrying back from the ISS in the loop."

Jesup nodded. Only one of the returning ISS crewmen was American; the other two were French and Russian.

"Colonel, I'll need help from your office to coordinate the press effort with ZetaComm," Ryerson said, "just so we're all singing from the same sheet music."

"Done."

7

USS Virginia

It first appeared like a flickering smudge of gray near the curved edge of the imaging chamber, a moving shape small and indistinct. In contrast, the holographic image of the ocean floor beneath *Virginia* looked solid and well defined—so much so that the remains of two shipwrecks had already been discovered. The smudge hovered for a minute, then slipped toward the acrylic and disappeared.

Three off-duty enlisted men were seated around the chamber, watching with rapt fascination. The men's normal duties required them to be in the torpedo room maintaining *Virginia*'s weapons and launching systems, and such proximity necessitated that they all be read into the black program and sworn to keep it secret. Once these men got a look at the magic Kilkenny and Grin were performing, there was no keeping them away when off-watch, even during the intermittent system crashes.

Instead of barring the door, Kilkenny and Grin welcomed the men and, when the acoustic daylighting system was up and running, employed their eyes in the search for the three submarines that *Virginia* was hunting.

"What *is* that?" Imran, a torpedoman's mate, asked, eyeing the smudge as it flickered back into view.

Kilkenny moved to the young sailor's side of the chamber. "Where?"

"That little cloud-thingy there."

Kilkenny studied the smudge for a moment. As with a wisp of smoke, there just wasn't enough substance to discern a form. Kilkenny looked at the center of the chamber; *Virginia* looked solid, though barely a quarter-inch long.

"Grin, what's our resolution?"

" 'Bout twelve miles. Why, you got something?"

"Maybe, or it could just be a burp in the system. It's pretty indistinct."

"We are grinding a lot of data. Where's your burp at?"

"Six miles astern."

Grin turned and arched an eyebrow at Kilkenny. "I don't speak navy, man. Gimme some numbers."

Kilkenny eyed the directional rings encircling the holographic submarine. "We're currently heading two-seven-zero. Look between zero-eight-zero and one-zero-five degrees."

As Grin typed, the wisp continued to hover near the edge of the chamber, moving perpendicular to the *Virginia*.

"Definitely something out there, though the return data's pretty funky. Is it close to a thermocline?"

As he asked the question, Grin keyed in a command. Several undulating, hexagonal grids appeared inside the chamber, dividing the holographic ocean into layers of warm and cold water.

"It's hovering right below the boundary of the layer we're in. But that shouldn't matter—we're getting a good solid image of the sea floor, and that's a couple layers down."

"Maybe it's a school of fish," a fire control technician named Billig offered.

"I'll zoom in on it," Grin said, "and see what we get."

Grin projected a three-dimensional grid into the chamber, dividing the holographic image into discrete cubes of space. The cube containing the Virginia was highlighted. Working back from the submarine through the lattice, he quickly selected the cube containing the cloudy gray smudge. The cube then slid to the center of the chamber and expanded to fill the space.

"I don't think it's fish," Kilkenny said. "The shape isn't fluttering or making sharp changes in direction. This looks more like a blob of something."

"Maybe it's in our baffles," Imran said.

"Baffles?" Kilkenny and Grin said in unison.

"Yeah," the twenty-year-old replied. "The spherical sonar array on our bow is isolated from the rest of the boat by a wall of acoustic blanking plates called baffles. These baffles keep all the noise on our side of the wall from overpowering the sensitivity of the sonar. They also create a cone-shaped blind spot for the array directly aft of the boat. If a sub really gets moving, then the noise from a cavitating screw can bleed out and widen the blind spot even more."

"But we're only making five knots," the fire control technician protested. "Our baffles shouldn't be that wide."

"What do you think, Nolan?" Grin asked.

Kilkenny caught sight of the dolphins pinned over the left breast of Imran's coveralls—a sign the young man was qualified in submarines and likely knew what he was talking about. "The E-three may be onto something."

Imran grinned.

"All our previous work was done with surface ships or small submersibles," Kilkenny explained to the crewmen. "We don't have any experience with screws the size of what's on the back of *Virginia*. Since we're getting the same raw sensor data as the control room, it stands to reason that whatever baffles them might baffle us."

Most of the crewmen laughed at Kilkenny's pun. Billig did not.

"Well, Torpedoman's Mate Imran, how do you propose we test your theory?"

"Clear the baffles, sir. That's what we'd do if we thought someone was trying to come up on our stern."

Kilkenny looked at the cloudy shape once more. Though vague, the form didn't look natural.

"Seaman, would you accompany me up to the control room? I need to have a word with the captain."

Johnston returned to the torpedo room with Kilkenny and Imran, the young seaman still beaming from the good word Kilkenny had put in for him with the captain.

During their absence, Grin had kept track of the slow-moving object and worked at trying to further define its true shape. At the moment, it looked like an elongated lozenge.

"So that's your possible contact?" Johnston said as he peered into the chamber. "Looks like a dust storm."

"Yeah," Grin agreed, "but one that's held that shape for the last five minutes."

Johnston looked at the lieutenant, who nodded. He then punched the talk button on the intercom.

"Control, this is the captain."

"Aye, sir," the XO answered.

"I want you to execute a one-eight-zero-degree starboard turn. Clear our baffles."

"One-eight-zero starboard. Aye, sir."

Johnston switched off the intercom. "Now maybe we'll see what this contact of yours is."

The vague form in the chamber rotated slowly in concert with *Virginia's* starboard turn. As it emerged from the turbulence of the submarine's baffles, the gray fragments coalesced into a hard curved surface.

"Holy shit!" the lieutenant blurted out.

"I'll be damned, Imran," Johnston said, his eyes fixed on the distinctive shape of an Ohio Class nuclear submarine. "You've done tagged yourself a boomer."

8

ISS
August 8

Kelsey pulled open the airlock hatch and leaned out into darkness. Two hundred twenty miles beneath the ISS, the Western Hemisphere was in shadow. Lightning flashed like strobes inside the swollen clouds of a storm front raging over the Central Plains and Kelsey thought of the tornadoes that would likely be spawned in the leading edge of that violent display.

Nature's presence on the planet below was evident at all times of day, visible in the interplay of land, sea, and air. Hurricanes, sandstorms, and wildfires were events of a magnitude easily viewed from orbit. The dust plume from a volcanic eruption on the island of Lopevi darkened the sky over an otherwise vividly blue expanse of the southwestern Pacific. Scientists were already predicting a slight dip in global temperatures as a result of the huge volume of ash billowing into the atmosphere.

Islands of light shone brightly on the darkened lands below. *San Francisco, Los Angeles, Phoenix, Mexico City*—Kelsey named them off in her head as they passed beneath her. An urban legend boasted that the Great Wall of China was the only man-made object visible from space. Kelsey had seen with her own eyes the fallacy of that claim, but it was at night that the extent of human activity was most apparent.

"I'm heading out," Kelsey announced.

"Watch out for that first step," Valentina warned. The punch line was unnecessary.

Kelsey rotated until she was facing away from the Earth, then pulled herself straight through the open hatch and up on top of the airlock. Carefully, she continued her ascent until she stood on the upper beam of the station's main truss. The large hexagonal framework extended straight out 175 feet to each side, ending in rotating segments that supported the port and starboard solar arrays. The entire assembly defined an area the size of two football fields placed side by side.

Running perpendicular to the main truss, six large modules formed the backbone of the ISS. Additional modules sprouted at right angles from connecting nodes in the backbone, providing the station with an impressive suite of research facilities and accommodations for up to seven residents. Russian-built modules composed the stern of the space station. The bow modules, mostly large cylinders, were built by the United States and the station's multinational partners.

Kelsey climbed down from the truss onto the U.S. Lab Module, then worked her way forward to Node 2. Research modules occupied three of the node's attachment points. The fourth, on the node's underside, was reserved for logistics modules, which the shuttle brought up to resupply the station.

Hand over hand, she pulled herself thirty feet up the

side of the vertically oriented Centrifuge Accommodation Module (CAM). This final ascent represented the culmination of years of research and planning by the small but dedicated group of scientists who had conceived and built the *Zwicky-Wolff* Dark Matter Array.

Like *Hubble* and *Chandra, Zwicky-Wolff* bore the name of a famous astronomer—in this case the eccentric, Swiss-American Fritz Zwicky, who in 1933 theorized the existence of dark matter in the universe. The second name on the array belonged to theoretical physicist Johann Wolff, who was murdered in the late 1940s. The recent discovery of Wolff's lost notebooks, along with his long-missing body, provided the array's scientists with tantalizing clues to the nature of Zwicky's enigmatic dark matter. Invigorated by Wolff's approach to the problem, they quickly secured several private grants and launched into a crash redesign of their orbital experiment. *Liberty*'s payload bay now held the result of that effort.

Atop CAM, Kelsey stood beside the slender mast installed during the previous shuttle mission. A series of alternating handholds ran up the length of the mast, and around its elevated base, a rigid framework anchored the slender structure to the end of the module. A thin bundle of cables ran out from the base of the mast to a connector port on CAM, providing a hard-wired power and data connection for the array.

"I'm in position," Kelsey announced.

"How's the view from the crow's nest?" Lundy asked.

Looking down the side of the module, she saw the orbiter's nose. *Liberty*'s commander waved at her through the flight-deck windows. She waved back.

Far below, the Earth still lay in darkness and the space

beyond was filled with more stars than she'd ever seen. A faint glow illuminated the curved edge of the Earth and she slid her protective visor down. Soaring out of the planet's shadow, Kelsey saw the first rays of the sun burst over the curved horizon. A thin line of brilliant light illuminated the edge and the sun, still rising, flared like a diamond set in a golden ring.

"Oh my," Kelsey said softly, awestruck.

In *Liberty*'s payload bay, Pete and Caroline removed the last of the restraints from *Zwicky-Wolff*.

"We're ready to move the array," Caroline announced.

Kelsey could feel her heart beating faster. From where she stood, only the upper portion of *Zwicky-Wolff* was visible. Lundy and Tosh were at *Liberty*'s aft station, controlling the orbiter's robotic arm. Molly remotely directed a larger, more advanced version of the Canadian-built arm mounted to the station.

Lundy studied the clearance between *Liberty* and the station. "Tosh, it looks pretty damn tight out there. Try not to ding anything."

Tosh laughed. "My father said the same thing when he was teaching me how to parallel park."

"Did it help?"

"Nope. I popped the clutch and scratched the bumper on his RX-7."

Tosh watched the monitors as he moved the arm into position, relying on Lundy to pass on any visual cues from the astronauts in the bay.

"Almost there," Tosh said expectantly, the screen filled with the image of a grappling point on the array.

The end of the RMS soundlessly touched the grappling point.

"How's it look out there?" Tosh asked.

Caroline looked critically at the robotic arm's grip on the array. "No good, Tosh. The RMS only got a partial hold."

Tosh released the array, pulled the robotic arm back a foot, and adjusted the alignment. The robotic arm then glided forward, slipped around the grappling point, and clamped on tightly.

"That get it?"

"Contact is solid," Caroline replied. "I'm moving out of the way."

Caroline floated to the empty rear of the cargo bay. During the grappling maneuver, Pete had positioned himself alongside the Japanese Experimentation Module (JEM) to observe the handoff between the two robotic arms. Both astronauts watched as Tosh lifted the spiny object out of its cradle. The mockup in Houston bore only the crudest resemblance to the real array. Even in its collapsed state, the precise engineering that went into fabricating the dynamic structure of *Zwicky-Wolff* was obvious.

Those with a view of the extraction held their collective breath as the array passed through the narrow gap between *Liberty* and JEM with just a foot to either side. Once clear of the payload bay doors, Tosh had ample room to maneuver the array for the exchange. He rotated the arm's elbow and wrist joints and extended the entire assembly upward. Kelsey thought *Zwicky-Wolff*, fastened to the end of the reedy arm, resembled a silver-white chrysanthemum.

Tosh locked the RMS and pulled his hands away from the controls. "I'm in position, Molly. Ball's in your court."

"I'm moving in," the ISS commander replied.

The station's robotic arm unfolded from the main truss and reached out toward the array. With no clear observation point, Molly was operating by cameras and cues from the spacewalkers. Pete guided Molly to a grappling point opposite the one held by the shuttle's arm, then inspected the connection.

"Clean lock on the array," Pete announced.

"Roger, that," Molly replied. "*Liberty,* we have *Zwicky-Wolff* and are ready for handoff."

"Initiating handoff," Tosh said. "Stand by."

Liberty's RMS released its hold on *Zwicky-Wolff*. The shuttle pilot then retracted the robotic arm, folding it at the elbow as he pulled it back into the payload bay.

Pete followed the arm's retreat. "*Liberty,* RMS is clear."

From where Kelsey stood, *Zwicky-Wolff* was less than twenty feet in front of her. Slowly, Molly rotated the station's arm about its base, lifting the array in a semicircular arc upward. Kelsey scaled the mast, moving into position to secure the array. Repositioned, the robotic arm extended upward, lifting the array up over the mast.

"Molly, you need to rotate the RMS wrist about ten degrees counterclockwise," Kelsey advised.

Molly studied the image from the camera mounted on Kelsey's Primary Life Support System (PLSS) backpack. The array's mounting strut was out of line with the mast. "I see it."

The array began to slowly rotate above Kelsey.

"Good . . . good . . . and hold there. Now let's bring it down."

Kelsey was careful not to move during this maneuver, providing her crewmates with a clear view.

"A little more, and . . . hold there."

The RMS stopped moving. Kelsey locked her foot restraints onto one of the mast handholds, then located the cable couplings and linked the array to the station.

"Are you getting a signal?" Kelsey asked.

"Yes," Molly replied. "Connection is good."

Using a thirty-six-volt pistol grip power tool, Kelsey then fastened the array's mounting strut to the top of the mast. On Earth, setting these same six bolts would take less than five minutes, but wrapped inside nine layers of spacesuit while working in a microgravity environment turned the job into a thirty-five-minute test of patience. After setting the bolts, Kelsey checked the torque on each of the precision-engineered fasteners. She felt a trickle of sweat running down her back, the sun of her second orbit during this spacewalk bearing down on her.

"The array is secured to the mast," Kelsey said.

"Retracting RMS," Molly replied.

When the arm was clear, Kelsey released her foot restraints and, hand over hand, descended the mast. After resetting her restraints on the top of CAM, Kelsey opened the control panel inside the mast's support framework. The two buttons inside were large, selected for use by someone with thickly gloved hands. Only one of the buttons was illuminated.

She depressed the first button. Slowly, the mast telescoped upward, raising the array high above the station. As each of the mast segments locked into place, a light on the panel display switched from red to green. When the fourth segment reached full extension, the second button lit up.

"Over seventy years ago," Kelsey began, "Fritz Zwicky's observations of how galaxies moved led him to theorize that as much as nine-tenths of what composes the universe is unknown to us. The bright, luminous matter we see in the heavens around us is only a small fraction of what must really be out there. The rest is dark and mysterious. This array, named in honor of two pioneers in the search for a theory of everything, was designed to allow us to see into the darkness and allow us to learn more about this creation that we inhabit."

Kelsey depressed the second button. High above her, dozens of tiny electric motors switched on in the joints of the array and the structure began to unfold. Based on Hoberman spheres, the collapsed form of the *Zwicky-Wolff* array blossomed into a glittering sphere nearly one hundred feet in diameter.

"It's huge," Pete blurted out, impressed with the array's deployment.

"It has a nickname, you know," Kelsey said.

"What?" several voices asked.

"Gifted as he was, Zwicky was not the easiest fellow to be around," Kelsey explained. "He was fond of calling people *spherical bastards* because they were bastards every way he looked at them. During the design of the array, that name sort of stuck."

9

USS Virginia
August 9

"We're losing it again," Kilkenny said.

Grin left the workstation and joined Kilkenny by the imaging chamber. Bit by bit, the hologram deteriorated until the cylinder was clear and empty. This had become an all-too-frequent condition during the past few days, one that was devouring every moment of their time in search of a solution.

"I thought we had it," Grin said, frustrated.

"There's simply too much raw data for our rig to handle."

"I'm beginning to think you're right."

As they stared into the empty chamber, their thoughts wrestling with an elusive mathematical foe, Johnston entered the torpedo room, followed by a couple of enlisted men from the galley. He waited for a moment, but neither Grin nor Kilkenny seemed to notice his arrival.

"Looking for a glimpse of the future in that crystal ball of yours?" Johnston asked.

"Oh, sorry, Cap'n. We didn't see you come in."

"Obviously. I must say, gentlemen, you both look like

something we'd scrape out of the bilge. When was the last time either of you got some sleep?"

"I took a fifteen-minute nap about ten hours ago," Grin replied.

"Pitiful. Look, I work my crew hard, but they still get eight hours in the sack. Sleep deprivation can kill a sub just as easily as a torpedo. I notice you guys didn't make it to the captain's table tonight, so I had the boys whip up something to go. The coffee's decaf."

"Thanks," Kilkenny said.

Johnston turned to the enlisted men, who'd finished setting out some sandwiches and a pot of coffee. "You're dismissed."

The crewmen nodded and left.

"Dig in, gentlemen," Johnston ordered as he poured himself a cup.

Virginia's captain sipped his coffee and looked into the empty chamber. Submarine warfare could accurately be described as a game of Blind Man's Bluff, where opponents could hear, but not see each other. These two civilians had brought a bit of scientific wizardry onboard, a glimpse of a technology that might one day provide the U.S. Navy an immense advantage over its adversaries.

"So, where are you at with this? Can you get it running again?"

"Running?" Kilkenny replied. "Sure, but for only short periods of time. Our setup wasn't designed to handle the amount of acoustic data we're pulling out of your passive array."

"All right, but can you fix it so it can run full-time?"

Grin nodded. "It's a math and memory problem. Tough, but solvable."

"Well, if it's any consolation, you did help us tag all three of the subs we were sent out to find."

"At least we earned our keep," Kilkenny said.

"More than that. I'm putting my report together on this experiment. Despite technical difficulties, I'm convinced acoustic daylighting is an asset the navy absolutely must acquire. If I had any say in the matter, you'd get whatever you needed to finish the job."

10

Long Beach, California
August 10

"NASA is definitely going after the ZetaComm satellite," Moug reported.

"When?" Skye asked.

"Tomorrow."

"That doesn't make any sense. ZetaComm would be better off collecting on the insurance and building a new one. Bringing this one back for repair and a second launch—it's just throwing good money after bad."

Skye leaned back in her chair, arms crossed, pondering this development.

"Regardless if it's a smart-money move or not, they're doing it," Moug said. "Maybe NASA still feels it has something to prove."

"If they retrieve that satellite, what they might prove could shut this company down and send the both of us to jail. I just hope *Zeus-1* has enough fuel left to take care of this."

"Are you going to make another pass at the satellite?"

Skye shook her head. "A few more holes won't stop them from picking it up."

Moug studied his employer carefully. In the years that he'd been with her, he'd known C. J. Skye to be a person who never shrank from doing what had to be done, no matter how unpleasant.

"Owen, we always knew it might come to this someday," Skye said.

"Another shuttle," Moug sighed. "This could shut NASA down for good."

"They'll recover," Skye replied confidently. "They always do. On the plus side, it'll keep them out of commercial launches for a while."

"And we'll be there to pick up the slack. It's decided then?"

Skye nodded.

"Then I'll get to work on collecting the data for our intercept."

11

Pearl Harbor, Hawaii
August 10

"Is this one of the guys responsible for tracking my boat?" Granskog asked sternly as Kilkenny entered the paneled conference room.

Commander Mike Granskog stood beside a long oak conference table. The table was covered with large naval charts—plots of submarine movements tracked by *Virginia.* The wiry commander's balding pate stretched tightly over the top of his head like a drumskin, the slack bunched in thick ripples on his furrowed brow.

At the head of the table sat Rear Admiral Jack Dawson, Kilkenny's former CO and the man currently in charge of Naval Special Warfare. When Kilkenny left the service, only the temples of Dawson's close-cropped Afro showed any sign of gray, but just two years after achieving flag rank, a field of salt-and-pepper gray had spread across the admiral's head like kudzu.

"He is," Dawson replied, leaning back in his chair with the satisfied smile of a coach whose underdog team had just pulled off an upset.

"How the hell did you do this?" Granskog demanded.

"You figure out a way to hack into the fleet's computers after we returned to port?"

"Sir," Kilkenny answered, "I can assure you the *Virginia's* plots are legitimate. Once we located your boat in the exercise area, we were able to keep tabs on it most of the time."

"Mike, calm down," Dawson said. "The means used to track your boat is experimental, and, for the moment, compartmented."

"I drive a boomer for a living, so I'm naturally averse to the idea of anybody being able to follow me when I'm at sea. Hiding at depth is what keeps me and my men alive and able to do our job."

"I understand," Dawson replied. "SEALs work under the cover of darkness, too. What Kilkenny is working on for us is a way to increase a sub's situational awareness without compromising its stealthiness."

"Well, I'm all for that. It just would've been nice to know there was a fourth boat involved in the exercise."

"Back in the bad old days, would the Russians have let you know something like that?"

Granskog almost snapped back an answer, but quickly realized it would be better to keep his mouth shut.

"That'll be all," Dawson said.

"Aye, aye, sir," Granskog replied.

With a quick exchange of nods, Granskog departed.

"He didn't seem too happy about the project," Kilkenny said.

"Mike's a damn good sub driver. He's just pissed 'cuz *Virginia* tagged him during the exercise. Cost him a case of Bombay Sapphire. By the way, where's your buddy Grin?"

"Sacked out. We burned a lot of midnight oil over the past few days."

"It shows. You two did a good job out there."

"Thanks. I think we proved acoustic daylight on a sub is doable, but it's going to take a lot more work to turn it into a reliable onboard system."

"Nobody expected a flawless performance first time out of the chute—I just wanted you to prove the concept. You did. Now the navy can talk real dollars with that consortium you work for and really figure out what it'll take to rig our ships for acoustic daylight."

"My father'll be pleased to hear that," Kilkenny said.

"He was. I spoke with him shortly after *Virginia* pulled into port."

"Bet he's already got the lawyers and accountants churning out the paperwork."

Dawson smiled. "I don't doubt it. He's also agreed to loan you and Grin to the navy for a couple more weeks of evaluation."

"Oh."

"Don't worry. By evaluation, I mean dog and pony show. I want to take some of the brass out on the *Virginia* and let them see this thing in action."

"And get a few more big guns backing you up," Kilkenny said.

"All part of the game." Dawson leaned back in his leather chair with the back of his head cradled in the palms of his hands. "And speaking of games, just a reminder that security's sphincter rating is going to jump by about a factor of ten in a couple days. We got company coming."

"Company?" Kilkenny said, puzzled.

"The Chinese. They're running a couple of their

Russian-built destroyers down our side of the Pacific on a goodwill tour. Pearl is their last stop before sailing back east—part of their reward for yanking the leash a bit on North Korea."

"I'll pass the word to Grin."

"Good, because we got your project bottled up real nice right now, and I'd kind of like to keep it that way for as long as possible."

Kilkenny nodded. "Loose lips sink ships."

12

Liberty
August 11

Sixteen hours after undocking from the ISS for her return flight home, *Liberty* drew close to the NRO's damaged satellite. *Oculus* was spinning slowly, end over end—a billion-dollar piece of orbital debris.

Pete looked through the upper windows at their quarry. "She sure didn't get very far."

"At least it's not our fault," Caroline replied.

"What do you think, Pete?" Lundy asked.

"I think it's going to be a pain in the ass. If we can't stabilize that spin, the show's over."

"We can't go at it from underneath," Caroline said, "but look at the way it's rotating. It's all in one plane."

Tosh studied the tumbling satellite carefully. "She's right, it's spinning like a fan. We come at it from the bottom, we get all chopped up, but if we pull *Liberty* around in front—"

"—we can get a clean shot at its center of gravity," Lundy said. "If we get you close, can you grapple it?"

"Probably," Pete replied, "but I won't know till I get there."

"Good enough for me. Suit up, you two. Tosh and I'll bring the bus around."

After the spacewalkers had floated down to the mid-deck, Lundy nodded to Tosh. The pilot initiated a program uploaded by Jesup to *Liberty*'s computer as part of an in-flight data upgrade. The program instantly deactivated the link between the orbiter's closed-circuit television system and the communications system.

"*Liberty*, this is Houston," Capcom's voice crackled in Lundy and Tosh's headsets.

"This is *Liberty*," Lundy replied, expecting the call. "Go ahead, Houston."

"INCO is showing a fault in your CCTV system."

"Checking on that, Houston." Lundy and Tosh went through the motions of checking for a system fault. "Roger, Houston. CCTV downlink is offline. We still show onboard CCTV active. Are we still a go on satellite retrieval?"

"Roger, *Liberty*. You are still a go," Jesup confirmed. "You'll just have to do without us looking over your shoulder."

Caroline stood in the payload bay, *Liberty*'s nose pointed down at the Earth below. The orbiter's robotic arm extended straight up from the port side of the bay, aimed like a spear at the slowly spinning satellite. Pete stood at the end of the arm, his feet secured to a small metal platform, his arms outstretched.

Tosh piloted the orbiter while Lundy watched the approach through the upper observation windows, making minute adjustments along the way. Though similar, this approach was far more difficult than docking with the ISS.

"How's it look, Pete?" Lundy asked.

"Right on the R-Bar."

Hanging out in space, Pete was moving toward the satellite at one-tenth of a foot per second. To keep from getting dizzy, he kept his eyes focused on the center point of the spinning satellite. *Oculus* wasn't rotating very quickly, but it still had several times more mass than the spacewalker.

"Five feet," Pete estimated, calling out the distance for Tosh. "Three . . . two . . . and hold."

Tosh fired the maneuvering thrusters and brought the orbiter to a dead stop. The satellite was now spinning within arm's reach. Pete's body tensed like a snake preparing to strike. In his mind, he tried to slow the satellite down into still images, looking for the perfect spot to latch on.

He lunged forward. One hand struck the flat side of the satellite, the other missed entirely. The bulky suit had thrown off his timing. The satellite swept around and a piece of metal framing struck his wrist.

"Shit," he cursed, recoiling.

"You okay?" Caroline asked.

"Yeah, I'm fine," he replied bitterly. "I'm going for another try."

On his second attempt, Pete grabbed hold of the main framing struts. The satellite continued rotating and his arms turned with it, his left forearm crossing over his right like a twist-tie. The torque strained at his wrists and shoulders and he felt himself being pulled out of the foot restraints. He held on until he had to let go. Beads of sweat covered his forehead as he gulped for air.

"I think you slowed it down," Caroline said.

"A little."

Pete's third grab slowed the rotation even further, and his fourth arrested the spin completely. He held tightly on to the satellite, panting, afraid that if he let go it might somehow begin spinning again.

"You okay?" Caroline asked.

"Just a little beat up. Preparing to secure the satellite to the RMS."

Pete removed his foot restraints from the end of the robotic arm, then swung himself around the side of the satellite. "I'm clear, Tosh. Go ahead and snag it."

Tosh switched on the camera at the end of the RMS and saw a clear view of *Oculus*'s foil-covered side. He panned the camera until he saw the grappling point on the satellite's frame. Slowly, he guided the arm forward until it lightly touched his target, then he grabbed on tight.

"Good latch," Pete reported. "You can reel it in."

"Hang on, Pete. I wouldn't want to leave you out there."

Sailing 220 miles over Asia, *Zeus-1* waited, its elliptical orbit carefully adjusted to bring it into range of the shuttle at precisely this moment. The spacecraft was nearing perigee, the point when it was closest to Earth, barely 180 miles above the surface. Roughly the same altitude as *Liberty*.

As *Liberty* soared above Malaysia, Tosh carefully retracted the RMS back toward the payload bay. Pete worked his way down from the middle of the errant satellite toward the propulsion unit. There he found a charred, gaping wound in the craft's side.

"I can confirm that this bird had a big blowout."

"What do you see?" Lundy asked.

Pete moved closer to the damaged area. "There's a huge hole in the skin of the propulsion unit, the metal looks scorched. Something must've sparked in one of the tanks when they switched on the booster and set the whole thing off."

When the satellite was twenty feet from the payload bay, Tosh momentarily stopped retracting the RMS.

"Hang on, Pete," Tosh said. "I gotta line the bird up before I bring her in."

"I ain't going nowhere."

Looking at the charred wound, Pete had no sense of the movement as he rotated with the satellite. He pulled his head just over the opening and gazed inside the craft. The spherical oxygen fuel tank was mostly intact, save for the rupture in the lower hemisphere. The tank's aluminum skin peeled back in a radial pattern around the opening.

Must've been a weak spot in the metal, he thought.

The symmetry of the blast opening struck Pete as odd—it was too perfect. As he stared into the hole, he caught a flicker of movement. Another spot of light whizzed by. Stars.

The two objects *Zeus-1* had been tracking gradually merged into one. The killer satellite was now ahead of the orbiter, the spacecraft's black-tiled underside an inviting target at such close range, its altitude nearly matching that of its prey. Gyros spinning, *Zeus-1* took steady aim.

Liberty's heat-resistant ceramic tiles offered little protection against the focused intensity of the high-energy laser. The beam ripped through the equipment bay into the middeck, where it narrowly missed the returning leader of the previous ISS expedition. Passing through the flight deck, the beam severed Lundy's forearm, vaporizing flesh and bone.

"Son of a . . ." Lundy said, reaching for his damaged limb.

Before the shuttle commander could complete his pained expression, the laser drilled through the top of the crew compartment and passed, somewhat diminished, into space. As quickly as it had struck, the bright pulse was gone.

Warning alarms blared, combining with the shrill whine of the pressurized atmosphere escaping through two deadly breaches. Blood oozed out between Lundy's fingers and a stream of crimson droplets was drawn into the escaping flow of air.

Tosh turned away from the aft station, his eyes following the blood trail from Lundy's arm to the hole in the ceiling. A second blast from *Zeus-1* struck the pilot in the abdomen before exiting through the starboard upper observation window.

The temperature inside the crew compartment plunged as the air grew thin. Two of the returning astronauts fought to plug the holes in the middeck while the returning ISS commander scrambled through the interdeck access.

"We are losing atmosphere!" the balding cosmonaut shouted as he emerged onto the flight deck, his voice barely audible in the din.

Then he saw what had happened to the *Liberty*'s commander and pilot. Tosh floated in a fetal position, doubled over in pain and coughing up blood. Lundy, one arm useless and bleeding, was frantically searching for something to stem two of the breaches in *Liberty*'s hull. The cosmonaut raced to his aid.

"Oh my God!" Caroline shouted.

Liberty's warning alarm rang loudly over the spacewalkers' headsets. Pete looked up from the damaged satellite and saw two gray-white plumes spouting from *Liberty*'s brow.

A third shot struck the aft fuselage, lancing the spherical tank containing *Liberty*'s supply of liquefied oxygen. The rear of the orbiter disintegrated in the fury of two back-to-back explosions as first the oxygen, then the hydrogen detonated. The nozzles from the three main engines spiraled away like paper cups caught in a gale.

Shards from the exploding tanks sprayed through the payload bay. Several struck Caroline, slicing through her helmet and spacesuit, while others were embedded in the payload bay doors and the airlock. She died almost instantly.

The vertical tail was the largest fragment to emerge from the fireball engulfing *Liberty*'s aft fuselage. Pete couldn't hear the twin explosions—the vacuum of space erasing any sound—but the tail's impact on the far side of *Oculus* was impossible to miss.

Liberty's tail crushed the lightly built satellite, wrapping the spacecraft around its leading edge, locking the two together. Even though his chest was protected by his spacesuit's rigid upper torso, Pete felt like he'd been struck squarely by a three-hundred-pound linebacker. The blow loosened his grip on the satellite's frame and flung him spinning into space.

The RMS held fast to the satellite through the impact and pulled the entire tangled mass at its end in a sweeping arc that ended with a collision that shattered *Liberty*'s port wing.

Pete quickly reached around his left to the base of his PLSS, grabbed the control module for his SAFER unit, and brought it around front. The module consisted of a joystick and a display. Manipulating the joystick, he fired a short series of nitrogen bursts from the SAFER and brought himself to a stop. He then surveyed the extent of the damage done to the orbiter.

Liberty was slowly rolling end over end, the last wisps of air sputtering from four distinct holes. The crew cabin was now as cold and inhospitable as space. In the payload bay, Caroline lay grotesquely entangled in the struts supporting the docking airlock, her body broken and still. Looking aft, he saw wreckage in place of the orbiter's propulsion systems.

She's falling, Pete realized as the damaged spacecraft passed beneath him.

The explosion had acted like a full burn from the main engines, robbing *Liberty* of her precious speed and pushing her down toward the Earth.

13

Houston, Texas

"INCO, anything?" Jesup yelled.

"Negative," the communications officer replied. "We're not receiving any signals from *Liberty*. We've lost contact."

Pacing, Jesup slammed his clipboard against his console. The rendezvous with the errant satellite had been textbook perfect. Then, as the crew was reeling the captured bird in, all hell had broken loose aboard *Liberty*.

"Eecom, what happened up there?"

"The data I have indicate a sudden loss of cabin pressure at 19:22:47," the emergency, environmental, and consumables manager replied. The woman continued scanning the information on her screen as she spoke. "I'm not seeing any problems with the systems, even after the pressure drop. It might be an impact."

"Shit!"

"Flight, the media wants to know what's happening," the public affairs officer reported.

"Shit!" Jesup wheeled around to the PAO. "Tell 'em we're having trouble communicating with *Liberty*, but nothing else until we know more ourselves."

The PAO nodded and relayed the current mission status to the reporters in the press room.

"Security, clear the observation gallery," Jesup ordered.

"Flight? I think I got something" EGIL called out.

"Yeah, Eagle?"

"Just before we lost contact, there was a temperature spike in the LOX tank."

"How big a spike?" Jesup asked, leaning over the man's console.

Temperature sensors mounted on the tank containing the *Liberty*'s supply of liquid oxygen recorded a sudden change from minus 298 degrees Fahrenheit to nearly zero just before the data feed was lost. At the last recorded temperature, the cryogenically chilled fuel would have instantly boiled into a gas. The pressure exerted by the rapidly expanding gas inside the tank would have been explosive.

"Big enough," EGIL replied.

"Any malfunctions in the cryo system?"

"Negative. The spike is the only sign of a problem."

Jesup checked the time index on the data feed. *Liberty*'s main computers had continued transmitting several seconds after the temperature spike, reporting null data from the propulsion systems. The time index for the spike read 19:22:52.

"Eecom, say again when *Liberty* lost pressure."

She reread the time index from her screen. Jesup rechecked the index on Prop's screen.

"The crew compartment lost pressure *before* the tank heated up," Jesup mused aloud. "Damn."

He looked at the control room's main screen. *Liberty*'s projected path put her over the Pacific on a line headed toward Northern California. He returned to his post and hit his phone's speed dial for U.S. Space Command.

"INCO, anything at all from *Liberty?*" he shouted as the line rang.

"Negative. She's gone quiet."

Tim Heshel answered Jesup's call before the second ring. "Fred, I do not like what I'm seeing right now."

"Do you have a track on *Liberty?*" Jesup asked somberly.

"Yeah. I hate to say this, but she's coming down awful fast."

"Where?"

"Best guess? Draw a line across the middle of the U.S. Whatever survives reentry will land within a hundred miles either side. What happened?"

"We're still trying to figure it out. Everything was going great, then wham. Preliminary indications look like she took a hit."

"No way. You and I went through this when we cleared the window."

"I know, but just the same you better recheck your logs and lock down your data. It's going to to be *Columbia* all over again."

14

Liberty plunged into the atmosphere above the Sierra Nevada Mountains, inverted and breech. The wreckage of the vertical fin and the captured satellite tore away first, ripping the robotic arm from its track, followed quickly by the payload bay doors. Caroline's body disappeared in an instant, consumed by the hellish fire of reentry. And soon after, *Liberty* shattered into pieces. The crew compartment sheared away, taking the external airlock assembly with it. Friction and heat then tore these components apart, exposing the interior of the crew compartment. Everything combustible inside was incinerated.

The fireball was clearly visible in the blue sky over Tennessee. Boaters and swimmers in Lake Cumberland stopped to view the unexpected celestial display, then wonder turned to horror with the still-fresh memory of another funeral pyre that too recently had burned across the Texas sky.

Pete was somewhere over Colorado when he finally lost sight of *Liberty*'s fiery descent. Tears streamed down his face as he prayed for the souls of his lost crewmates, but he allowed himself only a moment's grief.

After regaining control with the SAFER, he made a check of his EMU. He found no leaks in the spacesuit and his PLSS also appeared undamaged. The satellite he'd clung to had saved his life, but the question was for how long. Pete was currently the fastest human alive, but eventually friction would rob him of his speed and, like Icarus, he would fall from the heavens. His only consolation was that he'd be dead long before his body burned in the fire of reentry.

A veteran spacewalker, Pete knew his EMU systems better than the people who engineered them. His most critical problem was consumables—the twin tanks in his PLSS contained enough oxygen to last him possibly nine hours. After that, he would suffocate and die.

"Well, Pete, what are you going to do?" he asked himself. "You gonna just sit there like a wuss and wait for the end or are you going to go down swinging?"

With a quick burst from the SAFER, he reoriented himself to face in the direction he was traveling. In the distance, he saw the unmistakable shimmering of the largest object in orbit and his only hope of survival: the ISS.

The space station's altitude was roughly forty miles higher than his and both were circling the globe in the same direction. Pete knew it was possible to get ahead of the ISS while in a lower orbit, then boost himself into position for a rendezvous, as the shuttle did. The deadly variable in the Pete's survival plan was time.

15

Long Beach, California

News stations around the globe were all replaying the same snippets of amateur video, the same awful image of fireballs streaking across a cloudless sky, the remains of an object disintegrating in the Earth's upper atmosphere. Then came the carefully worded statements from the Public Affairs Office at the Johnson Space Center, a terse confirmation that during the retrieval of a commercial satellite contact with *Liberty* had been lost.

Skye turned away from the monitors and gazed out her office windows at the pier where *Aequatus* and *Argo* were moored. Both vessels were marvels of modern engineering and as technologically advanced as almost anything afloat.

The glistening white *Aequatus* was slightly wider than a football field and twice as long. Beneath her main deck, a cavernous hold ran the full length and breadth of the ship. Up to three Skye-4GR rockets could be assembled and fitted with payloads and prepared for launch in the hold, though at present only one lay inside the world's only floating rocket assembly facility. The ship's five-story superstructure could accommodate 240 crew, technicians, and guests and housed the mission control facilities for launches at sea—the purpose for which this unique ship had been designed and built.

In its first incarnation, *Argo* had searched for oil in the Gulf of Mexico. It was one of the largest self-propelled, semisubmersible vessels in the world and could accommodate sixty-eight crew and technical personnel. Eight massive columns supported the white and gray launch platform, which was two-thirds as long as *Aequatus* and twice as wide. The black columns, in turn, were borne by a pair of black pontoons, each as large as a Seawolf Class submarine. An elongated hangar jutted out from atop the platform like a large head, giving the lumbering craft the look of a mechanical eight-legged sea monster.

Skye ran through the checklist in her mind. Over the next few days, technicians would run a full diagnostic on the rocket and its payload. Once the rocket was fully prepared for flight, the stern doors of *Aequatus* would be opened and the two-hundred-foot-long launch vehicle would be rolled out on rails and onto *Argo*'s transfer hoist. The huge lifting mechanism would then climb back into place with the rocket, forming the floor of the launch platform's climate-controller hangar.

"It had to be done," Moug offered reassuringly.

"That knowledge doesn't make my actions any more palatable," Skye replied. "But this is the course I've chosen, and I will see it through."

"Your defensive strategy was sound."

"This isn't a game to me, Owen. This company is my life. I'll do whatever is necessary to ensure its survival."

Moug nodded. "The debris field extends well off the East Coast, making most, if not all, of *Liberty* unrecoverable. Also, any immediate search effort will have to deal with a tropical storm moving north from the Bahamas."

"It won't stop them from looking. The Chinese navy hasn't given up trying to find the remains of *Shenzhou-7.*"

"I'm not worried about what NASA or the Chinese might find. There's not enough left of either spacecraft to piece together what really happened."

"It will remain a mystery for conspiracy theorists," Skye said. "I wonder what they'll say."

16

Dahlgren, Virginia

"Sir," Alana Taggert called out, "I'm tracking something you might want to take a look at."

"I'll be right there, Lieutenant," Heshel replied.

He cradled the phone and left his windowless office with a cup of old coffee. Right now he needed a decent jolt of caffeine and hoped that someone had a fresh pot on in the Tracking Center.

The explosion that destroyed *Liberty* had doubled Heshel's normal duty shift as he and his staff searched for anything in orbit that might have brought the spacecraft down. While most of the orbiter had burned up during reentry, hundreds of fragments, ranging in size from a few inches to several feet, still circled the globe. Space Command had to tag each and analyze its orbit.

"What do you got?" Heshel asked.

"A fragment from *Liberty* is closing on the ISS."

"How big?"

"About seven feet long."

Heshel studied the enlarged image on Taggert's monitor. The two track lines were on a southeast course, heading toward the African coast.

"Altitude?"

"One-eighty-seven."

"That puts this thing about thirty-three miles under the ISS."

"Its altitude is increasing."

"Increasing?"

Taggert nodded. "Probably picked up some positive-Z from the explosion. That's what I wanted you to see. The two tracks are coincident at the moment, but the fragment will pull ahead in another couple orbits."

"Then there's no cause for alarm."

"True, but after what happened today—"

"I understand. Anything else that might cause ISS a problem?"

"No, the rest of the track is clear."

17

In Orbit

Passing over the west coast of Africa, Pete was well into his second solo orbit of the Earth. At most, he had seven hours of oxygen left. He looked up and saw in the distance the bright sunlit glow of the ISS, at the moment the most welcome object in his personal cosmos. It was nearly above him. Catching up with the station by riding the lower orbit had turned out to be easier than he'd expected. Then he remembered Lundy's golf analogy for orbital rendezvous: *Drive for show, putt for dough.*

Getting to this point was like a solid drive off the tee that had left him with a good lie on the fairway. More a matter of brute force than surgical precision. To *putt for dough,* Pete had to close the distance. During his first lap around the planet, he had managed to gain about six miles of altitude.

"Thirty-five miles. No wind," Pete mused as he gazed at the ISS. "I think I'll use a seven iron, see if I can put it on the green."

He flicked his wrist and fired the SAFER. Tiny jets of nitrogen gas erupted from the nozzles on his backpack, pushing him on an upward angle at the pace of a slow run.

* * *

Kelsey floated inside *Zwicky-Wolff* making careful adjustments to one of the array's constellation of detectors. The delicate work seemed an exercise in frustration due to thick inflated gloves that surrounded her hands. But she was thankful for the work as it kept her mind off the tragedy that had struck *Liberty*. People she'd spent a year training with were now dead.

As she labored, her thoughts drifted back to another array—this one in a salt mine deep under Lake Erie. Over a year ago, she had conscripted Nolan to help her upgrade the several thousand photomultiplier tubes that lined the walls of a six-story-deep cube of water. The job required several hours' dive time and the tedium of the work was only broken by Nolan's playful nature. Even when they were growing up together, he had possessed a Zenlike ability to find satisfaction in whatever he was doing.

Kelsey finished the adjustment and closed the housing on the detector. Looking at the Earth, she caught sight of the Hawaiian Islands and thought of him. As hard as she'd worked to realize this lifelong dream, a part of her already looked forward to returning home and resuming the rest of her life.

"C'mon, baby," Pete urged. "Just a little closer."

His body ached, stiff from over eight hours of inactivity. He had had to limit his movements during his orbital trek because of Newton's First Law of Motion. Unrestrained in microgravity, any movement of his arms or legs might put him into spin, and to halt the spin he would have to waste some of the SAFER's precious nitrogen propellant, all of which he needed to pull this rendezvous off. Pete knew his attempt to reach the ISS was a long shot of lotteryesque proportions, but he did all he could to keep his odds from deteriorating any further.

What had started out like a shining point of light in the distance had, in five orbits, grown larger and more substantial. Distinct elements of the station were now clearly visible. It was the most beautiful thing he'd ever seen.

Pete took a sip of water—his mouth parched from breathing bottled air—and began plotting his next move. Only a few short bursts remained in the SAFER, leaving him with only one real chance for success.

The ISS was, he guessed, less than a quarter-mile above him. At this moment, he would have given his right arm for a laser range finder and access to *Liberty*'s computer. He drew an imaginary line down the main axis of the station, then extended it another hundred feet in its forward line of travel. When he found his mark, he twisted the joystick and squeezed another burst of thrust from the SAFER.

". . . o yo . . . py? O . . . r."

The crackle of static and broken syllables startled Kelsey. Other than her regular radio checks, all she'd heard in the last two hours was the sound of her own breathing. She stopped work, straining to listen.

"ISS . . . c . . . py? . . . ver." The signal sounded stronger, but the voice was just above a whisper.

"This is ISS. Over."

"Tha . . . k God. Kels . . . y, is . . . at you?"

Kelsey paled. The voice she heard belonged to a dead man. "Pete?"

"Kelsey," Molly's voice blurted in. "Who are you talking to out there?"

"She's talk . . . g to me," Pete answered weakly.

"Pete!" Kelsey's said excitedly, her voice a near shout. "Where are you?"

"Hundred feet," he gasped, ". . . front of station."

Kelsey turned around and saw a tiny figure rising up in space ahead of the ISS.

"Low on air," Pete continued. "SAFER gone."

Kelsey tethered her tools and grabbed the control module for her SAFER. "I'm going after him, Molly. Meet me at the airlock with a med kit."

"I'll contact Mission Control—"

"No!" Pete croaked, cutting her off. "Can't tell Houston."

"But we must," Molly countered.

"Do as he asks for now," Kelsey pleaded. "Let's just concentrate on getting him aboard."

"Very well," Molly acquiesced. "We'll be ready for you at the airlock."

Kelsey picked a point in Pete's line of travel and fired her SAFER.

"Pete, I'm coming. Just hold on."

"I . . . air . . . gone . . ."

"Hold on, Pete. I'm almost there."

Pete didn't reply. Kelsey sped down from the array, hoping she hadn't misjudged his rate of ascent. It took less than a minute to close the distance, and Pete was coming up fast. She fired the SAFER to stop, then reached out to grab his arm, but his spacesuit was too thick for her gloved hand to find purchase. Her attempt caused Pete to spin forward, his ascent unchanged.

Desperate, Kelsey wrapped both her arms around Pete's legs. She had him—upside down—but now they were both ascending and slowly rotating. She pulled her right hand back and used the SAFER to halt all their motion relative to the ISS.

"Pete, can you hear me?"

No answer.

She carefully maneuvered Pete so he was facing her. Droplets of condensation clung to the inside of his visor. His eyes were closed, his lips parted and tinged with blue.

"I have him," Kelsey announced. "We're coming in."

"Understood," Molly replied.

The two minutes it took to fly back to the station's airlock and close the hatch seemed like an eon. The display on Pete's suit reported a negligible amount of oxygen. Kelsey prayed it was enough to stave off death or permanent damage.

Molly and Valentina watched through the observation window as air repressurized the chamber. Kelsey stripped off her gloves and moved quickly to remove Pete's helmet. It detached from his space suit with a sucking hiss. Pete's face had turned ashen gray.

"Breathe, Pete, breathe," Kelsey implored, lightly slapping his cheeks.

The change came slowly at first, and then Pete's skin grew noticeably warmer in color. He coughed and gasped, like a drowned man revived. Kelsey braced her feet and held him so he wouldn't tumble into a bulkhead. He continued to shake, his chest wracked with spasms, his eyes wide and glassy.

"It's all right, Pete. You made it. I don't know how you pulled it off, but you made it."

18

As soon as the airlock equalized with the station, Molly and Valentina opened the hatch. Kelsey, still in her EMU, cradled Pete in her arms. The unconscious spacewalker's head dripped with sweat and condensation. Valentina quickly detached Pete's spent PLSS, then pulled him through into Node 1 where she and Molly had more room to remove the rest of his spacesuit. The two women worked quickly, then Valentina, the expedition's medical officer, began tending to her patient.

Kelsey had her helmet off by the time Molly floated through the hatch to assist her.

"Bloody miraculous," Molly said as she removed the PLSS from Kelsey's back.

Kelsey pulled off her gloves, her hands quivering. "I'm still shaking. When I heard his voice, it was like . . ." Her voice faltered, unable to capture the words to describe her emotions.

"Let's get the rest of that off you," Molly said sympathetically.

Though officially listed as a one-person job, donning or doffing the EMU was actually quite difficult without a second pair of hands. Once Kelsey was out of her suit, the two women glided into Node 1.

"How is he?" Kelsey asked.

"Unconscious, but stable," Valentina replied. "His airway is clear and he doesn't appear to have suffered any physical injuries."

"Prognosis?" Molly inquired.

Valentina shrugged. "It depends on how long he was deprived of oxygen."

"He was unconscious when I reached him," Kelsey said, "but we spoke just a moment before. It couldn't have been more than a couple minutes until I had him in the airlock."

"Hypoxia is a very tricky condition. If we got to him soon enough, he'll recover fully. Otherwise, there could be complications. For now, I think we should move him to the Hab and make him comfortable."

"Then we should contact Mission Control," Molly said.

"Pete said we shouldn't."

"That could be the hypoxia," Valentina offered. "It creates a state much like drunkenness."

"He sounded pretty emphatic about it," Kelsey countered, "and I think we should wait until he comes around to find out why."

Molly considered this, then turned to Valentina. "Do you need to consult with Surgeon?"

"*Nyet.* There's nothing else to be done."

"Molly, as far as Mission Control knows, Pete died with everyone else on *Liberty.* Waiting a little while before contacting them won't hurt anything."

"What about his family?"

"For the moment, I think his wishes override every other concern."

"Very well, then," Molly decided. "We'll wait till Pete comes around."

* * *

Pete lay in a sleeping bag, fastened to the wall of the Habitation Module. Nearby, Kelsey floated, reading an e-book while watching over him. From their first meeting, Kelsey had thought of the stocky Hoosier as a physically imposing man. It amazed her now to see how much of that perceived strength the ordeal in space had robbed him of.

"God, my neck hurts," Pete rasped, his voice barely above a whisper.

"Easy, Pete," Kelsey said softly. "Do you want some water?"

Pete nodded. Kelsey lifted a squeeze bottle up to his mouth.

"Take it slow."

Pete gagged on his first attempt to swallow. A few errant droplets escaped from the corner of his mouth. Kelsey blotted at them with a cloth before they floated away. She then switched on the station intercom.

"Val, Molly. He's awake."

"I was in space, running out of air," Pete recalled, trying to piece events together. "How did I—"

"Shhh. I was outside when you arrived. I pulled you in."

"*Liberty*. Everyone's dead."

"We know," Kelsey said softly. "Mission Control told us shortly after it happened. A terrible accident."

Pete shook his head. "Deliberate."

Kelsey's face blanched. Just then, Valentina and Molly entered the module from Node 1, the Russian gliding straight to the end of the module to examine her patient. Kelsey moved to the middle of the module where Molly waited.

"Molly," Kelsey said in a low voice, "Pete just told me something very disturbing."

"What?"

"He said whatever happened to *Liberty* was deliberate."

"Are you serious? How could that be?"

"I don't know."

"Do you know where you are?" Valentina asked as she fastened a pressure cuff to Pete's arm.

"Space station," Pete replied hoarsely.

"What day is it?"

"Mission elapsed time—day ten, maybe eleven. How long was I out?"

"About four hours," Valentina answered with a trace of a smile—her patient had demonstrated both memory and cognitive function. "I'll get you something for the pain and you should continue to rest for a while. I think you'll be fully recovered in a few days."

Overhearing Valentina's prognosis, Kelsey and Molly moved to the end of the module.

"Is your patient ready for a few questions?" Molly asked.

"*Da.* I think we got to him before there was any lasting damage."

"Pete, what happened?" Kelsey asked.

"Satellite—the one we launched before docking here. It didn't make orbit. We went to retrieve it, bring it back for repairs. Caroline was in the bay. I was out on the end of the arm to make the grab. We got it, and while Tosh was pulling it in, I found out why it didn't make orbit. Cryo tank blew. Strange, too."

"How so?" Molly asked.

"The tank blew out on opposite sides, I could look right

through it. And the holes, not that big and perfectly round. Like something shot right through it."

"What about *Liberty?*" Kelsey asked.

"It was while I was checking out the satellite that something happened in the crew compartment—I don't know what, but I could hear the alarms going off over my headset. The hull was breached—I saw two plumes shooting out the flight-deck roof. She was bleeding atmosphere fast. A second later, I got knocked off the satellite and went tumbling into space. By the time I recovered from the spin, *Liberty's* whole tail section was gone and she was heading straight down."

"What makes you suspect this was deliberate?" Molly asked. "Couldn't *Liberty* simply have been hit by something in orbit?"

Pete shook his head. "Once, maybe, but not three times. And whatever hit her went in one side and out the other. A piece of space junk couldn't do that."

"He's right," Kelsey said. "Even at orbital velocity, a projectile crashing through one side of *Liberty* would've lost a lot of its kinetic energy, assuming it even survived the initial impact in one piece."

"Like gun shot to the head," Valentina concurred. "The bullet gets flattened against the skull before it punches through. Once inside, it doesn't have enough energy left to exit other side, so it just rattles around in the brain."

"That is a truly revolting image," Molly declared.

"Unfortunately, it is one I saw many times in emergency room."

"Disgusting or not, it illustrates my point," Kelsey continued. "A solid projectile would lose a lot of its energy to deformation and fragmentation. The initial impact would have been devastating, but there shouldn't be enough residual velocity for it to continue straight through the flight-deck floor and out the other side. Only a focused beam of high-energy laser could do that."

"Are you suggesting that an energy weapon has been placed in orbit?"

"That's one possibility. I've seen proposals for ground- and air-based lasers as well, though none that are beyond rudimentary testing."

"I think we're making some very large leaps here," Molly said, "and with only one person's word to go on. Begging your pardon, Pete, but there could be a multitude of explanations to account for what you saw, or thought you saw, before the explosion."

"I know what I saw."

"Perhaps, and perhaps not. I think it best we contact Houston and give them at least one piece of good news today."

"No," Pete said emphatically. "*Liberty* and that satellite were destroyed for a reason."

"And what might that be?"

"I don't know, but if I saw something I wasn't supposed to, letting the outside world know I'm here could be dangerous."

"Pete," Molly said, her tone softer, "I don't mean to sound like I'm belittling your powers of observation, but based on what you've told us, you didn't have time to take anything more than a cursory glance at the satellite. And what you saw of *Liberty* was fleeting at best."

Pete thought for a moment. "What about my helmet camera? It should have a record of everything I saw."

"But then Mission Control should've seen it as well,"

Molly countered. "And we've received no warning from them about a space weapon."

"Houston didn't see any of the EVA. *Liberty*'s CCTV and part of the comm system went out while Caroline and I were getting prepped," Pete explained.

"We have to take a look at that video before making any decision about contacting Houston," Kelsey advised.

"Do it," Molly agreed.

Kelsey shot up to Node 1, then turned ninety degrees and pulled herself into the airlock. Both spacesuits were stowed in racks against the wall. She retrieved Pete's helmet, still fitted with work lights and a digital video camera, and removed the unit's flash memory card.

"Got it," Kelsey announced on her return.

She slipped the card into one of the wall-mounted computer stations. The screen flickered, then a still image of the ISS taken from a distance appeared. In it, Kelsey saw herself en route to Pete. The others hovered around her, watching the monitor.

"Did you leave your camera on the whole time you were out there?"

"I must've," Pete admitted. "After all that happened, I guess I forgot to turn it off."

Kelsey checked the card's statistics. "Pete, there's over nine hours of video here. You've got a full record of what has to be one of the greatest survival epics in history."

"Trust me, most of it is pretty boring," Pete replied. "What you want to see is in the first hour."

Kelsey reset the time index to 00:00 and fast-forwarded through the video in time-lapse stills.

"Start there," Pete said.

The still image showed the charred foil covering the

side of the satellite. Moving at normal speed, they peered with Pete into the blasted propulsion unit.

"Hold it there," Pete said. "That's what I was telling you about."

The still image showed the aluminum skin of the tank splayed open like the withered petals of a scorched metal flower. The work lights on Pete's helmet shone down into the empty hold of the tank, and on the opposite side was a similar forced opening.

"That's odd," Kelsey said. "Take a look at the ends of these shards."

She zoomed in tightly on the ends of scorched flower petals, panning them slowly, one by one. The sides of each petal were jagged—indicative of the blast that had violently torn the metal—but the tips all ended in smooth, concave arcs.

"If you bend them back into place—" Valentina mused.

"—they would form a circle," Molly concurred.

"More precisely, an ellipse," Kelsey said. "A perfectly elliptical hole."

"That ain't no manufacturing defect," Pete said, relieved the evidence bore him out.

"A metal-to-metal collision wouldn't make a nice clean hole like that," Kelsey said, "but a laser would."

"Let's see the rest of it," Molly ordered.

The destruction of *Liberty* unfolded exactly as Pete had described it. The three women watched in horror as the wounded orbiter plunged downward, knowing they'd just watched the death of six fellow astronauts.

Pete looked away, having relived the moment too many times already.

When *Liberty* disappeared from view, Kelsey turned off

the replay. "I think Pete's interpretation of these events is valid. Those holes in *Liberty* were definitely not caused by micrometeorites or space junk."

"I'm convinced," Molly said, "but we still must tell someone what we know. Mission Control has to see this video."

Pete shook his head. "You saw what happened to *Liberty,* Molly. God knows who's behind this, but if word got out about me and that video—"

The threat hanging over all their heads was unimaginable.

"We've got to get this information into the right hands," Kelsey said, "without broadcasting it to the world and painting a big bull's-eye on the station. I think I know how to do it."

19

Pearl Harbor

After a dozen hours of near-comatose sleep, Kilkenny arose just before dawn and set out from the hotel on a ten-mile run. A steady breeze off the ocean cooled him as he ran, shaking off the previous days of confinement aboard *Virginia.* By the time he looped back to the hotel, the sun was cresting over the Koolau Range and the temperature was starting to rise.

When he reached his room, he found the message light on his phone blinking—it was from Grin. He returned the call.

"Great, you're back," Grin said, relieved. "Have you seen the news?"

"Nope." Kilkenny sat on the edge of the bed and removed his Nikes. "What's going on?"

"I don't know the details, just turn on your TV."

Grin was the kind of guy who took most of what he saw or heard in the news with a certain jaded cynicism—especially politics. The last time Kilkenny had heard this tone in his friend's voice was on September 11. He grabbed the remote and switched on Fox. They were cycling to the top of the news rotation. Lead story: *Space Shuttle Liberty Destroyed.* Kilkenny's heart sank.

"Oh my God."

"Yeah," Grin said, echoing his friend's concern.

Kilkenny turned up the volume and carefully listened to the report. The space beat reporter in Houston quickly ran down the facts as they were known, summarizing what had been a very successful mission up until the disaster that claimed the lives of all seven people aboard. France and Russia joined the United States in mourning the lost men and women of *Liberty.*

"You okay?"

"Yeah, it's just for a second there—"

"I know. I thought the same thing. Can you get word to her?"

"I don't know. NASA's probably swamped right now."

"Tell you what. Meet me downstairs. We'll grab a quick bite and head over to the lab for a little Grin-at-sleight-of-hand-dot-com."

"You're going to hack NASA?"

"If that's what it takes."

"Give me five minutes."

Kilkenny and Grin entered their makeshift computer lab, a small space in one of the recently renovated office buildings on the naval base. As their computers booted up, Grin switched on his iPod. The plaintive opening chords of the Chieftains album *Tears of Stone* wailed from the tiny speakers.

Nine days of e-mail awaited Kilkenny when he launched his computer—some of it junk, most of it work-related or personal. Skimming through the listings, one immediately stuck out.

"She beat us to it."

"Who?" Grin asked.

"Kelsey. She sent an e-mail. It's dated just a few hours ago."

Grin rolled his chair over to Kilkenny's desk. "Well, open it."

Kilkenny selected the message. A warning appeared on his screen that the message was encrypted.

"NASA lets her do that?"

"Sure, and we both have security clearances. It's only for personal communication."

"Mash notes, eh?"

Kilkenny refrained from comment and typed in his key to unlock the message. A bar graph along the bottom of his screen quickly filled, displaying the percentage of information decrypted. In a blink, the gibberish was replaced by readable plain-text.

Nolan,

I'm sending you this file because I know you will discreetly get it into the right hands.

By now, you've heard what happened in Liberty. It wasn't an accident. I'm certain of this because Pete Washabaugh survived the attack and barely managed to make it here alive. Attached is a portion of the video record from his spacewalk that clearly shows what he saw.

We've watched the video and are convinced that someone deliberately attacked Liberty and murdered her crew. We also believe the weapon used is an energy beam, and maybe some image enhancement of this video can verify that. We don't know who is behind the attack, but we think it has something to do with the satellite that Liberty was sent to retrieve. The video clearly shows the satellite was also attacked, which is why it failed to make orbit.

My crewmates and I believe our lives would be endangered if word of Pete's survival and his video record became general knowledge. That's why I'm contacting you, Nolan. We need your help.

All my love,
Kelsey

"Well, that was certainly no French postcard," Grin said. "But at least she's okay."

"Yeah, let's take a look at the clip."

Kilkenny selected the attached file. Immediately, a window containing a multimedia program filled the screen. The clip showed Washabaugh's inspection of the damaged satellite and the destruction of *Liberty*. The last frame froze with *Liberty* spiraling down toward the Earth.

"Damn," Grin said soberly.

"It's never easy watching something like that—knowing at that moment people are either dead or dying."

Kilkenny closed the video clip viewer. Kelsey's plea for help remained in the center of his screen. He hit the reply button.

Kelsey,

I understand. I love you too.

Nolan

20

Xiyuan, China
August 12

Huang Zhanfu moved purposefully through the gallery, the soles of his black tasseled loafers tapping softly on the polished marble floor. Artwork from various periods in China's long history adorned the walls, a collection impressive in the quality of the pieces and their estimated worth. Any museum would be proud to house such a display, but this gallery never opened to the public. Few, outside senior party officials and those who worked for the Ministry of State Security, even knew of its existence—and the security force that protected the *Goujia Anquan Bu*'s well-hidden compound were tasked with keeping it that way.

As Huang entered the anteroom, the minister's executive assistant lifted the phone and announced his arrival. He then rose and met Huang at the door to the minister's office.

"Chief Huang," the man said with a respectful nod, "the minister will see you now."

The ornate wooden door glided open silently and closed behind Huang with a barely audible click. That such a massive object could pivot with such ease impressed the head of the ministry's Tenth Bureau, a man who specialized in matters of science and technology. The door, like every other surface enclosing the office, was thick with soundproofing and electromagnetic shielding—a vault for some of the nation's most carefully guarded secrets.

Huang glanced out the ribbon of windows that ran along one side of the large office. In keeping with the position, the minister's office possessed a splendid view of one of the capital's most treasured landscapes: the Summer Palace.

Tian Yi sat and watched as Huang approached. At fifty-nine, the minister was a decade Huang's senior. Before his appointment as minister, Tian had held Huang's post, and it was his handling of intelligence-gathering operations in the United States during the nineties that had made him a clear favorite for the top job when the previous minister retired. Tian then tapped his young protégé as his successor in the Tenth Bureau.

Both men wore crisply tailored business suits, Tian in a solid, dark blue and Huang in a lightweight summer gray. They exchanged bows and Tian motioned for Huang to take a seat.

"So, what is this urgent matter that we need to discuss?" Tian asked.

"The American shuttle."

Tian sighed. "Two tragedies in so short a time."

"Yes, but I suspect the Americans believe theirs was not an accident."

The hairless freckled skin covering Tian's head tightened as his eyes narrowed. "Continue."

"Our agents monitoring activity at the Pearl Harbor

naval base in Hawaii intercepted two interesting communications. The first was an e-mail sent by Kelsey Newton to Nolan Kilkenny."

"I have heard those names before."

"The operation against Moy Electronics," Huang offered.

"Ah," Tian replied, recalling the failed attempt to secure American encryption technology.

"Newton is an astronaut, currently serving aboard the International Space Station. She is also Kilkenny's fiancée. Kilkenny works for a technology consortium and is currently working on an undetermined project with the navy—all we know is that it has something to do with the new submarine *Virginia*. A few hours after the shuttle exploded, Newton sent an encrypted message to Kilkenny. Our cryptography section is currently working on the message, but all they have been able to determine is that it contains a very large file."

"Sounds like nothing more than a private exchange between lovers, perhaps something pornographic to *comfort* this Kilkenny during his woman's long absence."

"I don't believe so. According to records from the internal network and telephone switchboard at Pearl Harbor, within minutes of opening Newton's message, Kilkenny placed a call to Langley, Virginia. He dialed the direct line to the office of your counterpart at the CIA. At this moment, Kilkenny is onboard a military aircraft headed toward Washington. He did not return to his hotel room to pack for this trip."

"Why do you believe this has something to do with their shuttle?" Tian asked.

Huang had conversed this way many times with Tian.

When he was a new recruit, the minister saw promise in him, honed his intellect, and taught him the skills, both analytical and political, needed to succeed in the world of intelligence. Tian had taught him that intelligence is like the ancient game of Wei Ch'i, where the ability to think many moves beyond the current play is absolutely necessary for victory. Now, he was probing Huang, seeing just how far his student had followed this line of thinking.

"While your suggestion that Newton's attached file might contain inspirational imagery is an interesting one, I doubt Kilkenny would wish to share such material with the head of the CIA. And if he was that kind of man, forwarding the attachment would have saved both the time and expense of his hasty flight to Washington. Based on the reaction we have seen so far, it is clear the Newton's message contains something of great importance to the American government."

"A reasonable conclusion, but how have you divined that the contents of this message relate to the shuttle incident?"

"It's the most plausible theory," Huang replied. "Newton has been in space too brief a time to have performed any scientific work. On the same day that a shuttle is lost, Newton sends an encrypted message to a person she trusts. This implies that she did not trust the open channels at NASA with the contents of her message; therefore the message must have nothing to do with her duties aboard the station. You taught me that secrecy and urgency are often the companions of bad news—the destruction of a shuttle is bad news."

"But the loss of the shuttle is no secret."

"True, but the reason for the loss is."

"And why should we be concerned?" Tian asked. "The Western news networks will dissect this event for months, and in the end NASA will release an official finding."

"Our official finding in the *Schenzhou-7* inquiry left much unanswered and our space program remains grounded," Huang replied, somewhat bitterly. "The engineers could find no sign of a fault in any of the spacecraft's systems leading up to the moment contact was lost. While a collision with a micrometeoroid was listed as the probable cause, analysis of our launch window shows it was clear of such dangers. The loss of a second spacecraft in orbit, so soon after our accident, strikes me as curious. Newton's message and the American's reaction to it have amplified that curiosity."

Tian considered what he'd heard carefully and could find no fault in Huang's reasoning.

"What do you propose?"

"Our first task is to decode and analyze Newton's message. Cryptography estimates several days to a week to accomplish this. As a secondary line of inquiry, I recommend that we begin surveillance of Kilkenny in hope that his movements may reveal a clue to his intentions."

"Approved. Keep me informed of your progress. And Huang . . . good thinking."

21

Palmdale, California

Inside the clean room, Anson Rainey observed as the engineers responsible for the satellite's power systems made their final inspection. Like Rainey, they all were dressed in white sterile suits, surgeons of a sort working in an operating room far cleaner than any hospital and shielded for all forms of external electromagnetic radiation.

Zeus-2 was a long and slender spacecraft, its outer skin a dull black composite that reflected nothing save its purpose. It was a weapon and Rainey had created it.

This was the second satellite constructed by the small team of elite engineers who composed Skye Aerospace's secretive Defense Systems Group. The first, a prototype, had gone into orbit in January 2001. There, it proved the essentials of Rainey's elegant design to Pentagon skeptics.

Rainey remembered the day C. J. Skye paid a visit to the DSG facility and announced that the government had awarded Skye Aerospace a lucrative contract to build the orbiting portion of the nation's nuclear missile defense shield. The champagne flowed and bonuses were handed out as Skye toasted the groundbreaking work of her talented engineers.

While the money was great, and he appreciated the praise of his employer, neither was the driving force behind Rainey's work on the Zeus project. What motivated him was proliferation. In an era when the United States and Russia were dismantling ICBMs, long-range missiles and various weapons of mass destruction were blossoming, for the most part, in nations where the government ruled by the barrel of a gun. Duty was a quality instilled in Rainey by his father, and that he was using his mind and skills to protect his country was a source of great pride.

Daddy would have been right proud, Rainey thought, *that his paunchy, nearsighted son would engineer a way to protect the good old U. S. of A.*

"Power systems are go, boss," the lead power engineer reported.

"Nice work, ladies and gentlemen," Rainey called out. "*Zeus*-2 is now certified ready to fly. Let's get it buttoned up and prepped for the trip to Long Beach."

22

Washington, D.C.

The driver left Peng Shi off near the corner of Seventeenth Street and Pennsylvania Avenue, then merged back into the flow of Washington traffic where he would circle until called upon. Dressed in khaki pants and a yellow golf shirt, Peng easily blended in with the people milling about the heart of the Washington. With an expensive digital camera dangling from his neck and a camera bag off his shoulder, he was mistaken by most people for a Japanese tourist.

When the order for this surveillance came in, Peng quickly set aside his normal duties at the embassy as a junior attaché with the office for economic development and leaped at the chance to do some fieldwork. Peng gleaned two important facts from the subject background material provided by the ministry: Nolan Kilkenny was currently involved in high-tech venture capitalism and had previously served with distinction in the United States Navy's Special Forces.

That same brief also led Peng to believe that his subject's initial destination would be the CIA's sprawling campus in Langley, Virginia. Instead, the government car sent to collect Kilkenny from Andrews Air Force Base brought him directly to the Old Executive Office Building, right next door to the White House.

Completed in 1888 as office space for the navy and the Departments of State and War, the OEOB's current occupants included senior White House staff and the vice president. While the purpose of Kilkenny's visit was still unknown, the message he brought with him had clearly found an audience at the highest levels of the American government.

Peng found a spot on the opposite side of Seventeenth Street from which to observe the main entrance to the OEOB. Feigning an interest in the building's overly ornate French Second Empire styling, Peng raised his camera and squeezed off a rapid succession of frames, capturing his subject as he moved up the granite stair.

Kilkenny stopped at a security checkpoint just inside the building and was quickly granted entry.

They're expecting him, Peng noted.

"Hello, Nolan."

Kilkenny had just passed through the security at the main entrance of the Old Executive Office Building when he heard the familiar, sultry voice. He quickly located Roxanne Tao standing near the information desk, waiting for him. She was dressed in a sleek black blazer and skirt with a matching silk blouse. Her long black hair was done up in a twist and a pair of simple golden hoops dangled from her earlobes.

"Did you get my suit?" he asked.

Tao nodded. "Your father went through your closet, I made sure it all matched."

"Thanks. He's as color-blind as I am."

"I'm surprised you didn't have one with you."

"I was working on a submarine with Grin. Not much call for formal attire."

"Still, weren't you a Boy Scout or something—*be prepared* and all that?" Tao asked sarcastically. "Here. I had an interesting time getting it through security. I told them I was a delivery girl for a Chinese Laundry."

"You look more like a lobbyist," Kilkenny said as he relieved her of the garment bag.

He then disappeared into the men's room to exchange the rumpled casual attire he'd worn during the long flight for something more appropriate to the level of this meeting. He returned five minutes later shaved and clad in a charcoal-gray suit and white button-down shirt accented with a Jerry Garcia tie.

Tao carefully appraised his transformation. "Much better."

Peng studied the Asian woman who had met Kilkenny in the lobby and found her arrestingly beautiful. After handing Kilkenny the garment bag, she remained in the lobby waiting. Peng took advantage of the situation and captured her image with the precision optics mated to his Canon EOS-10D. When Kilkenny returned, the pair moved into the building's interior and out of sight.

And now, I wait, Peng thought.

Leaning up against a lamppost, he scrolled through the images stored in the camera's memory. Most were worthless, but a few clearly captured Kilkenny and the woman. He selected two images—one of the woman head on, the other in profile—and uploaded them through a thin cable into his digital phone. Seconds later, the image files were streaming through the air into a computer inside the PRC embassy on Connecticut Avenue where a facial recognition program would attempt identify the woman.

Kilkenny and Tao descended to the lower level, where their ID cards permitted them access to the tunnel leading to the White House. They were met at the checkpoint on the opposite end by a thin, silver-haired man, impeccably attired—CIA Director Jackson Barnett.

"Quite a bombshell you've uncovered, Nolan," Barnett said as he shook Kilkenny's hand. "This way."

Barnett led them through the warren beneath the executive mansion to a guarded situation room. Inside, Kilkenny saw five people but recognized only Darcy Oates from her regular appearances in the news. The president's national security advisor was seen by both friends and foes of the current administration as one of the brightest people serving the president and a serious contender for the top job a few years down the road. Barnett gave Oates a nod.

"Let's begin, shall we," Oates said, cutting through the low buzz of conversation. "I believe some introductions are in order."

Everyone took their seats with Oates at the head of the dark oak conference table. From her left sat Ben Kowalkowski of the NRO, Tim Heshel of U.S. Space Command, and Linda Ryerson and Fred Jesup of NASA. Barnett, Tao, and Kilkenny sat on her right. FBI Director Ethan McRae sat on the opposite end.

"The purpose of this meeting," Oates began, "is to discuss the incident involving the space shuttle *Liberty*."

"My people are still trying to determine the cause,"

Ryerson jumped in quickly. "A full integral investigation is under way, but it's only been two days since the accident. It's still too early for anything conclusive."

Ryerson looked rattled: The abrupt shift into crisis-management mode had clearly affected her. Jesup nodded in agreement with his boss. The darkened folds of skin beneath his eyes bespoke the hours of sleep he'd forgone since the loss of *Liberty.*

"I appreciate the efforts NASA is making to thoroughly investigate this disaster," Oates continued, "but not the interruption. Recent evidence has come to light that points to a deliberate rather than accidental cause. If true, this matter clearly moves into the realm of national security and everything we discuss today falls under the Official Secrets Act. Director Barnett, if you please."

Barnett wiped his wire-frame bifocals, rose, and walked over to a large wall monitor.

"What you are about to see was received yesterday by my associate, Mr. Kilkenny," Barnett began, his voice a smooth Carolina drawl. "I believe you'll find it, as I did, rather disturbing. It's a brief clip, so please hold your questions until the end."

The lights in the room dimmed and the monitor filled with an image of a satellite spinning against a dark, star-filled background. The shallow white curve of an astronaut's protective helmet arced across the bottom of the screen.

Having seen the clip several times, Kilkenny instead watched the reaction of the other people in the room. Jesup was the most visibly affected by hearing once more the voices of *Liberty*'s crew—people he considered friends—then witnessing the manner of their deaths. The clip ended and the room lights came back up.

"W-where did you get this?" Jesup stammered.

"That's the one piece of good news that I can provide today," Barnett replied. "As you can see in the clip, astronaut Pete Washabaugh was outside the shuttle at the time of the attack. He survived the destruction of *Liberty* and, in a display of survival heroics comparable to Shackelton, managed to rendezvous with the International Space Station."

"Son of a gun," Jesup said with a broad smile. He then turned to Kilkenny. "Why did Pete send this to you?"

"He didn't," Kilkenny replied. "Kelsey Newton did."

"Who?" Kowalkowski asked.

"Dr. Newton is a member of the current expedition crew aboard the ISS," Ryerson answered.

"She is also my associate's fiancée," Barnett added. "Upon recovering Washabaugh from space, Dr. Newton and her crewmates quickly realized the gravity of their situation and wisely sought a secure means of letting us know something terribly wrong had transpired. While not in our employ, Mr. Kilkenny does have a working relationship with the agency that to date has proven quite useful."

"What I don't understand is why anyone would attack our shuttle," Ryerson said. "And how did they do it?"

"The how is easy," Kowalkowski answered. "Star Wars."

"Star Wars?"

"Under Reagan it was called Star Wars," Kowalkowski explained. "Later it evolved into NMD, but whatever the name, the idea was still the same. Every missile defense concept has always included some form of space-based weapon—either energy beam or kinetic."

"Are you saying that *Liberty* was destroyed by an American missile defense weapon?" Ryerson asked, barely masking her anger.

"The United States has not deployed any form of space-based missile defense system," Oates replied firmly. "Nor has the government authorized recent testing for any part of our NMD strategy. Miss Ryerson, the answer to your question is an emphatic *no*—the United States did not shoot down *Liberty*."

"Ma'am, I didn't mean to imply that at all," Kowalkowski said to Ryerson. "My point was some form of space-based weapon is the likely mechanism of this tragedy. I have no knowledge regarding who actually pulled the trigger."

"Kelsey believes that the weapon used was an energy beam—a laser," Kilkenny offered. "Getting back to your first question, Ms. Ryerson, whoever did this wasn't after the shuttle, initially. They were after that communications satellite."

"Oh, shit," Jesup blurted out before he could stop himself.

"You care to explain that deduction?" Kowalkowski asked suspiciously, ignoring Jesup's outburst.

"Sure." Kilkenny checked his notes and punched a time index into the computer connected to the wall display. The damaged side of the satellite appeared on the screen. "This is what Washabaugh saw when he retrieved the satellite. Note that both sides of this tank are blown out and that the openings are exactly opposite each other. There's no way those ruptures are the result of metal fatigue or an *Apollo 13*–style explosion inside the tank. Something burned a hole straight through and ignited the fuel."

"Dr. Newton is a well-respected physicist," Barnett

added. "This image was enough to convince her that an energy weapon had been used to disable this satellite. What she saw of the damage inflicted on *Liberty* served only to bolster that opinion."

"So *Liberty* was attacked because we sent it to retrieve that satellite," Jesup concluded.

"That appears to be the most plausible scenario," Kilkenny replied.

"Which then raises the likelihood of a security breach," Barnett said.

"How so?" Tao asked. "I knew *Liberty* was launching that satellite—it was on CNN."

"Oh, that's right, Roxanne," Barnett said. "You and Nolan haven't been briefed on the satellite's true nature. Colonel, would you do the honors?"

"Ma'am, what you saw on the news was our cover story. The satellite *Liberty* took up was the first in a new generation of reconnaissance satellites, code-named *Oculus*. These new birds were designed to replace our aging *Lacrosse* radar imaging satellites. Since we don't want anyone to know about these new ones, we're mixing our launches in with those for a commercial constellation being put up by the shuttle for ZetaComm. ZetaComm also happens to be the contractor for our satellites."

"Convenient," Kilkenny said.

"Both sides do benefit from this arrangement."

Tao turned to Barnett. "So, someone who knew about *Oculus* must have leaked that information."

Barnett nodded.

"Colonel, how many people knew about your covert launch program?" Oates asked.

"Outside the NRO, somewhere in the neighborhood of

thirty, mostly ZetaComm technicians involved with prepping the satellite for launch and a few key people at NASA. I can have my staff pull together a current list of names."

Jesup's face reddened, still angry at being left out of the loop regarding his shuttle's payload.

"That'll be a starting point for us," McRae said. "We'll put together a task force out of Quantico to run down those leads."

"Good," Oates said. "The other half of this investigation falls to the CIA—identifying which nation may have placed a weapon system in orbit."

"Feel free to correct me if I'm wrong," Kilkenny said, "but isn't the attack on *Liberty* an act of war?"

Oates studied Kilkenny carefully before answering. "Any provocative act, taken at the wrong time, could be construed as an act of war. Our flying U2s over the Soviet Union, and the subsequent downing of one of those planes, could have easily been seen in that way."

"But isn't there a sort of international gentlemen's agreement about spy satellites? We don't shoot down theirs and they don't shoot down ours."

"Yes, but in the decades since that quiet understanding was reached, several other nations have acquired the ability to place technological assets into orbit. Some of these nations are ruled by people for whom the term *gentlemen* does not apply."

"I think we're getting a little ahead of ourselves," Barnett interjected. "Above us are four people aboard a space station, and somewhere in orbit with them is a weapon that could end their lives. We must find out whose hand guides that weapon, and our efforts must be both quick and quiet. We must act as through we suspect nothing, pretending that what happened two days ago was a tragic accident. Whatever action the president decides to take in the pursuit of justice, we here must not forget that four more lives depend upon our efforts."

23

Dahlgren, Virginia

"—and here in the Tracking Center is where we keep tabs on pretty much everything in orbit, right down to stuff about the size of a baseball," Heshel explained as he led Kilkenny and Tao back to his office.

Bright orange cards hanging from Kilkenny's and Tao's necks identified them as visitors to the facility. Military and civilian personnel working at U.S. Space Command all wore photo IDs with embedded chips that permitted or denied access to areas depending on the person's clearance. Heshel swiped his ID through the reader by his office door, then held it open for his guests.

"Last count, we were tracking nearly ten thousand objects," Heshel continued.

"And you know where everything is at any given moment?" Tao asked.

"Pretty much. Coffee?"

Both Kilkenny and Tao shook their heads as they sat down.

"How do you do that?" Tao asked.

"I'll show you."

Heshel jockeyed his mouse around a pad decorated

with the image of an F117A. As he rapidly clicked away with the pointing device, one of his workstation monitors filled with an image of the Earth.

"That's the Fence," Heshel said, referring to a thin, transparent plane of pale yellow that extended from the southern United States straight up into space.

"How far up does it reach?" Kilkenny asked.

"About fifteen thousand miles."

"Aren't there satellites higher up than that?"

Heshel nodded. "Geosynchronous orbit is 22,300 miles up, directly over the equator. That's prime real estate—mostly big telecommunications satellites."

"How do you police the area in between?" Tao asked.

"Optically, with a network of ground-based telescopes. That's also how we keep tabs on all the smaller junk in orbit—stuff down to the size of a pebble. We estimate there's around four hundred thousand objects in orbit, all zipping around at over seventeen thousand miles per hour. Getting hit by any of that stuff is guaranteed to ruin your day."

"With everything that's up there," Tao said, "it sounds like we're looking for a speck of dust in a whirlwind."

"True, but fortunately, what we're looking for should be considerably larger than a baseball," Kilkenny said, "which should narrow the field."

"Considerably," Heshel agreed. "There's only somewhere in the neighborhood of a few thousand objects that meet the criteria of what we're looking for. Also, your weapon will likely be in a lower orbit, putting it in range of the Fence."

"Why is that?" Tao asked.

"You put a satellite in geosynchronous orbit when

you want it to always be in the same spot on Earth. That way you can point a receiver up at one spot in the sky and forget it—like the small dish I have at home to watch TV. For something like a spy satellite or this weapon we're looking for, you want flexibility, so you shoot for a lower orbit and move your bird around as needed."

Kilkenny studied the image on the wall monitor, imagining objects orbiting the planet. "So, you don't have continuous real-time coverage of everything in orbit."

"No," Heshel replied. "But we really don't need to. When an object crosses our sensors, we know exactly where it is at that moment. Orbits being what they are, it's not hard to extropolate where something's going."

"What about the satellites that move?" Tao asked.

"That's the exception to the rule, but even those birds can only go so far."

"So, how do we proceed?" Tao asked.

Kilkenny studied the image on the monitor further, then motioned toward the white board on Heshel's wall. "May I?"

"Sure."

Kilkenny cleared the board and drew a large circle. "This is the Earth, and this"—he said, adding a small triangle above the circle—"is *Liberty.* Since we believe we're dealing with a laser, the weapon must have had a direct line of sight with the shuttle."

He drew two lines, at a tangent to the Earth, extending down from the triangle. "Anything above these lines can see *Liberty,* anything below can't, which eliminates it from our list of possibilities."

"That still leaves a lot of space," Tao said.

"Yes, but we can narrow the list even further by looking at the attack on the spy satellite as well."

Heshel crossed his arms and leaned back in his chair, pensive. "It's doable, but that's going to be a hell of a lot of data to parse through. I'm not sure I have the resources here to do this quickly without somebody noticing."

"Just get me the data on everything you were tracking at the time of both attacks," Kilkenny replied, "I'll take it from there."

"What happens to old satellites?" Tao asked. "The ones that no longer function."

"If they're in geosynchronous orbit, they get moved down into a junk orbit to make room. The rest are just left where they are. Eventually, all of them come down. Why?"

"I was just thinking about target practice."

"Target practice?" Heshel questioned.

"Yes. If you were placing a new type of weapon in space, you'd want to test it, wouldn't you? Make sure that it works?"

"Lady's got a point," Kilkenny said. "Have you lost any other satellites?"

"A few die every year. Most are obsolete, but some get zapped by heavy solar activity or micrometeoroids."

"Can we get a list of those that appear to have failed suddenly?" Tao asked.

"Sure. You just want the military and government satellites?"

"No, I think we should take a look at everything until we have a better idea of what we're looking for."

"How far back?" Heshel asked.

Tao looked at Kilkenny. "Ten years?"

Kilkenny nodded. "That should get us back to a time before this weapon was launched."

"I can get you some of the data on the military satellites, who owns what and when they went up, but our files on the commercial birds are pretty thin. If you want details on any of those, you should check with Lloyd's of London. They're one of the larger satellite insurers."

Kilkenny nodded, then turned to Tao. "After we're done here, let's give Barnett a call to set something up."

Heshel quickly wrote down a list of specifications, then picked up his phone. "Lieutenant, could you step into my office?"

A moment later, Alana Taggert presented herself at Heshel's door.

"At ease, Lieutenant," Heshel said, then he introduced Kilkenny and Tao.

"Pleasure to meet you," Taggert said.

"Lieutenant, these folks are working with NASA to get a better idea of the hazards posed by debris in orbit."

"*Liberty*?" Taggert asked.

Heshel nodded, then tore the top page from the legal pad and handed it to Taggert.

"I want you to pull this information together for these folks."

Taggert quickly skimmed the list, checking the date range. "Some of this will have to come out of the archives."

"I understand, but make it happen ASAP. This is your top priority."

Taggert worked into the early evening, assembling the decade's worth of information that Heshel had requested. In the end, the data set she culled filled a stack of CDs, which she hand-delivered to Kilkenny and Tao at their hotel in Washington.

Kilkenny had offered her a late dinner as compensation for her efforts. While tempted—she found the red-haired young man was easy on the eyes—Taggert dutifully declined the offer. In truth, she was tired and wanted nothing more than to go home, strip off her uniform, and slip into a cool shower.

She pulled off the highway near Shiloh and located a pay phone at a gas station.

"Yes?" Moug answered.

"Something's come up I thought you should know about," she said.

"Go on."

Taggert described the visit by two NASA consultants to the Dahlgren facility and their request for information about failed satellites.

"Did they make specific mention of any particular satellite?"

"No. The impression I got was that this was more of a broad survey. What happened with *Liberty* has a lot of people at NASA spooked, so they're checking to see if collisions with orbital debris might be more common than the statisticians have led them to believe."

"A fishing trip."

"Probably, but the reason I called is that many of the satellites we've discussed in the past are on the list I gave them. I just thought you'd like to know."

"Give me the names of these two people and where they're staying."

"Nolan Kilkenny and Roxanne Tato. They're at the Hyatt near Capitol Hill."

After she hung up, Taggert returned to her car and thought about a vacation she might take with her next payment.

"How are things in our nation's capital?" Grin asked.

Through the earpiece, Kilkenny could hear the White Stripes rocking in the background.

"Hot and muggy, which is why all the pols leave town this time of year."

"Leaving only the mosquitoes to suck your blood."

"Exactly. I got some data I need you to slice and dice for me."

"In the immortal words of Leonard Cohen, *I'm your man.* Whatcha got?"

"The full specs on the data are in a text file in a folder marked *Orbital Survey.* It's in my directory and flagged for your access. Basically it's a huge block of information about every piece of equipment in orbit since the mid '90s. I want you to create a model based on this data."

"How many objects we talking about?"

"About ten-K at any given time. Almost all of it will be satellites with predictable orbits."

"Doesn't sound too tough. What am I looking for?"

"Start with *Liberty* and the satellite it launched. I've listed exact times and locations for the two attacks. What we're looking for is any satellite that had a clear line of site for both. I worked out some rough geometry on how to deal with this problem, but I defer to your mathematical skills to pull it off."

As he spoke, Kilkenny heard the staccato fire of Grin's fingers on his keyboard.

"Uh-huh," Grin replied absently as he skimmed through

Kilkenny's notes on his computer. "If there's ten thousand objects in orbit, then with only two points of reference, we're still going to end up with a pretty big list."

"Roxanne and I are working to whittle it down a little more, but we gotta start somewhere."

24

Xiyuan, China
August 13

"You wished to see me, Minister?" Huang said respectfully as he entered Tian's office.

"I did, indeed. Take a seat."

Tian leaned forward, his elbows set squarely on the desktop. As Huang sat down, he noticed that the minister's gaze did not lift from the opened file atop his desk, his attention focused on a pair of photographs. After a moment, the minister shook his head and sat up.

"Have you seen this?" Tian asked, spinning one of the photographs around for Huang.

Huang looked at the image and nodded. "That's the woman who met Kilkenny in Washington. Has she been identified?"

"Yes."

Tian slid the second photograph to Huang. It was clearly that same woman, but where the first image presented a woman of high refinement, the second was clearly one of the masses.

"We've been looking for her for almost two years. Her name, or at least the name we knew her by, is Chen Mei

Yue. Her presence in Washington confirms our belief that she was an illegal operative for the CIA. A very good one—in some ways we still have not recovered completely from her activities."

"Is any action to be taken?"

Tian shook his head. "Against the rules of the game. But, now that we know where she is . . ."

Tian kept the rest of the thought to himself as he slipped the photographs into a thick file. Huang recognized the file's color-coding and realized that in being told the woman's cover name, he had been made privy to a highly classified secret.

"Any progress with your investigation of the American shuttle incident?" Tian asked.

"Kilkenny made two stops of interest in Washington. The first was to an office building adjacent to the White House where many of their president's senior staff have offices."

"I am familiar with that building from my posting in Washington," Tian said. "Your estimate of the importance of Newton's message appears correct. Any idea with whom he met?"

"Other than that woman, no, sir. Our agent was unable to maintain contact with Kilkenny after he entered the building."

"And the second stop?"

"The U.S. Space Command facility in Dahlgren, Virginia—this is where their navy keeps track of objects in orbit and determines safe windows for space launches. The woman accompanied him there and, at this moment, they are both en route to London."

"London?"

"Yes, and we are maintaining our surveillance."

"Good. So, what do you make of this?"

"Kilkenny went to Washington with information relevant to the cause of their shuttle's destruction. This information was placed before senior members of the American government and it apparently has caused the launch of a second line of inquiry."

"This has an odd feel to it, Huang. The Americans analyze their accidents in public—almost as a form of entertainment. If Newton's message supported an accidental scenario, I have no doubt it would have been released to the media by now. This covert investigation bolsters your theory of a deliberate cause. If so, then the question becomes who?"

"A question I am certain the Americans are most interested in answering." Huang paused to consider his words.

"What's on your mind, Huang?" the minister asked.

"*Shenzhou-7.*"

"I would not look too deeply into this matter for answers to our own loss. Our nation is new to space travel, and both Russia and the United States lost men in their early days. It is a difficult and dangerous activity. Even if their shuttle suffered some form of sabotage, the odds of mounting two operations with that kind of complexity are unimaginable."

"There are two ways to attack an enemy," Huang replied. "From the inside, and from the outside."

25

London
August 13

The overnight flight from Washington put Kilkenny and Tao in London late in the following morning. In a courtesy normally extended to persons bearing diplomatic credentials, they were escorted through customs by a representative of the British government, then collected by a driver from the U.S. Embassy and taken to their hotel.

That afternoon, their driver pulled up to the curb at 1 Lime Street. Towering above them, an elegant composition of glass, concrete, and stainless steel—the landmark headquarters of Lloyd's of London. The late-modern cathedral to capitalism was a far cry from the seventeenth-century Thames-side coffeehouse on Tower Street run by Edward Lloyd.

They presented their identification at the main entrance and were quickly processed by building security and issued visitor identification cards. From there, they entered the Room—an open volume of space encompassing most of the ground floor and several levels of overlooking galleries above. A twelve-story atrium soared high above them, and as they walked into the center of the ground floor, they passed the columned structure under which hung the famed Lutine Bell. Recovered from the British warship *Lutine,* which sank in 1799 off the coast of Holland, the bell was hung in Lloyd's for two centuries, ringing twice to signal good news, such as the safe return of a ship, and once for bad. Most recently, it had tolled a single time for the shuttle *Liberty.*

The blended sounds of conversations, office machines, and movement surrounded them with a continuous pulsing hum. Like the building's facade, the interior spaces were exquisitely detailed—every element was part of an elegant, well-crafted machine of commerce.

Following the directions they'd been given at security, they crossed the trading floor and arrived at the MATS area, where brokers and underwriters serviced the needs of the marine, aviation, transportation, and space industries. They were met by a tall, thin man with graying temples and an impeccably tailored suit.

"I see you made it," Devon Fleetwood said warmly, "not much trouble getting here, I hope? Traffic's usually quite thick this time of day."

"Not at all," Tao replied, accepting Fleetwood's offered hand.

Introductions made, Fleetwood led them back to his box—a rectangle of space surrounded by low panels of richly stained wood.

"Please have a seat," Fleetwood said, "and do pardon the mess."

Kilkenny looked around the box as he sat down—other than a few stray files on Fleetwood's wood and steel desk, the space could have been an installation at MoMA.

"Early this morning," Fleetwood began, "I received a telephone call from Sir Daniel Long, who, in addition to requesting that I schedule this meeting, asked me to pass along his regards."

"On both counts, thank you," Kilkenny replied.

"I take it you are a personal acquaintance of the minister's?"

"I met Sir Daniel a few years ago, during my last visit to London."

"Well, how may I be of help to you? Sir Daniel indicated that you have an interest in satellite insurance."

"Indirectly," Tao said. "We're looking into the loss of the shuttle *Liberty.*"

Fleetwood's mouth dropped into a slight frown. "Oh, the incident with your shuttle. Quite tragic. Been a blow to the industry as well."

"How so?" Kilkenny asked.

"Insurance, like any investment, is based on risk. We, the insurers, base our premiums on the level of risk we are being asked to take. The industry as a whole has enough capacity to absorb the loss of a few satellites each year without raising our premiums, but what happened to *Liberty* has hit our little niche in the market like an earthquake. When our followers get nervous, premiums go up."

"I think you lost me with the followers," Kilkenny admitted. "I'm used to thinking about insurance as it relates to my car. I sign up with one company, pay my premiums, and make a claim when something bad happens. Isn't that how it works with satellites?"

"Yes and no," Fleetwood replied. "Your auto is a small part of a very large pool of vehicles. The premiums you pay are based on the type of vehicle you own, your driving record, and where you live. Those are the risk factors your insurer uses when quoting you a price. With satellites, the risk in monetary terms for an individual satellite is quite large and ownership of the spacecraft changes as it moves from the factory into space. To deal with this complexity, we provide separate policies for the different owners and distinct periods of time. Pre-Launch covers satellites and rockets while they are still on the ground. Launch insurance covers from launch through to satellite separation and Post-Separation insurance follows the satellite to its intended orbit and through in-orbit testing. In-Orbit coverage lasts for the service life of the satellite once it is in place and functioning properly. Other policies cover just the satellite transponders, loss of incentives to satellite manufacturers if their product fails to perform properly, launch risk guarantees, and third-party liability."

"And that's what Lloyd's provides?" Tao asked.

Fleetwood shook his head. "You're still thinking of Lloyd's as a monolithic insurance company. We're really much more like a marketplace. Any time you're dealing with a very expensive property—be it a satellite, an oil tanker, or a fleet of aircraft—you're talking about a risk that's far too large for a single insurer to handle alone. That would be putting all your eggs in one basket. Each of the underwriters here in the Room represents a syndicate of individuals or corporations. These syndicates take on a portion of the risk and, if nothing goes wrong, are rewarded with a share of the profits."

"And if a claim is made," Tao said, "they bear the burden of liability."

"Precisely. Instead of shares of ownership, members of our syndicates assume shares of risk. It's our members that provide the financial capacity to service our industry."

"This capacity you're talking about, just how large is this market?" Kilkenny asked.

"As with the stock market, the amount of money available varies. During the late nineties, the industry as a whole had roughly $1.3 billion in capacity and could provide up to $400 million of coverage for a single launch. A recent string of satellite failures and the secondary effects of nine-eleven drove a lot of money out of the market. Present capacity is about half what was available ten years ago, and premiums with some insurers are 50 to 75 percent higher."

"Doesn't a shuttle cost about two billion?" Kilkenny asked.

"I believe so, but the U.S. government self-insures its shuttle fleet as well as its scientific and military satellites. Our industry only covers commercial payloads."

"Like the ZetaComm satellite," Tao offered.

Fleetwood nodded. "I don't know how that's going to affect NASA's stance on commercial payloads. They stopped carrying them aboard the shuttle in '86 after *Challenger,* and only returned to the field after completing construction of the ISS, albeit on a limited basis. From our point of view as the insurer, the ZetaComm loss is currently in review and, once a cause is determined, we'll see whether or not the coverage applies."

Kilkenny shot a quick glance at Tao, then returned his attention to Fleetwood. "Since you can't send a claims investigator into space—"

"Not that I haven't considered it, from time to time,

but there's another issue," Fleetwood joked. "Please continue."

"—I assume you study all the communications between a satellite and its ground control?"

"Precisely. In most cases, we have partial communications with the satellite, from which we can deduce a specific component failure. One line of satellites suffered from faulty controller systems while another's solar panels degraded quickly over time. With ZetaComm, all we have to go on is a brief bit of telemetry before it went silent."

"I think that gets us to why we're here," Kilkenny said. "We're looking for any information you may have on other satellites that have failed, for whatever reason, over the past ten years."

"Is there anything specific you are looking for?" Fleetwood asked, intrigued.

"There's some concern at NASA that *Liberty* was struck by either a micrometeoroid or a fragment of man-made space debris. We're looking for more hard data to help in understanding the nature of the problem."

"I see," Fleetwood replied, not really buying Kilkenny's explanation. Orbital collision was one of several risk factors assessed by the MATS Group.

"Here are the specifics," Tao added as she handed Fleetwood a list.

Fleetwood perused the list. "Shouldn't be a problem pulling this together. When you're finished with your survey, I do hope you'll share the results with us. We're always interested in anything that might have an effect on determining risks."

* * *

Ernst Unger casually approached the MATS area, a friendly smile on his weathered face. He was compact and ruggedly built—a mountain climber, when time permitted, with dark eyes and wavy black hair.

"Good afternoon, Amanda," he said warmly, his English almost devoid of a German accent.

"Ernst, you scoundrel," the receptionist flirted. "Where have you been hiding?"

"Hiding?" Unger replied, playing along. "It is my cruel employer who keeps me away from your loveliness."

"Silver-tongued devil. So, what brings you to town?"

"Business, as usual. I was in the neighborhood and thought I would stop in and say hello to Devon, but I see he has visitors."

"Yes. He's tied up at the moment with a couple of Americans. A last-minute sort of thing. I don't really know how long they'll be, but he asked that I clear the rest of his afternoon."

"I see. Well, this was just a social call and I have a few other stops to make. Just let him know that I came by."

"Will do, love."

Unger left as Amanda keyed a message notice into Fleetwood's e-mail. Outside, he walked a short distance up Lime Street and slipped into the passenger seat of a BMW X5. From where he sat, he had a clear view of the embassy car that had brought Fleetwood's visitors.

In addition to Lloyd's files, Fleetwood called in favors with his counterparts at the other lead insurers and, in a matter of a few hours, had amassed a detailed list of the world's space-based assets. Highlighted in the database were those assets which, for any reason, had failed and the results of the insurer's investigation into those claims.

"Well, this ought to give Grin something more to chew on," Tao said as they departed Lloyd's.

"A lack of raw data isn't one of our problems. I just hope we don't end up spinning our wheels on an overload of irrelevant information."

Tao understood Kilkenny's frustration. In a desperate search for leads, they were groping blindly for anything that might aid them in their search for the weapon used to murder six astronauts and to identify those responsible for placing it in space. Tao also knew that Kelsey Newton's presence aboard the ISS only fueled Kilkenny's anxiety.

As they approached the embassy car, the driver stepped out and opened the door.

"While you were inside, I received word that Jackson Barnett would like you to call him," the driver reported. "You can use the secure phone in the car."

Kilkenny took the slip with Barnett's number and, as the car pulled out into traffic, punched in the digits and switched on the speaker. The driver had already raised the glass between the front and rear compartments.

"So, how's London?" Barnett asked.

Kilkenny and Tao both knew the CIA chief wasn't inquiring about the weather.

"Fine, sir," Kilkenny replied. "We got what we came for."

"Good. I received a call from Heshel earlier today. It seems that after you two had left for London, he realized that he'd missed something in your search."

"We didn't get *all* the satellites?" Tao asked.

"Yes, you did, and that's the root of Heshel's problem.

The search he ran for you was too narrow. It only covered satellites."

"What else is up there—" Kilkenny's question died in midbreath, his mind racing through to assemble an answer. "Manned spacecraft?"

"Heshel was thinking about Roxanne's idea of target practice," Barnett continued, "and there's one item, a rather large one, that didn't make it onto your list—*Mir*."

"That went down back in what, spring of 2001?" Kilkenny asked.

"On the twenty-third of March, to be exact. Heshel was present at the Russian control center outside Moscow when they brought it down. Officially, everything went picture perfect."

"And unofficially?" Tao asked.

"The way Heshel tells it, a lot of his comrades went straight to the bar after the last bits of the old station hit the Pacific. Which leads to a change in your travel plans. Instead of coming back here, you two are going to Moscow. I want you to meet with a man named Yuri Zadkine. He was in charge of bringing *Mir* down."

Unger's BMW followed several lengths behind as the dark-blue embassy car moved west along High Holborn toward Oxford Street—a direct route back to the U.S. Embassy. In the rear seat, one of Unger's men manipulated a joystick controller, keeping the infrared laser concealed in the satellite radio receiver mounted atop the SUV aimed at the rear window of the embassy car. Through his headset, Unger clearly heard every word of Kilkenny and Tao's conversation with Barnett.

As the car pulled up to the embassy on Grosvenor

Square, Unger motioned for the driver to move on, breaking contact both visually and electronically. He then pulled off his headset and selected a number from his cell phone's memory.

"It's Ernst," Unger announced as soon as Owen Moug answered. "I don't think these two you're interested in are consultants for NASA."

"What have you learned?"

"Kilkenny is former Navy Special Forces. He did a six-year hitch, then left the service to work for a high-tech investment consortium headed up by his father in Michigan. A few years ago, he was involved in bringing down a ring of industrial spies here in London. His traveling companion is a bit more enigmatic. Tao heads the Michigan branch of a small venture capital firm that is, in part, funded by the CIA. They do business together."

"So what are they doing in London?" Moug asked, impatiently.

"I'm getting to that. When they arrived here, MI6 waltzed them through Customs, stopping only long enough to get their passports stamped. They're being chauffeured around in embassy cars, but have only made one stop of interest. They paid a visit to Devon Fleetwood at Lloyd's."

"Shit."

"It gets more interesting. I don't know the substance of their conversation with Fleetwood, but during their ride back to the embassy, we captured a phone conversation between them and Jackson Barnett, the director of the CIA. In addition to looking at satellites, Barnett is sending them to Moscow to talk with a Russian, a man named Zadkine, who was responsible for deorbiting the *Mir* space station. There apparently was a problem with

Mir that relates to something Barnett referred to as *target practice.*"

"Keep on them, and assemble a team. I don't like where this inquiry is heading."

Peng and his driver watched the BMW SUV glide past the U.S. Embassy. They'd spotted it trailing after Kilkenny and the woman now identified as Roxanne Tao on the A23 heading into London from Gatwick Airport. The driver of the vehicle had expertly maintained subtle contact with his quarry, and was noticeable only because Peng had the advantage of observing the movements of both vehicles. The Chinese agent and his driver took full advantage of the second tail, using it to further mask their own surveillance.

Outside Lloyd's of London, Peng photographed one of the men from the second car and transmitted the images to a ministry computer in the embassy. Whoever the man was, Peng noted in his report to the ministry later that evening, he carried the appropriate credentials to gain admittance and freely move about inside the Lloyd's building. The man had also visited the same area of the trading floor as Kilkenny and his associate, an area the Lloyd's of London website identified as serving the insurance needs of the satellite industry.

Peng's report ended with some ticketing information gleaned from an airline network, indicating the American investigation was now heading toward Moscow.

26

Korolev, Russia
August 14

The midmorning flight out of Heathrow put Tao and Kilkenny on the ground at Sheremetyevo 2 Airport outside Moscow at four in the afternoon. Regardless of what their watches said, their internal clocks were still struggling with the shift of eight time zones. Both had slept as much as possible to moderate the effects of jet lag.

As in London, Barnett's advance calls greased their arrival and in little more than the time it took to deplane, they were in another embassy car cruising down the northern arc of the Moscow Ring Road.

The driver brought them to a modest dacha in the northern periphery of Korolev, a small city on the outskirts of the Russian capital. The house was a simple, one-story wooden structure with a detached outbuilding. A battered Giguli sat parked on the gravel drive and a mature grove of birch and pine covered the property. The dense foliage visually isolated the home from its distant neighbors.

"Will you be needing a translator?" the driver asked.

"I don't think so," Kilkenny replied. "We were told he speaks English."

As they approached the front door, Kilkenny and Tao heard jazz playing from behind the house. They followed the music to the outbuilding at the end of the driveway.

"The Bird—Charlie Parker," Tao said, picking out enough of the melody. "The man has taste."

"Grin's tried to turn me on to jazz, but so far it hasn't stuck. Says I'm a philistine."

"He's right."

Kilkenny ignored the jibe and knocked on the door. The music quieted and Kilkenny knocked again. Footsteps followed and the door opened a few inches. The man eyed them warily, but said nothing.

"Yuri Zadkine?" Kilkenny asked.

"Da."

"Andy Heshel sends his regards."

As Zadkine considered what Kilkenny had said, his face softened and he opened the door a little further. "You are Americans?"

"Yes. You weren't told we were coming?"

"Someone may have tried to contact me. Phone rings, but I don't always hear it."

"May we come in?" Tao asked.

"Oh, I forget my manners. Please."

The interior of the outbuilding contained a large open space on the ground floor and what Kilkenny presumed was an attic storage room above. The room was large enough to shelter two cars, but Zadkine had it equipped with an array of tools and equipment.

Zadkine pulled a pair of wooden folding chairs off hooks in the wall and set them down for his visitors, then perched himself atop a low stool at the workbench. He was dressed in worn coveralls and his hands were stained with grease. The outbuilding had the musty metallic odor of an old machine shop.

"Sit, sit," Zadkine said as he picked up a blackened piece of metal from the workbench and began rubbing it with a solvent-soaked rag. The fumes were strong, but Kilkenny noted thankfully that the windows were open. "So why has my old friend Heshel sent you to see me?"

"It has to do with *Mir*," Tao said softly. Heshel had warned them it was a sore subject for the proud engineer.

"What else could it be? Heshel was there. And he stood up for me; not that it did any good. Officially, *Mir* came down perfectly—a triumph of Russian science."

Kilkenny glanced at Tao, nodded for her to continue. "Sir, we want to know what really happened when *Mir* came down."

"All hell broke loose is what happened," Zadkine replied bitterly.

"Did something hit *Mir*?" Kilkenny asked.

Zadkine stopped cleaning the part and glared at Kilkenny defensively. During the internal review of the *Mir* reentry, Zadkine had espoused the theory that the space station had been struck. The physics of the matter seemed to bear him out—to indicate that only a collision with an object of significant mass could have pushed the station into an uncontrolled spin. Those presiding over the inquiry—political appointees rather than scientists—rejected Zadkine's argument in the belief that such a collision was a statistical improbability. In the end, they found Zadkine responsible for the near-disaster and his career in the Russian space industry was finished.

"Heshel said something happened during the final

deorbit burn," Kilkenny continued. "That *Mir* began tumbling. What could have caused that?"

"According to the review board, the cause was my incompetence. *You were in charge, Yuri,*" Zadkine ranted. *"You fucked up and the thing almost smashed into Chile, Yuri.* Now I'm out on my ass. No job, no pension. Disgraced."

Kilkenny looked at Zadkine squarely. "The review board wasn't there. You were. You're an engineer, tell me what you think happened to the station."

Zadkinc continued to stew, his eyes darting back and forth between Kilkenny and Tao. He found no sign of accusation in his visitors; their curiosity appeared genuine and even urgent.

"Why do you want to know about this bit of ancient history?" Zadkine asked, his tone softening.

"Liberty," Kilkenny replied.

Zadkine closed his eyes, saddened. Then he leaned forward and collected his thoughts.

"*Mir* was in last orbit. Up to this point, everything went well. I called for final burn from Progress."

"What is Progress?" Tao asked.

"Unmanned spacecraft. We use them to send supplies up to station and bring back garbage. Last one went up empty to bring station back. Progress engines fired, *Mir* slowed down and began to enter upper atmosphere. Then all electrical systems on station failed and we lost contact. We switched over to computers on Progress and discovered station was tumbling end over end. When it finally entered the atmosphere, its trajectory was far outside target area. Several large pieces of station land just off coast of South America."

"Couldn't hitting the atmosphere have caused *Mir* to tumble?" Tao asked.

"Given the station's configuration, yes, but *Mir* began spinning before it entered the atmosphere. Had we not fired Progress engines, the station would have remained in orbit for at least another week. I have studied the telemetry, and I am convinced that one of the modules—either Kvant-2 or Kristall—was hit with great force. The collision disrupted station's electrical system and started spin."

"Can we have a copy of the data and your analysis?" Kilkenny asked. "I'm certain the U.S. government would value your insights as a expert consultant and compensate you appropriately."

Zadkine lowered his head, but couldn't hide the flush of embarrassment that reddened his face. Of all that he'd lost after *Mir*, the respect of others for his abilities and his experience as an engineer was by far the most painful.

"If my analysis will help, of course you are welcome to it. But how is what happened to *Mir* relevant to *Liberty*?"

"We're not sure that it is," Tao replied.

A faint knowing smile curled the ends of Zadkine's mouth. "Ah, but I sensed there is hypothesis you are trying to test. Unfortunately, my government was unwilling to investigate mine."

"How could they?" Kilkenny asked.

"Recover the evidence," Zadkine answered matter-of-factly. "Six large pieces of *Mir* lie in ocean off coast of Chile. Just looking at what's left of station should be enough to determine whether or not it was struck."

Tao looked at Kilkenny, who nodded back. It was a good suggestion. Zadkine caught the exchange and hoped he correctly understood its meaning.

"Something I find odd, though," Zadkine continued. "The shell of low Earth orbit surrounding the planet is a very large volume of space, which makes the probability of two objects running into each other very small—at least that was the argument used against me."

"Very small doesn't mean impossible," Tao countered.

"No, it doesn't. But the probability of two spacecraft being destroyed in accidental collisions in so short a span of time, well that is something for mathematicians to chew on, eh? Being a product of Soviet system, I find myself wondering if a deliberate action has perhaps overcome the improbabilities."

Looking for a way to deflect this line of reasoning, Kilkenny caught sight of the part in Zadkine's hands and the collection of pieces of the workbench.

"What are you rebuilding?"

"A piece of history," Zadkine replied. "This was my hobby, until I lost my job. Now it helps to keep me sane. I just started work on this one, but, here, showing is better than telling."

Zadkine set the nearly clean gear on the workbench with the other engine parts and motioned for Kilkenny and Tao to follow him to the back of the building. There he pulled a protective tarp off an antique motorcycle.

The bike's rigid tubular frame and wide split tank were painted light green with a dull matte finish. The sides of the tank bore the bright-red star of the Red Army. A tin box off the right front fender held ammunition, the leather sleeve on the left was for the rider's rifle. The polished steel of a 45°V Twin engine glistened beneath the tank and fish-shaped exhaust tubes ran along the bottom of the frame straight back.

"May I?" Kilkenny asked.

Zadkine nodded.

Kilkenny grasped the handgrips and climbed into the brown leather saddle. The spartan machine was nothing like the high-tech motorcycles he was used to. Instrumentation consisted solely of a speedometer mounted over the center of the fuel tank and switches for lights and ignition. Along the left side of the split tank, Kilkenny saw the gearshift set in a notched slot guide. He experimented, trying to imagine steering the bike one-handed while changing gears.

"How do you shift?"

"Carefully," Zadkine replied knowingly, "This is called a suicide shift, because you have to take your hand off the grip to use it."

"Definitely not for the faint of heart."

In the center of the tank, Kilkenny found an engraved plate listing the daily instructions for maintaining the motorcycle. The instructions were in English.

"Is this American?"

"*Da.* 1942 Harley-Davidson WLA. Under Lend-Lease program, your President Roosevelt sent many motorcycles to Russia to fight Germans in Great Patriotic War. This one was still in running condition when it was brought to me a few months ago."

"It looks like it just rolled off the assembly line."

Zadkine beamed. "I have a lot of time on my hands these days. That collection of parts over there is 1939 Zÿndapp, German army motorcycle. Legend says it was captured in Stalingrad."

"What are you going to do with them?" Tao asked.

"Oh, they're not mine. I just restore them. They belong

to a Canadian who does much business in Moscow. A business associate presented him with one of the first motorcycles I restored and he fell in love. On his last visit, he rode off with a 1942 Indian. He was a very happy man."

"I can see why. You do beautiful work."

"I must," Zadkine replied, "this is now my livelihood."

27

Unger's driver, Nikita, had no trouble following the embassy car to Korolev, but this was not a testament to the man's tradecraft. The embassy car made no effort to shake off or even detect their surveillance. Instead, the driver's biggest problem had been to remain unnoticed as traffic thinned on the rural roads of the Moscow suburb.

Leaving the driver and car down the road, Unger approached Zadkine's home through the thick woods accompanied by Stefan and Jurg. All three of the local men he'd hired were former KGB, now plying their trade as security consultants to the Russian *mafiya*. None had struck Unger as exceptionally bright—why else would the Russians have let them go?—but their current employer vouched for their ability to follow orders. The Russians were dressed in slacks with open-collared shirts and loose-fitting jackets, which concealed their weapons. Unger was dressed similarly, but with a sense of style that left him looking less like a thug.

Stefan crept close to the outbuilding. Using hand signals, he indicated that three people were inside. The embassy driver had remained with his car and was seated behind the wheel reading a book.

Unger signaled for the Russians to remain in place. The

two men nodded. He pulled a Stechkin APS fitted with a sound suppressor out of his shoulder holster and chambered a round. Then, with his arms held behind his back, he casually walked up the gravel drive toward the car and rapped on the window. The driver hit a button to lower the glass and Unger bent to face him.

"Excuse me," Unger said in Russian, "but my car has broken down and—"

As he spoke, Unger flipped the safety off, swung the pistol up, and fired. A nine-millimeter bullet cratered the young man's face, the dampened sound of the gunshot completely masked by wind rustling through the birches. The driver slumped back in his seat, his head hanging limply to one side.

Cover the outbuilding, Unger signaled, then he moved on to the house.

The interior was small and cluttered with stacks of books and engineering journals. In a corner of the sitting room, he saw a small table covered with a collection of framed photographs. Some were of a family—a young Zadkine with a woman and young girl—others of just the woman.

Unger swept the other rooms, but found the house empty. It appeared that Zadkine lived alone. According to the very brief report hastily generated by his people, the engineer was a widower of several years and father of one child—a daughter—who resided in Denmark. Unger was pleased to see the old man hadn't taken up with anyone else.

In a back room, he found a computer surrounded by reams of printouts. One wall of the room was covered by images of *Mir* and diagrams describing impact angles and trajectories. An engineering postmortem.

Among the clutter, Unger saw a half-consumed pack of cigarettes, an ashtray, and a cheap plastic lighter. He flicked the lighter. A tall colorful flame leaped up from the igniter. Flames quickly spread across the paper that littered the room, consuming years of work and turning it into ash.

Not sharing Kilkenny and Zadkine's enthusiasm for vintage motorcycles, Tao decided to step out of the stuffy garage for a breath of air. Just outside, she detected a faint acrid scent, then saw the trails of black smoke leaking out of Zadkine's house.

"Fire!" she shouted. "The house is on fire!"

A bullet splintered the wooden door frame just inches from Tao's head. She dropped as a second shattered a dirty pane in the door, jagged fragments of glass raining down on her.

"Get down!" Tao shouted as she scrambled on elbows and knees back inside the garage.

Ignoring Tao's warning, Zadkine rushed to the doorway, fire the only thought in his mind. Kilkenny leaped off the motorcycle, moving to intercept him. At the doorway, Zadkine stopped, then staggered back a few steps before dropping onto his knees. Kilkenny caught him as he crumpled backward and dragged him out of view. Two crimson blooms spread in the fabric of Zadkine's shirt. He grabbed hold of Kilkenny's arm stared up at him urgently.

"*Mir, Liberty,*" Zadkine's voice was low, his breathing coming in labored gasps. "You suspect . . . weapon?"

"Yes."

The look of relief on Zadkine's face caught Kilkenny by surprise.

"Considered possibility myself . . . after *Mir* destroyed," Zadkine rasped, his collapsing lung filling with fluid. "Did not offer as explanation. Unthinkable."

What are those fools doing? Unger thought when he saw his hired gunmen moving toward the outbuilding, pistols drawn.

Unger fired a shot through the grille of the embassy car, then two more through the tires on the driver's side of the car. The Crown Victoria slumped to one side and a puddle of radiator fluid pooled onto the ground beneath it. Unger inflicted similar damage to Zadkine's car, then moved to the rear of the outbuilding.

Peng reached the edge of the clearing surrounding the home just as two men opened fire. He couldn't tell if Tao was injured, but the old man who'd appeared seconds after her in the doorway clearly was. In the area in front of the house, the man he'd spotted following Kilkenny in London disabled the two cars parked in the drive, then moved around the far side of the house.

Kilkenny must be close to discovering the truth, Peng quickly deduced. *I cannot allow my investigation to stop here.*

Reaching inside his jacket, he pulled out a pistol.

Tao kicked the door shut and moved to Kilkenny's side. "How is he?"

"Not good. See anything out there?"

Tao shook her head. "Nada."

Kilkenny looked around the workroom. "They'll be coming for us. We need a weapon."

"Rifle," Zadkind rasped weakly, pointing toward the back wall. "In cabinet."

"Take him," Kilkenny said.

Tao eased her arms under Zadkine's head and shoulders as Kilkenny pulled free. He grabbed a maul from the workbench and, with a single swing, tore the padlock and hasp from the cabinet door. Inside he found an old leather rifle case, which he pulled out and set on the floor. The case contained a World War II–era Tokarev SVT40.

"I just hope this antique still works," Kilkenny grumbled.

He lifted the semiautomatic rifle from the case and quickly familiarized himself with it. The restored rifle looked factory-new; only the character dings in the wood stock hinted at a long history of combat. Kilkenny loaded the ten-round magazine, slipped it into place, and chambered a round.

Unger made a wide circle around the dacha, pistol held with both hands in front of him. Clearing the far side, he saw Stefan and Jurg sidling against the outbuilding, cautiously approaching the door.

Fucking Russian idiots, he fumed.

He'd planned to use the fire to draw Kilkenny, Tao, and Zadkine out into the open, into a killing zone. Instead, his men had attacked at the first sign of movement, losing the element of surprise while allowing their prey to find defensive cover. They had no idea what that old engineer might have in there.

Slipping into the woods, Unger moved quickly to the rear of the outbuilding. The ground there sloped steeply away from the structure, so much so that through the windows he could only see the ceiling inside. He noticed the windows were open, but just a few, and the foliage beneath them showed no sign of recent damage.

At least nobody has escaped.

Stefan ducked and quickly moved beneath the shattered window to the hinge side of the door. Fragments of broken glass crunched beneath his rubber-soled shoes. Flanking the door, he nodded to his partner. Jurg spun out from the wall, raised his leg and drove his foot into the door stile. The old wood splintered and gave way.

Kilkenny heard the gringing crackle of glass and aimed the Tokarev at the door. A flicker of a shadowy movement, then the door shuddered and flew open. The man leading the assault dropped low, sweeping his weapon left while his partner stood over him searching to the right. Kilkenny squeezed off two rounds, striking the lead man just above his eyes. Then the sixty-year-old rifle jammed. The second man in the doorway drew a bead on him and two shots rang out.

Kilkenny saw the muzzle flash, but felt nothing. The man in the doorway toppled sideways as if struck by an invisible force.

"Nolan?" Tao called out.

"I'm fine," Kilkenny replied, not quite believing it himself.

"Scheisse!" Unger hissed through clenched teeth when he heard the door being forced, followed by four distinct pops.

Jurg and Stefan were armed with suppressed pistols identical to one he carried, so what he'd heard must have been directed at them.

Moving more quickly than before, he looped back the way he'd come, keeping a careful eye on the outbuilding.

Zadkine slumped in Tao's arms, his breathing almost imperceptible. He was dying.

The bodies of the two dead men lay heaped in the doorway. Neither moved at all. Cautiously, Kilkenny approached the opening. Within his limited field of vision, he saw no one else outside. The low roar of the fire consuming Zadkine's home was the only sound to be heard. Bright yellow-orange flames filled all the windows, and a thick column of black smoke rose into the sky.

Kilkenny palmed one of the dead men's pistols, discarded the suppressor, and slipped the weapon into his waistband. Then he collected the other. A hasty search of the two men provided additional clips for both weapons. Kilkenny retreated from the door and moved to the corner where Tao cradled Zadkine.

"I don't think he has much time," Tao said softly.

"I know." Kilkenny handed her a pistol and one of the clips. "Here. I'll recon and see if I can find our driver—that guy just saved our lives. If it's clear out there, we'll be back with the car."

Tao accepted the weapon with a nod and Kilkenny slipped out the door.

* * *

Unger watched as Kilkenny stepped over the bodies of the dead Russians. He was now armed with one of their pistols, which he held expertly in a modified Weaver stance. Out in the open, Kilkenny dashed from tree to tree, quickly covering the distance between the outbuilding and the embassy car. Unger moved closer to the forest edge, cautiously paralleling Kilkenny's movements.

Peng remained motionless, his breathing slow and calm. The man he had first encountered following Kilkenny in London was passing just a few feet away, stalking his prey yet unaware of the eyes watching from beneath the broad-spread boughs of pine.

What the hell? Kilkenny thought.

Their driver was dead, the young man's face marred by a single shot fired at point-blank range. Whoever had done this had caught the young man unaware, a blood-stained paperback still in his hands.

If it wasn't you, then who just rode in like the cavalry and saved my butt?

Kilkenny pushed the swirl of questions to the back of his mind and focused on what he needed to do right now. Standing by the damaged embassy car, he did a three-sixty sweep for any sign that the two dead men weren't here alone. He saw nothing but trees. Keeping his attention on the woods, Kilkenny reached through the car's open window and patted the driver's jacket. He found a cell phone in the man's right breast pocket.

* * *

"Nikita," Unger said softly into a handheld radio. "Bring the car."

"Da," the driver replied.

Kilkenny heard the crunch of gravel and dropped into a crouch beside the embassy car. Through the trees, he saw the dark shape of an automobile moving up the drive. He caught a flutter of movement in the woods to his left. He turned, his eyes tracking with the Stechkin's sight, and found a target—a dark-haired man zigzagging through the trees, his weapon drawn, racing toward the driveway. Kilkenny squeezed the trigger and the pistol bucked in his hands—a brass casing spiraled in the air, arcing toward the ground.

The shot flew wide, gouging the side of a birch. As Kilkenny adjusted his aim, the man fired back. Two rounds thumped into the rear of the embassy car, shattering the tailight just inches from Kilkenny's head. As he ducked behind the car, he heard the distinct crack of a pistol firing from the opposite side of the clearing.

The first two shots drilled into the bole of an ancient pine to Unger's left, an impossible shot from Kilkenny's position behind the embassy car. Unger shifted his gaze and saw a muzzle flare for a third time, just inside the far edge of the woods, and heard the report. It felt as if someone had reached out from behind, planted a meat hook into his left shoulder, and yanked back hard. The bullet struck just below the collarbone and chipped his shoulder blade on its way out. The wound burned and his arm went completely numb. Unger grunted loudly; the pain was blinding.

Regaining his balance, Unger aimed at where the fire had come from, but saw no one. His eyes began to water and he could feel his outstretched arm quivering—early signs of shock. A single thought managed to surface through the mental confusion: *Kilkenny!*

He saw a shadowy bulge in the sloping curve of the trunk, possibly the top of a man's head. If their positions were reversed, Unger knew that he would seize any lull in an opponent's attack as an opportunity to take control of the fight. Defensively, Unger shot at the embassy car. The rear window exploded into pebbled fragments. Nikita was almost up to the loop at the end of the driveway. He ran toward the dark-gray Mercedes, squeezing shots off to cover his escape.

The roaring house fire washed out what little noise the suppressed weapon made, but the sound of bullets shattering glass and punching holes through the sheet metal of the embassy car kept the shooter's intentions in the forefront of Kilkenny's mind. Pebbles of safety glass rained over him like the jackpot from a pachinko machine. The dark-haired man was firing at a steady rate, just enough to keep Kilkenny pinned down.

As the Mercedes rounded the last bend in driveway, the driver slowed, but showed no sign of stopping. Five more shots fired in rapid succession hammered into the trunk and rear bumper. Kilkenny heard a car door slam, then two more rounds ripped into the embassy car as the Mercedes sped past and back down the drive. He took aim at the fleeing car but, through the trees, could find no target. A few seconds later, the car disappeared from view.

Kilkenny popped open the trunk and retrieved a government-issue first-aid kit. As he ran back to the outbuilding, he spotted a man near the forest edge tracking him with a pistol. Unlike the others, this man was Asian, and though he had a clear shot he showed no sign of taking it. Kilkenny stopped and kept his hands out in the open. The Asian gave a curt nod, then turned and quickly disappeared into the woods.

28

"Here," Kilkenny said, handing Tao the embassy driver's cell phone and the first-aid kit from the car. "Do what you can for him and call for help."

Tao found the sterile dressings and pressed them down on Zadkine's wounds. The man was ashen and unconscious. "What's happening?"

"Looks like we were hit by a four-man team, but I think we're safe here for the moment," Kilkenny replied. "Our guardian angel gets credit for an assist with those two by the door, but the others are heading down the road. Both cars out there are useless."

"Guardian angel? What are you talking about?"

"I only got a brief look at the guy, but we owe him our lives. Funny thing about him, though, I kind of got the impression he's not one of ours."

As he spoke, he opened the large hanging door at the front of the outbuilding and rolled the Harley outside. Kilkenny took a quick glance around the workroom—no helmet or goggles. He slipped on his Oakley sunglasses and, trying to recall Zadkine's brief review of the motorcycle's idiosyncrasies, turned the ignition and stomped on the starter.

The engine sputtered but failed to catch. *Retard the*

spark when starting, he remembered Zadkine saying. Kilkenny did, and the War Hog's 740cc-knucklehead engine ignited, a throaty rumble reverberating from the tailpipes. Kilkenny pressed down on the clutch, shifted into first gear, and pointed the Harley toward the road.

On their way in, Kilkenny had noticed that the country roads near Zadkine's dacha were in rough shape—the winters here were easily as brutal as those in Michigan. The suspension-mounted saddle on the WLA dampened some of the shock, but the worst of the potholes still jarred his spine.

Kilkenny twisted the throttle, pushing the Harley as he grew accustomed to its ride. The War Hog was a different animal entirely from the crotch rockets many of his buddies in the service rode. As he shifted into third, his right arm rigidly holding the handlebar steady, a rut caught the front wheel and jerked it to the side. The sudden change in direction caused the bike's tail to slew left. Kilkenny stood up in the saddle, grabbed both handgrips, and righted the War Hog.

Suicide shift is right, Kilkenny thought, thankful he hadn't dumped the bike.

After fleeing the dacha, the Mercedes slowed to a pace more appropriate for the rough condition of the road. The cloud of road dust kicked up by the car's tires obscured the view behind like a mud-brown fog.

Unger had stripped off his jacket and was using it as a compress on his shoulder wound. The jarring bumps in the road multiplied the throbbing pain he felt.

"How much farther to the main road?" Unger asked.

"Little more than a kilometer," the driver replied. "Do you want me to drive faster?"

Just then, the car bottomed out against a deep rut. Unger groaned, his whole body shaken.

"*Nyet.* Just get there without beating me to death in the process."

Designed for abusive battlefield conditions, the War Hog fared better on the country road than the Mercedes sedan. Kilkenny rode motocross-style, standing high in the saddle, using his arms and legs as shock absorbers. He slowed when he encountered a thickening cloud of dust in the road. The dried particles of earth stuck to his sweat-soaked skin and clothes, covering him with a layer of grit. Kilkenny couldn't hear the Mercedes over the Harley's signature rumble, but knew it had to be just ahead.

"Someone is coming up behind us," Nikita said. In the mirrors he saw nothing, but the rising sound of an approaching motorcycle was unmistakable.

Unger heard the low rumble of the flathead engine, but glancing back, he saw only dust.

In the thickening cloud, Kilkenny saw the shadowy form of the escaping Mercedes. The car was in the center of the narrow road, jockeying right and left to avoid the most jarring potholes.

Kilkenny moved to the right side of the road and closed distance. The dust-covered rear quarter panel of the sedan became clearly visible. He steadied himself on the Harley and, left-handed, pulled the pistol from his waistband. A slight twist on the throttle pushed the motorcycle up alongside the car.

"The fool is trying to pass us," Nikita grumbled.

Unger opened his eyes and looked out window as Kilkenny pulled up with a pistol pointed right at him.

"Krake!" Unger cursed.

Unger grabbed the steering wheel and pulled it to the right. The passenger window touched the barrel of Kilkenny's pistol just as it flared. The shot punched high through the glass and struck Nikita in the meat of his left thigh. He growled and pressed the accelerator to the floor.

Kilkenny dropped the pistol and fought to keep the War Hog upright. Dozens of tiny stones strafed him and the motorcycle, projectiles thrown back by the sedan's rapid escape. His Oakleys took several sharp bits of gravel that otherwise might have blinded him.

After a brief struggle, Kilkenny regained control of the Harley and resumed his pursuit. He stifled the persistent cough in his throat and rode on through the particle-laden cloud.

Visibility improved just a few yards onto the paved roadway. Ahead, the gray sedan was speeding away. Kilkenny revved the War Hog to full throttle, squeezing every ounce of power he could from the rebuilt engine. The knucklehead gave all that it had, but it had been built for strength, not speed, and topped out at sixty-five miles per hour.

Kilkenny wove dangerously through the steadily increasing traffic, but the race between the Mercedes and the

Harley was a mismatch. After only a few miles on Outer Ring Road surrounding Moscow, he lost sight of the dusty gray sedan. Unfortunately, even in the free-for-all of Russian highways, the sight of an ancient Red Army motorcycle slaloming recklessly through traffic was more than enough to attract the attention of the State Traffic Police.

29

A uniformed officer retrieved Kilkenny from the lockup, where he'd spent the past few hours in the company of several drunks, and escorted him to an interview room. The man stood by the door and motioned for Kilkenny to enter.

The room was dimly lit, the walls bare of ornament and in need of a fresh coat of paint, the floor covered with dingy sheet vinyl. Kilkenny sat in one of four wooden chairs placed around a metal table. The table was bolted to the floor.

Ten minutes later, the door opened and admitted a squat bull of a man with black wiry hair and a bushy eyebrow that crossed his forehead in a thick, uninterrupted line. The man barked an order at the officer standing guard by the door. Very quickly, the man removed the restraints from Kilkenny's wrists and ankles and retreated from the room. Kilkenny smiled warmly at the director of the FSB.

"Nolan Seanovich, so good to see you again," the man said.

"And you as well, Igor Sergeevich."

Igor Sergeevich Fydorov turned one of the chairs around and straddled it, resting his arms on the back.

"First you come to Moscow to deal with a criminal oligarch, then a corrupt general. And now we find you playing cowboy on our highways." Fydorov sighed. "You made our evening news, no mention of your name or nationality, of course."

"I'm sure Jackson Barnett will appreciate that."

"He did. And you were smart to keep your mouth shut while you were in here. Delicate business is best handled through appropriate channels."

"What's the word on Zadkine?"

"Dead, I'm afraid. With immediate attention, he might have survived. By the time the ambulance arrived . . ." Fydorov's voice trailed off with a shrug. "Your associate, Miss Tao, is fine and waiting for you at the U.S. Embassy."

"Good."

"I must admit, I'm a little puzzled by this whole affair and I'm beginning to think that, maybe, our mutual friend Barnett has been somewhat less than forthcoming about the purpose of your visit to Moscow."

"Oh, what has he told you?"

"That you wished to discuss an incident that occurred during the deorbit of *Mir* with the man in charge of that operation."

"That's true."

"Ah, but not why. Would you care to offer any theory you may have as to why someone would want you, your associate, and this apparently harmless retiree dead?"

"I have no idea. Roxanne and I are looking into what happened to *Liberty*. We'd heard something similar happened when *Mir* came down and just wanted to compare notes with Zadkine."

"That's what Barnett told me."

"It's the truth."

The left half of Fydorov's unibrow curled upward. "I have been in the intelligence business long enough to know that a bit of the truth can often be a better cover story than an outright lie. I have no doubt that you are investigating possible causes for what happened to your shuttle, but I remind you that Russia also lost a man up there. We, too, are very interested in what happened."

"Our experts believe that *Liberty* was destroyed by a fragment of orbital debris," Kilkenny said in a carefully measured tone. "I cannot speculate on any hypothetical scenarios that may differ from that line of inquiry."

Fydorov listened carefully to Kilkenny's words, then remembered that the young man's fiancée was currently aboard the International Space Station. Kilkenny wasn't simply looking, he was hunting.

"I understand. Do not concern yourself about this incident with the motorcycle—it never happened. Full dossiers on the men you killed will be delivered to the embassy before you leave the country, including any past and present associations. We will continue investigating the attack on you and Zadkine and will relay everything we uncover. I wish you success in your inquiry."

Kilkenny was relieved Fydorov didn't press any harder. In their past two encounters, the FSB chief had shown himself to be a trustworthy man, and it bothered Kilkenny to leave him out of the loop.

"Would it be possible to get the final telemetry on *Mir*'s reentry, as well?"

"I will see to it."

Both men stood, and Kilkenny walked around the table

and extended his hand. Fydorov accepted, then clapped his other bearlike paw on Kilkenny's shoulder and looked him in the eye.

"I swear to you, Nolan Seanovich, my country is not involved with the destruction of *Liberty*."

30

Near midnight, on what had been an exceedingly long day, a marine guard escorted Kilkenny to the secure conference room in the basement of the U.S. Embassy in Moscow. Tao was there waiting for him.

"How are you?" she asked.

Kilkenny slumped in one of the high-backed chairs. "Whipped, but nothing a day or two of rest won't cure. You?"

"Same. I tried to get some sleep, but I still see Zadkine dying in my arms. I have too many images like that in my head."

Kilkenny said nothing, but nodded his understanding. They both carried scarred memories of things they would prefer to have never known.

"Satellite feed coming in now," a voice announced through an overhead speaker.

The large monitor covering the end wall of the room switched on, first with a blue test screen. Two windows then split the long screen into equal halves. Legend strips along the bottom of the screen showed the transmission feeding the window on the left originated in Langley, while the one on the right came from Pearl Harbor. A moment later, life-size images of Jackson Barnett and Grin filled the windows. Kilkenny smiled at the sight of Barnett, nattily attired in a suit and tie, juxtaposed with Grin in his cut-off jeans, sandals, and a floral print shirt loud enough to make a blind Hawaiian squint.

"You appear in rather good spirits for someone who just spent several hours in a Russian jail," Barnett commented.

Kilkenny tried sobering his expression. "Just glad to be alive, sir."

"Morning all," Grin said warmly despite his evident fatigue. "How are things on the other side of the world?"

"Dark," Tao replied.

"Burning the midnight oil?" Kilkenny asked.

"By the barrel," Grin replied. "But it's nothing a little caffeine and the right mood music can't handle."

"How was your conversation with Zadkine?" Barnett asked.

"Brief," Tao answered. "As Heshel told you, something happened during *Mir*'s final orbit that caused it to go into an uncontrolled spin. Mission Control, then headed by Zadkine, lost control of the station. Since it still ended up in the ocean, the deorbit was publicly deemed a success. The unpleasant part was swept under the rug and Zadkine lost his job."

"Doesn't sound too fair," Grin opined.

"It wasn't," Kilkenny agreed. "Zadkine's an engineer. He understood how an object like *Mir* moves in space—basic laws of motion stuff. He studied the telemetry and worked out some likely trajectories for collisions that could have caused what happened."

"Where you able to get his data?" Grin asked.

"No. It was probably in his house, which was burned to the ground."

"Too bad. I would have liked to compare notes with the man."

"You would have liked him," Kilkenny said. "A Charlie Parker fan."

"Cool."

"Mr. Grinelli," Barnett said, reasserting control over this meeting, "would you care to bring Roxanne and Nolan up to date on your efforts?"

"Sure thing. I worked over the data you two sent me pretty much like we discussed and came up with a lot of possibles. For example, both hits took place over the Eastern Hemisphere, so everything in geostationary orbit over that side of the world is a suspect."

"I get the idea," Kilkenny said. "The list is long."

"Yeah, but it's a start. I then took what you and Roxanne picked up at Lloyd's and repeated the process for every satellite whose failure could not be determined with 100 percent certainty. You'd be surprised at just how many have just blinked off one day without any prior hint of trouble. Sunspots and micrometeoroids seem to be the favored causes of sudden death."

"And did that narrow your list?" Tao asked.

Grin nodded. "To zero."

"Zero?" Kilkenny repeated, surprised.

"Yep. There's not one satellite in orbit that could've taken out all the others."

"Could there be more than one?" Tao asked.

"I thought of that and ran a few different combinations just to see what might pop up. I got a few groups of two or three that fit the profile, except they belong to different countries. I kind of have my doubts that China and Taiwan are in cahoots to zap our spy satellites."

"An international conspiracy of this nature does seem rather unlikely," Barnett agreed.

"Exactly, but I checked the background on these satellites just for kicks, and all of 'em look legit. A couple even went up on American-built rockets."

"Maybe we're looking at too broad a time frame," Kilkenny suggested.

"That's why I like you," Grin said. "Great minds think alike."

Tao rolled her eyes. "Such humility."

"And handsome, too," Grin added. "I reran my analysis, but in discrete increments of time, starting from *Liberty* and stepping back to each previous satellite failure."

Grin paused, a broad, self-satisfied smile twinkling inside his goatee.

"He's got that *ain't I brilliant* look on his face again," Kilkenny said.

"You found it?" Tao asked.

"No. A few steps back from *Liberty* and a list of possibles again drops to zero. What I found is the time period that our killer sat has been operating, and it's all because of your astute suggestion, Roxanne, that someone with a new weapon would do a little target practice before using it for real."

"Care to explain that?" Barnett asked, "Preferably in English."

"Looking at all these dead satellites over time, I realized that the number that die each year has been increasing."

"Yeah," Kilkenny said, "but the number of satellites in orbit has gone up, too."

"But not as fast," Grin countered. "I've got enough historical data, thanks to you two, to statistically model the birth and death rate of our orbiting population of satellites. Up until a few years ago, both rates were fairly steady, just as you'd expect. Then the rate of satellite death spiked, and it has been up ever since."

"And if you exclude the government satellites," Kilkenny hypothesized, "the rate drops back to normal?"

"That's the thing. *Oculus* is the first noncommercial satellite to go down in a couple years. And nearly all the others died, as expected, of old age. The spike in the death rate is totally a result of commercial satellite failures."

Kilkenny slumped back in the chair, arms crossed tightly over his chest, puzzled by the results of Grin's analysis.

"So what you're saying," Barnett summarized, "is that whoever is behind all this is using commercial satellites as skeet, to warm up for downing our satellite. Is that essentially it?"

"No," Grin replied. "What the data suggest is that our initial premise is totally wrong. When I was first briefed on this, I was told only a handful of people knew *Liberty* was carrying a spy satellite, and the assumption was that security for that satellite had been compromised. What if that security had instead held?"

"Then whoever did this would had to have believed that *Oculus* was a commercial satellite," Tao replied.

"Which fits very nicely into the rest of my data."

"Commercial satellites," Kilkenny mused. "What is this, some kind of insurance scam?"

"If it is, it's the loopiest one I've ever seen," Grin replied.

"Commercial satellites are a very big business," Barnett offered. "There's well over $100 billion in hardware circling the globe at this moment and, as Grin pointed out, that number is on the rise. The world has become quite dependent on this technology."

Kilkenny thought about his pager, the GPS in his SUV, the Internet, even this three-way conversation—all of it reliant on satellites. "Can you pinpoint a start date on these attacks?"

"Based on the data I have, it looks like *Mir* was the first," Grin replied. "I think that one was Roxanne's target practice."

"An intriguing piece of analysis," Barnett said.

"Yes," Tao agreed, "but how do we proceed? We still don't know where the weapon is."

"We haven't found it yet because we aren't looking in the right place," Kilkenny said. "Grin, I've got a change in tactics for you."

"Shoot."

"Take a look at all the launches preceding the attack on *Mir*."

"How far back?"

"As far as the data you have, but I'd focus on the two years previous. Cross-ref the launches against the payloads—I want to know what's still up there."

"But we already know what's up there, and there were no winners in it."

"Which is exactly why I want you to look at the launches, too. We all know there's a weapon up there, but for some reason we can't see it. That means somebody has found a way to hide a satellite. But unless I'm mistaken, no one has come up with a way to hide a launch."

Barnett nodded. "We have satellites that do nothing but launch detection. If it's big enough to reach orbit, we know about it."

"Somewhere in those launches is a payload that's not on the books anymore. I'm betting that's where we'll find out who's behind all this."

"I'll arrange to get you that launch data," Barnett said as he jotted some notes on a legal pad. Then he looked at Kilkenny and Tao. "When do you think you'll be heading back?"

"We're not sure. Nolan and I have another stop to make," Tao replied, "this one to collect some hard evidence."

"What hard evidence?" Barnett asked.

"*Mir,*" Kilkenny replied.

31

Deep inside the compound off Druzhby Ulitsa, Peng sat in a room almost identical to the one in the Washington embassy where he'd received his orders to shadow Kilkenny and Tao. He was alone sipping a cup of tea in front of a dark flat-screen display after what had been a long day of unexpected developments. He thought about the report he'd submitted, and wondered about the reaction of his superiors. Peng expected nothing short of a reprimand for his role in the shootout.

"Secure connection with Xiyuan established," a voice announced through the speaker on the table.

The screen instantly glowed with the life-sized image of Directorate Chief Huang Zhanfu.

"Chief Huang," Peng said with a polite nod.

"Peng, I have been going over your report," Huang began.

And in light of your actions, Peng mentally finished the sentence, *your next assignment will consist of ten years' hard labor at a work camp in the western provinces.*

"What do you know about the man who was killed, this Zadkine?" Huang asked.

"Oh," Peng blurted, focusing his thoughts. "Just what I've read in the files here at the embassy. He was a senior engineer with the Russian space program, currently retired."

"He was sacked. Zadkine was in charge of bringing the Russians' *Mir* space station back to Earth. Something happened and *Mir* fell away off target."

"And Zadkine was found responsible?"

Huang nodded. "Unofficially, no definitive cause was found, through the possibility of an impact was considered. So, now we have three spacecraft, from three nations, all possible victims of an impact in orbit. Most curious, wouldn't you say?"

"Yes. Has the man I first spotted in London been identified?"

"A search of all known foreign intelligence personnel has failed to uncover a match. The technical staff is widening their search to include military and commercial security services and passport controls."

"And my orders?" Peng asked.

"You are to continue your surveillance, follow this wherever it leads."

32

Long Beach, California

Owen Moug was driving down Ocean Boulevard in a red Hummer H3, the breeze ruffling his dark-brown hair, when Iron Butterfly's "In-A-Gadda-Da-Vida" chimed out of his cell phone. It took a second longer for the call to connect—when it did, the red LED light glowed, indicating the call was secure.

"Yeah," he answered.

"It's Unger."

"Did you terminate that line of inquiry?"

"No, too many complications."

"What am I paying you for?"

"Fuck you!" Unger growled. "I got shot trying to do this job. Do you know what a Moscow doctor who doesn't ask questions costs? Those morons our mutual friend loaned us fucked the whole thing. I'm lucky not to be dead or in jail right now."

"Calm down, Ernst. We both understand the fog of war. What do you have to report?"

"Zadkine is dead, along with two of the men I brought with me. I don't know what he told his visitors, but any data he had in his home has been destroyed. Kilkenny and

Tao spent the rest of their stay safely behind the walls of the U.S. Embassy. A short while ago, they were escorted to Sheremetyevo and put aboard a plane."

"Back to the U.S.?"

"No, their end destination is Chile. You still want me to keep an eye on them?"

"Yeah. Send me their itinerary as well, so I can cover any layovers."

"Understood."

Moug ended the call, his mind mulling over Unger's report. As he continued down the highway, the former Air Force officer tried to extrapolate the line of the government's investigation.

Thirty minutes later, he pulled through the main gate of Skye Aerospace's Long Beach complex. Most of the buildings dated to the 1930s, when the Skye Tool Corporation launched a marine division. Decried by the critics of the day as starkly modern with their long, low silhouettes of glass accented with piers of masonry and sculpted concrete, the historic buildings were now viewed as prime examples of modern industrial architecture.

The Long Beach facility fell into neglect during the seventies and eighties, when the marine division exited the shipbuilding business, but was revived in the nineties and now served as the home port for Skye Aerospace's oceanic launch system, *Aequatus*.

"You are expected, sir," Skye's executive assistant said as Moug arrived at the CEO's suite. "Go right in."

"Good evening, Owen," Skye said, looking up from a financial report as he entered.

Moug nodded respectfully. "C.J."

"You look like a man who could use a drink."

"I'm fine. There was a problem in Moscow."

"What *kind* of problem?"

"The messy kind, but nothing that can be tied back to us. The two government investigators are unfortunately still alive."

"Did they speak with Zadkine?"

Moug nodded. "Briefly. He's dead along with a pair of hired Russians."

"The mess, I presume."

"Yes."

"Where are Kilkenny and Tao now?"

"In transit. They're traveling to Chile, though I don't know why."

"Hmmm," Skye mused, then it hit her. "They're going after *Mir*."

"You've got to be kidding. Whatever's left of that station is resting on the bottom of the Pacific."

"Only because no one has had a good enough reason to go look for it. Now it appears I've given them one."

"Don't second-guess yourself, C.J."

Skye glared back at him. "The final decision to fire on the shuttle was mine."

"I agree that taking down *Liberty* was a shitty thing to do, but *we had no choice*," Moug hammered the last words like a drumbeat. "They were going after the ZetaComm satellite. If enough of it was left to make it worth retrieving, then the odds are pretty strong they would've discovered what really happened to it."

"I know *why* it had to be done," Skye snapped back, "and rehashing it'll just give me a headache. The blood of those astronauts is on my hands."

"All I'm saying is we did the smart thing."

"Not if they're looking for *Mir.*"

"Even if they are, you're assuming there's enough of it left to be found, and that what is left can tell them something."

"What if that crucial piece of evidence *does* exist and they *do* find it?"

"Are you asking for my advice?"

"That is what I pay you for."

"We don't know that they're looking for *Mir.* If they are, then steps should be taken to make sure they don't find it."

"Another *tragic accident*?"

"If that's what it takes to protect this company, yes."

Skye turned from Moug and stared out her window at the empty pier. A few days earlier, *Argo* and *Aequatus* had departed, bound for the equator. In *Argo*'s hold was the next step in her company's future.

"Owen, I want you to handle this personally. Look into what they're doing. If it's *Mir,* I want to know why and I want them stopped."

"I understand," Moug replied.

33

Archipelago de Juan Fernandez, Chile
August 16

Over the past few days, Kilkenny's travels with Tao had drawn him back and forth across eight time zones and his circadian rhythm was hopelessly disconnected from any sense of place. As a consequence, Kilkenny was already asleep when the U.S. Navy Twin Otter lifted off from the runway in Santiago.

Two navy flight crews had ferried the De Havilland DHC-6 down from the States, arriving at the Chilean capital just ahead of its two travel-weary passengers. The hold of the plane was filled with the equipment Kilkenny had requested to aid in their search.

While awake, Kilkenny kept his thoughts centered on the problems at hand. He found comfort in the immediacy of things he could take action on because they helped keep his mind off Kelsey's situation. But she was there in his dreams, alone in the darkness, hunted by an unseen predator. And Kilkenny was unable to protect her.

His high-school swim coach, a wise old Basilian priest, had introduced him to the Prayer for Serenity following a particularly difficult loss. Intellectually, he accepted that some things he could change while others he could not, but still struggled, especially now, with the wisdom to know the difference.

The change in the pitch of engines roused Kilkenny from his slumber. They were descending. Below, the first glints of dawn sparkled on the blue waters of the Pacific. As the plane banked, he caught sight of the two eastern islands that composed the lonely volcanic archipelago. The third lay a hundred miles farther west.

The larger of the pair was a boomerang-shaped pile of rock roughly thirteen miles long and four miles across at its widest point. Off its southwestern tip lay the smaller Santa Clara Island. They had been known from the time of their discovery by Spanish pilot Juan Fernandez in 1563 as Mas-a-Tierra and Mas-a-Fuera, but the Chilean government had recently renamed the larger island and its distant sibling Isla Robinson Crusoe and Isla Alejandro Selkirk. The four years Scottish sailor Alexander Selkirk spent alone on Mas-a-Tierra provided the inspiration for Daniel Defoe's epic tale of survival.

Passing over the squat mountainous form of El Yunque—the Anvil—the pilot lined up the runway for his final descent into Punta de Isla airfield. As soon as the plane rolled to a stop, crewmen disembarked and secured the aircraft. A moment later, the two passengers were given approval to deplane.

"You Tao and Kilkenny?"

The voice—a New Jersey tenor—belonged to a swarthy fireplug of a man in a yellow squall coat, dungarees, and a denim baseball cap with the legend *R/V Sea Lion.* He wore his black hair long, pulled back in a ponytail, and a bushy black beard covered the lower half of his face.

"We are," Tao replied coolly.

"Thought as much, you two being the only ones not in uniform and all. I'm Guido Peretti, captain of the *Sea Lion.* My boss back at Harbor Branch pulled us off our survey to lend you two a hand."

"We appreciate it. I hope it hasn't caused you too much trouble," Kilkenny said, offering his hand.

"Nah. A couple of the eggheads are bellyaching, but when they saw the carrot and stick offered with regard to their grants, they came around. Let's get your gear offloaded and down to the docks. I was told this was a rush job, so I figured you'd want to get out to sea as soon as possible."

Peretti shot off a string of rapid-fire Spanish at a group of local young men who stood beside an old Ford pickup. Kilkenny caught the gist of what was said, including some of the profanities. The laborers quickly filled the rear of the truck with a collection of small crates and boxes, then drove off.

"They'll get all your gear aboard," Peretti assured them, "but before we head to the launch, there's somebody I think you'll want to meet."

Peretti drove through the small village of San Juan Bautista to a ramshackle home on the outskirts near the beach. At the sound of the jeep pulling up, Salvador Delmar appeared in the doorway, his arms folded across his chest.

"Buenos días, Salvador," Peretti called out.

The man nodded, but said nothing.

"Friendly," Kilkenny opined.

"Oh, he'll warm up." Peretti went to the back of the jeep and, from inside a backpack, retrieved a bottle of Havana Club Rum. "I just need to make a proper introduction."

Delmar grinned at the sight of the bottle and disappeared inside. He returned a moment later with four mismatched glasses that he set on the wooden table on the covered patio.

"Isn't it a little early to be drinking?" Tao asked.

"Depends on which time zone we're in," Kilkenny replied. "I, for one, could use a wee taste."

"And it would be impolite to refuse the man's hospitality," Peretti added.

Tao relented and sipped at the aged Cuban rum. It went down smooth and easy.

"I assume there's a reason why we're here, other than the charming company."

"*Qué?*" Delmar asked.

Peretti rattled off a short reply. Delmar leered at Tao, his gap-toothed smile two crooked rows of yellowed teeth.

"What did you tell him?" Tao demanded.

"Just that you thought he was charming."

Tao's glare turned icy.

"As to why I brought you here, it's to chat with Salvador. You see, when I found out what you were after, I remembered a story this old fisherman told me a few months back during one of our visits ashore. I'm sketchy on the details, so I figured we'd get it from the horse's mouth, so to speak."

Peretti then asked Delmar to tell him about the night that he saw the falling stars.

"*Sí, sí,*" Delmar agreed, taking another swallow of rum to lubricate his vocal cords before launching into his narrative.

Kilkenny and Tao listened politely as Delmar described what he had seen. From his hand gestures, they gathered that whatever the retired fisherman had seen had crossed the sky from west to east before falling into the ocean. Peretti let Delmar finish his story before asking any questions.

"Gracias, mi amigo," Peretti said after Delmar answered his last question. He poured the old man another glass, then turned to Kilkenny and Tao.

"One night a few years back, Salvador is out on his fishing boat when he hears what sounds like thunder, 'cept it doesn't stop like thunder does. It keeps on rumbling. He looks around to see what's making the noise and he sees five glowing objects falling out of the sky. Now, he's seen falling stars before, but they were always high up and never made a sound. These stars are noisy and heading right for him. One after another, they hammer into the water, each one closer than the next. One of 'em hits not a hundred meters from his boat and kicks off a wave big enough to knock his boat around and give Salvador a couple nasty bumps and bruises, and that scar on his forehead. At this point, he's figuring it was a plane, so he starts looking around for anything to salvage."

"No thought of survivors?" Tao asked.

Peretti shrugged. "The man's a realist. Anyway, he finds squat, except for these large patches of foam on the surface. Whatever hit the water went right down to the bottom. When he gets back here, he tells his story, but there's no report of any plane going down. Since he's got a history with the bottle, most folks figure he was just drunk at the time."

"And when did he say this happened?" Tao asked.

"On the twenty-third of March, 2001."

"The day *Mir* came down," Kilkenny said. "Can he pinpoint the area where he was that night?"

Peretti asked, and Delmar thought for a moment, then stepped back into his house. He returned and unrolled a sea chart on the table. The age-worn map was covered with notations, cryptic marks regarding his favorite fishing spots. It took Delmar a minute, but then he placed the tip of a gnarled finger on a mark north of the island. Beside the mark, Kilkenny saw precise notations of longitude and latitude.

"How'd he nail the coordinates?"

Peretti relayed Kilkenny's question and the old fisherman grinned.

"GPS."

34

Santiago, Chile

"Where are Kilkenny and Tao?" Peng asked as soon as the burgundy sedan pulled away from the airport curb.

The man seated beside him in the back of the embassy car was a few years older and dressed in a suit and tie. The abruptness of Peng's question struck him as impolite, but he dismissed the younger man's minor breach of etiquette as a side effect of his current assignment.

"The subjects are on an island a few hundred miles offshore," the chief of station of Chinese intelligence in Chile replied. "Radio intercepts seem to indicate they are mounting an ocean search of some kind."

"You have agents on the island?"

"No."

"No? Are you not aware of the importance of tracking Kilkenny and Tao? What arrangements have been made to maintain the surveillance?"

He is as impatient as an American, the chief of station thought. "None. The most recent communiqué from the ministry indicates that the surveillance has been canceled and requests that you be brought to the embassy immediately upon your arrival."

"What has happened?" Peng asked.

"I was provided with no further information. Perhaps Directorate Chief Huang will enlighten you when we reach the embassy."

Certain now that the Foreign Ministry was cloning the drab, windowless conference rooms in every Chinese embassy, Peng sat down and waited for the connection to be made. He had expected to see Directorate Chief Huang, to whom he had reported directly while on this assignment, but next to Huang sat Minister Tian.

"This is Peng?" Tian asked Huang.

"Yes, Minister." Huang replied.

Despite separation by half the globe, Peng felt the minister's eyes lock onto him as if he were in the room.

"You have uncovered an ugly situation, Peng, one which has infuriated the president and the state council."

"Oh?" Peng heard the wordless question escape from his lips and regretted the lapse.

"Explain it to him, Huang," Tian commanded.

"Your current assignment was based on an intercepted message and a bit of speculation on my part. The message was encrypted, but we knew the identity of both the sender and the recipient, and the Americans' reaction to this message was quite strong."

"If our leaders' concern has been aroused," Peng offered, "I assume that we, too, know the contents of this message?"

Huang nodded. "There is a saying that a picture is worth a thousand words. Watch."

Huang and Tian disappeared, replaced by a spectacular view of *Liberty* in orbit above the Earth, its payload bay opened wide with a long robotic arm extending out toward the screen. In the payload bay, an astronaut moved too slowly for the video to be running in normal time. But even in slow motion, the video barely caught the three focused beams of light that quickly flashed across the screen. They speared the doomed spacecraft and the destruction was total.

"A weapon," Peng said softly as the image faded and Tian and Huang reappeared.

"A most powerful weapon," Huang concurred. "Our engineering experts have also concluded that an attack by an energy weapon would explain some of the unusual data they received in the brief time before *Shenzhou*-7 was lost."

"I would have thought only the Americans capable of such a weapon, but then the attack on *Liberty* makes no sense."

"Our initial reaction as well, Peng," Huang said, having shared the younger man's confusion. "It was you who provided the key to unlocking thus puzzling situation. We have identified the man you discovered following Kilkenny in London and Moscow. His name is Ernst Unger, former German military officer of above-average ability, currently employed in corporate security by an American aerospace company."

"A company did this?" Peng was stunned.

"An intensely competitive company," Tian replied. "And yes, one with the means and the motivation to do what you have just seen."

Peng thought about his surveillance, and about Kilkenny and Tao on a remote island in the Pacific still searching for answers. "Will we share this intelligence with the Americans? Their loss is as great as ours."

"In time," Tian answered calmly, like a Wei Ch'i master who has already projected several moves to an end game. "First, an opportunity has presented itself, and we will take full advantage of it."

"Peng, prepare to leave as soon as possible," Huang ordered. "You are to be on the next flight to Hawaii."

35

As *Sea Lion* headed north out of Cumberland Bay, Tao and Kilkenny staked out a section of the stern deck and set to work on the equipment they'd brought with them. Both had changed into jeans and windbreakers; Tao had her long black hair twisted into a tight braid to keep the strands from flying around her face.

"I'll prep the tanks and fuel cell," Kilkenny said. "You test the batteries."

"Aye, sir," Tao replied, following his lead—this was, after all, Kilkenny's element.

She opened the first of the cases Kilkenny had indicated and found the several battery modules and a handheld tester. The process was straightforward—connect the tester to the positive and negative terminals.

"Batteries all show a full charge," Tao reported.

"Anything you need?" Peretti asked as he clambered down from the bridge.

"I have some tanks to be filled," Kilkenny replied.

"Tanks? I though you brought an ROV?"

Kilkenny shook his head. "None available for a couple weeks."

"Might take that long to find your wreckage, if we find it at all."

"But if we find it sooner, I'll check it out with the suit."

"You know, the water out here can get pretty deep."

"This rig's rated to five thousand feet. If it's deeper than that, we'll *commandeer* somebody's ROV."

Having been pulled off his own project to aid in this search, Peretti knew this wasn't idle talk. "Five grand—no shit?"

"No shit," Kilkenny said flatly.

"I'll send our dive master over to give you two a hand. She'll hook you up with whatever you need."

Two hours out, *Sea Lion* reached the southern corner of her primary search area—an elongated rectangle of ocean covering fourteen square miles. The point Delmar had indicated on his chart lay just inside the corner. The shallowest point in the search area was just over one thousand feet deep. Taking into account the speed at which falling pieces of *Mir* struck the water and the northerly current running along the coast of South America, the ship's resident oceanographer plotted a likely descent path for the wreckage.

"Why are we slowing?" Tao asked.

Compared to the quick sprint out to sea, the ship's speed had fallen to a relative crawl. Kilkenny looked up from the support frame they were assembling and saw two crewmembers at the stern lowering a slender torpedo-shaped instrument into the water.

"Guess it's time to mow the lawn," Kilkenny said.

"Excuse me?" Tao asked.

"Run a search pattern. That thing they just dropped in the water is a side scan sonar. Most people call it a fish because it's hooked to a cable off the stern of the ship and—you get the picture. We're going to drag the fish behind us underwater, which is why the ship has slowed. If the ship went fast, the fish would be skipping along the surface like a water skier. That reel back there will let out just enough cable to hold the fish about 120 feet off the bottom."

"So, metaphorically speaking, how does the ship *mow the lawn?*"

"When the sonar operator switches the fish on, it'll paint a thin strip of the ocean floor about six hundred feet wide—that's assuming Peretti's ordered a quick and dirty search of the area. If we were doing a detailed survey, we'd scan a narrower area by putting the fish closer to the bottom. Our search area is a big box and we're going to drive back and forth over the top of it, one strip at a time, just like mowing the lawn."

Tao's eyes narrowed. "A guy must have thought that one up."

"Probably," Kilkenny agreed, returning to his work.

By late evening, Kilkenny and Tao had reassembled and tested the HS5000. The atmospheric diving system (ADS)—more akin to a submarine than a conventional diver's wetsuit—consisted of a high-strength cast-aluminum exoskeleton mated with a transparent three-quarter-inch acrylic vision dome and an external backpack housing the life support, propulsion, and communications equipment. Each limb was segmented into separate rigid pieces connected by oil-filled hydraulic rotary joints, allowing the pilot a wide range of movement. The pressure inside the Hardsuit remained constant at one atmosphere—the same pressure found at sea level—eliminating the need for a lengthy postdive stay in a decompression chamber.

Peretti stood, arms akimbo, studying the bright yellow suit. "Looks like something out of an old science fiction flick."

"I know the one," Kilkenny replied. *"Forbidden Planet."*

"Well, as the saying goes, I got some good news and some bad news. Which do you want first?"

"Rox?" Kilkenny asked.

"We've had enough bad news," Tao answered. "Give us the good."

"Looks like Salvador wasn't too drunk that night and read his GPS correctly."

"You found *Mir?*"

"We're getting some strong returns—a good sign for hard, metallic objects. Spotted three pieces so far."

"What makes you think it's *Mir,*" Tao asked, "other than location?"

"I read a lot when I'm out at sea, and I remember this thing about craters on one of Jupiter's moons, and how a bunch of them were all lined up, like the moon had been strafed. The astronomers didn't know what to make of this until a few years back, when Shoemaker-Levy smacked into Jupiter."

"I remember that," Kilkenny said. "The comet had broken up into pieces during a previous pass of the planet."

"Yeah, then they came down, one after another. Bing, bang, boom. The three pieces we spotted so far are pretty much in a nice straight line, right down the alley. Got me thinking, maybe we caught a break. We'll continue running wide lanes, see if we find the rest. Then we'll do a tight pass, get better resolution over the whole site."

"How long will all that take?" Tao asked.

"We ought to be done early tomorrow afternoon."

"How deep is the wreckage?"

Peretti cast a wary eye over the Hardsuit. "Let's just say I hope they figured in a safety margin on your depth rating."

"What's the bad news?" Kilkenny asked.

"Weather's turning to shit on us. Storm front's coming through, nothing terrible, but the sea'll be heavy enough to keep me from pitching you over the side on the end of the crane. Chances are good you won't be diving at all tomorrow."

36

August 18

Kilkenny returned to the stern deck near dawn. A heavy layer of gray clouds blanketed the sky, but the seas were calm and the midwinter storm had petered to an intermittent drizzle. Peretti stood by the stern, watching a couple of crewmen service the ship's crane.

"Not a pretty morning, but the sea's decent enough to dive," Peretti said by way of a greeting.

"You found the other three pieces?"

Peretti nodded. "Little farther out than we expected, but pretty much in line with the first three. You wanna take a look?"

Kilkenny nodded and followed Peretti down to the electronics suite. Tao was already there, seated beside the sonar operator in front of a high-resolution plasma screen. Kilkenny stood behind her. On the screen he saw a long, roughly cylindrical shape partially embedded in the ocean floor. Using a mouse, the operator was taking critical measurements of the object.

"What are you looking at?"

"It's either the Core Module or Kvant-2," the operator speculated. "Both are about the same size."

Kilkenny looked closely at the ghostly image. "Looks like an old beer can from here. How far apart are the pieces?"

"About a mile from first to last." The operator switched to a wider image of the ocean floor. The bottom looked smooth, interrupted only by six mounds in a roughly straight line running southwest to northeast.

"What are the currents like down there?"

"Two to three knots, perpendicular to the line of the wreck."

"How do you want to tackle this?" Peretti asked.

"Start with this one," Kilkenny replied, pointing to the last fragment found, "and work my way back."

"When do you want to dive?"

"As soon as I can get in the water."

After a light breakfast, Kilkenny and Tao worked with the crew of the *Sea Lion* on deployment and retrieval procedures and shipboard dive operations. Fortunately, the ship's dive master, Joan Frores, had had experience with earlier models of the ADS while servicing oil rigs in the North Sea.

Kilkenny met Frores on the stern deck. He'd changed into a fleece sweatsuit for warmth, covered with an outer layer of Gore-Tex. A small flashlight hung from a cord around his neck and his head was covered by a lightweight stocking cap. Around his waist he wore a belly pack filled with snacks and emergency supplies. He slipped on a pair of clear, bug-eye glasses, similar to the ones worn by athletes. Thin rubber-coated cables ran from the end of each ear stem, joining behind his head into a single wire terminated with a USB connector.

"I have to say, I'm a bit squeamish about you diving without an umbilical," Frores opined. "I always liked knowing I had a firm grip on the lads when they were in deep water."

"I'll be fine," Kilkenny reassured her. "The wireless digital in the suit is just as good as an umbilical and the fuel cell will provide all the power I'll need. Besides, where would I have put a spool with a mile of cable on it, in my carry-on bag?"

Frores laughed. "Not likely. Well, let's get you buttoned up."

Using a hand crank, Kilkenny hoisted the Hardsuit's upper torso up off the lower torso/leg assembly. Out of the water, the cast aluminum suit weighed fifteen hundred pounds empty.

When the upper torso was clear, he climbed up the back of the support frame and eased himself into the lower half. That portion of the suit came up to his sternum.

"Oh no, Gromit!" Kilkenny exclaimed, recoiling in mock horror. "It's the *wrong trousers!*"

Frores stared, the reference completely lost on her.

"Wallace and Gromit?" he hinted.

Frores shook her head.

"It was an Academy Award–winning short," Kilkenny said, exasperated. "A claymation classic."

"Sorry, I'm not much for the cinema. Here's your scrubber."

"Bet she doesn't even like cheese," Kilkenny muttered to himself as he accepted the cartridge, again imitating Nick Park's hapless inventor.

Kilkenny fit the scrubber cartridge, which was filled with a granular CO^2 adsorbent, into place in the rear of the suit's waist. Unlike conventional scuba, in which the diver's exhaled breath is discharged from the regulator mouthpiece in a stream of bubbles—an open-circuit design—the HS5000 used a closed-circuit design. As Kilkenny breathed inside the suit, the CO^2 from his respiration would be scrubbed from the air by the adsorbent. Without the scrubber, Kilkenny would quickly suffocate.

"All set," Kilkenny reported.

"Tuck your wings in."

Kilkenny folded his arms over his chest and, as Frores lowered the upper torso, wriggled through the opening. The upper torso mated perfectly, setting down onto the oil-filled hydraulic joint. Kilkenny set the interior latches, then turned the upper torso—it rotated freely without a sound.

"Ready for the dome," Kilkenny said.

Frores climbed up the front of the support armature carrying the thick acrylic dome that would cover Kilkenny's head. She set it into place, then drove in three bolts at equidistant points around the dome's circular base. Inside the suit, Kilkenny hung an emergency mask around his neck and plugged his headset and goggles into jacks near the base of the dome.

"Radio check, test."

"Loud and clear, Nolan," Tao replied from the sonar room.

After Kilkenny set up the oxygen system, Frores attached a vacuum pump to the back of the suit and dropped the internal pressure one-half PSI below that of the outside. She watched the gauge carefully for several minutes, but the digital counter never wavered. The seals on the suit were all good.

Chin on his chest, Kilkenny studied the suit's familiar layout of controls and displays. System by system, Kilkenny powered up the suit. From the console, he tested his camera, external lighting, trim adjusters, and portable version of the experimental acoustic daylighting system. Inside the boots, Kilkenny's feet rested on actuated plates that controlled four thrusters mounted on the suit's backpack. Vertical controls were housed in the left foot, lateral controls in the right.

Kilkenny pushed his hands down into the articulated arms. In the end of each arm, he grabbed hold of a contoured handgrip. Flexing his wrist, he rotated the manipulator assembly through twenty degrees of movement. He squeezed on the grips, testing the operation of the manipulator jaws.

"All systems are good," Kilkenny announced.

Frores flashed him an okay sign, then waved over several other crewmen to roll the support stand bearing the Hardsuit into position near the crane. Kilkenny braced himself inside the suit as he was moved across the deck. They set him near the stern rail, facing out toward the sea.

Looking up, he watched Frores connect the crane cable to the lift attachment. She slipped the quick-release fastener down over the bullet-shaped casting and it locked in place. Then she motioned to the crane operator to gradually take up the slack, and the cable went taut. With the weight of the suit supported by the crane, Frores swung open the support stand, leaving Kilkenny standing free.

Frores looked one last time through the dome.

"Ready?" she shouted.

Kilkenny signed okay.

Slowly, the crane lifted Kilkenny off the deck and out

over the rail. They let him down easy—the surest sign of a skilled deck crew. Two divers were already in the cold sea, waiting for him. A red flag with a diagonal white stripe fluttered from the ship's mast. *Diver Down.*

When the water was chest-high, Frores stopped his descent. The suit bobbed in the light sea, weighing only seven pounds in the water. With a little slack in the cable, Kilkenny pivoted his left foot, firing the thrusters for descent. He slipped beneath the surface and was enveloped by blue-green water.

Kilkenny descended to ten feet, then waited.

Ka-chink.

The cable released and was quickly pulled up to keep it from drifting back into the Hardsuit.

"You're all clear," Tao reported over his headset. "Good hunting."

"Roger that," Kilkenny replied, and he began a controlled descent to the ocean floor.

He folded his arms over his chest to stay warm. After he passed through the surface layer, the water temperature around him rapidly dropped and was now near freezing. Other than the pale glow from his displays, Kilkenny was enveloped in complete darkness. He kept the external lights off to conserve power and busied himself with regular checks of the onboard systems.

"Approaching forty-five hundred feet," he called out.

"We copy that, Nolan," Tao replied.

"Switching on AD."

His goggles flickered, then filled with the image of the sea as if the water were transparent for miles. Schools of fish swam as if in midair. Looking up, he saw the *Sea Lion*'s keel, a dark tiny shape in a hazy field of acoustic scatter.

"*Sea Lion*, the view is tremendous."

"We see it," Tao replied, amazed. "Your video is coming through clearly."

With a slight adjustment of his foot pedals, Kilkenny tilted the suit forward slightly to get a better view of the approaching bottom. He felt an uneasy sense of vertigo, the computer-generated visual from the AD system showing nothing between him and gray field of rocks and silt below.

It's all mind over matter, he reminded himself. *If I don't mind, it don't matter.*

One hundred feet above the ocean floor, Kilkenny halted his descent and got his bearings. He was facing a few degrees north of due east. When planning this dive, he had factored in the drift caused by the deep ocean current, extrapolating backward from the site of the first piece of wreckage he wanted to survey to his launch point on the surface.

Kilkenny slowly rotated clockwise, panning the undersea landscape. To calculate shade and shadow, the AD software was programmed to assume the sun was at high noon over the equator. Turning south, he saw a projection of his own shadow on the uneven seabed. To his left, he saw a rounded, man-made shape totally out of place on the rock-strewn plain.

"*Sea Lion*, I've spotted the first piece of wreckage. Moving in to check it out."

"Roger, Nolan. We'll be watching over your shoulder."

The module was one of the smaller surviving fragments of *Mir.*

"I'm switching to external lights and video."

The rendered image in Kilkenny's goggles faded, replaced with a view of the real world outside his vision dome. Bits of particulate matter swirled like fine snow around him, disturbed by his thrusters. Bathed in the harsh light of two seventy-five-watt XENOPHOT bulbs, Kilkenny saw with his own eyes the scorched surface of the module.

It was roughly cylindrical, the center portion being as wide as it was long, with smaller diameter connections on each end. One end of the module was half-buried in the silt while the opposite end jutted upward. The exposed end looked as if it had been broken off—the metal was jagged and fractured.

"If this isn't part of *Mir*, I don't know what to make of it," Kilkenny said.

Tao glanced back and forth between the screen and a binder containing schematic drawings and photographs of the former space station, trying to find any identifying details. "I'd say you're looking at Kvant-1—the astrophysics module."

"I'll take that as a positive ID."

Kilkenny moved closer to the module, but was careful not to kick up any silt. It was blackened and covered with a fine layer of sediment. In her e-mail message, Kelsey had told him that she believed an energy weapon had struck both *Liberty* and the satellite. He slowly searched for any sign of a hole in the metal skin, but found none.

"That's all I can do where without rolling this thing over," Kilkenny said thirty minutes later. "I'm going to move on to the next one."

37

Owen Moug was seated inside his stateroom, reading a copy of Estleman's classic western *The Master Executioner*, when he heard a rap on the door.

"Come," he answered.

Unger entered. "The helicopter reports a positive visual sighting of *Sea Lion.*"

Moug looked up from novel. "Distance?"

"Ten miles."

"Have the captain move to intercept. Then tell the men to get ready."

Kilkenny's survey of the fallen Spektr module yielded the same result as Kvant-1. While it bore the scars of a fiery reentry and a punishing impact into the ocean, he found nothing to suggest that a high-energy laser had struck the module.

The third piece of wreckage from the station was more than twice the size of the first two. Switching back to acoustic daylight for the approach, he saw the module standing upright like a miniature Leaning Tower of Pisa. The lower half of the tower was a broad, squat cylinder that tapered into the upper segment. Portions of a further taper at the top on the tower remained, but whatever was attached there had been torn away.

"What's this one?" Kilkenny asked.

"Easy call," Tao replied, "that's the Core Module. There used to be a connecting node on top, where most of the other modules were tied in."

"That explains why it isn't there anymore—a victim of torque and sheer."

At depth, the HS5000 glided over the ocean floor at two knots—about the pace of a slow walk. It took Kilkenny thirty minutes to close the distance and begin his third wreck survey of the morning.

On first pass, Kilkenny immediately noticed one side of the module was buckled inward, almost flattened. Some of the charred metal on that side had broken or chipped away.

"This might be where it struck the water. At the speed it was traveling, it would've been like hitting concrete."

Moug sat in the bow of the launch as it pulled alongside *Sea Lion*. Unger and five men accompanied him on the short trip over from the yacht.

"Permission to come aboard," he called up to Peretti and the two deckhands who stood waiting by the starboard rail.

"Granted," Peretti answered.

Lines were passed and Moug climbed up the ladder onto the deck and introductions were made.

"I apologize for not having contacted you," Moug explained, "but our radio's gone out. We're heading into Valparaiso and I wanted to let the marina know when to expect us and to make arrangements for repairs. Would it be possible to use yours?"

"Certainly. Follow me."

Unger remained on the stern deck with four of the men as Moug followed Peretti inside. The fifth stayed with the launch.

Under artificial light, Kilkenny's field of view shrank down to a sphere no more than five feet in diameter. After the clarity of acoustic daylight, he found the restricted view of the real world almost claustrophobic.

He'd started from the top of the Core Module and slowly circled his way down the blackened tower. Just past the midsection taper, Kilkenny discovered a silver-dollar-sized hole in the module's smooth aluminum skin.

"I'm at the lower half of the module. Were there any external attachments in this area?"

Tao checked the reference binder. "Doesn't look like it. I'm seeing solar panels on the upper half, but nothing that far back."

Kilkenny moved closer to the hole. Though the edges were charred, he could see that it was elongated, slightly out of round. The HS5000's powerful lights, mounted near Kilkenny's waist, cast a dark shadow into the hole. And the closer he came to the module, the less he was able to see.

"I'm going to try something," Kilkenny announced as he switched off the external lights.

Bracing himself against the front of the upper torso, Kilkenny switched on the small flashlight that dangled from a cord around his neck and directed a tight beam into the hole. He adjusted the position of his head, trying to minimize the reflected glare of the vision dome's concave interior. Then he saw it. The hole wasn't a surface mount—it went straight through to the interior.

"Are you seeing this?"

"Seeing what? Everything went dark as soon as you killed the lights."

"This is what we came for. I'm seeing layers inside. This hole goes right through the module."

Kilkenny pulled back from the module and turned his exterior lights back on.

"What are you doing?" Tao asked, once again able to see what was in front of Kilkenny.

"Checking the other side. That hole was at a downward angle so—"

Kilkenny lowered himself onto the seabed, tiny clouds of silt spiraling around him, disturbed by the spinning blades of the thrusters. Carefully, he searched for the hole's mate on the module's opposite side.

Peretti led Moug to the radio room. The operator, a young man in his early twenties, was trying to eke a stronger signal out of a distant Latino music station.

"Sparks, we got a guest who needs to make a—"

Before Peretti could finish his order, Moug pressed a Glock pistol into his back and pulled back on the trigger. The nine-millimeter bullet exploded in Peretti's heart and the man staggered forward. Moug pushed him aside and fired twice more into the radioman's forehead.

Two loud pops interrupted Unger's idle chat with one of the deckhands.

"What the fuck was that?" the deckhand asked, trying to identify the source of the noise.

Unger unholstered his pistol and fired point-blank into the back of the crewman's head. A gory spray of bone and brain erupted from the man's face, his left cheek and eye destroyed by the exiting projectile. Propelled by the force of the blow, the man toppled forward and crumpled face-first onto the deck.

"That was the sound of your ship being seized," Unger replied.

Following Unger's lead, his men drew out their weapons and took control of the stern deck. Two shots silenced the remaining deckhand before he could sound a warning. Unger holstered his pistol and signaled to the man in the launch. The man handed up six Uzi SMGs, then joined his comrades on deck. Unger left two men to guard the stern deck and motioned for the other three to follow him forward.

Room by room, they collected the researchers and crew and escorted them to a hold in the bowels of the ship. Tao and Frores were kept under guard in the electronics suite, both seated and bound. It took less than five minutes for Unger and his men to take control of *Sea Lion.*

"That one's Tao," Unger reported as he led Moug into the electronics suite.

Moug studied Tao for a moment and found her much more attractive in the flesh than the photographs he'd seen of her. His attention was repaid with an icy stare. Frores's anger was far less restrained, her face flushed and tense.

Moug then walked over to the console where the two women had been monitoring Kilkenny's dive. On the main screen, he saw a video image shot over the left shoulder of the HS5000. A bright spot of light slowly traveled over a curved sheet of badly damaged metal. He thumbed through the binder on the desktop and confirmed what they were after.

"When I came aboard, I noticed this ship was flying a *Diver Down* flag," Moug said calmly, again watching the video display. "Since we haven't located your associate, I think I can guess where he is. Unfortunately for him, that's where he's going to stay."

"You animal!" Frores exploded. "You can't leave the man down there. He'll die."

"That's the point."

"Got to be here somewhere," Kilkenny muttered, his eyes darting over the blackened aluminum skin. "Bingo."

The second hole was a mirror image of the first and Kilkenny would have bet that the two lined up perfectly, with laserlike precision.

"*Sea Lion*, I've found the second hole!"

Nothing.

"*Sea Lion*, do you copy? Over."

Again, no response.

Kilkenny checked his computer—it was still receiving data from the ship and the signal was strong. Looking for a simple cause for the problem, he checked his headset and found the jack was firmly connected.

"*Sea Lion*, do you copy? Over."

"This is *Sea Lion*," Moug replied. "We hear you loud and clear."

"Who the hell is this?" Kilkenny asked, not recognizing the voice.

"Not important. Have you found what you're looking for down there?"

"Where's Roxanne?"

"She's here."

"Don't tell him anything!" Tao shouted.

Unger backhanded her across the face, splitting her lip. A trickle of blood ran down her chin. Frores lunged headlong into Unger, driving him back into the wall. Pinned, Unger grabbed two handfuls of Frores's curly salt-and-pepper mane and drove his knee up into her face. Dazed, she staggered back. Unger drew his pistol and placed two bullets into the top of her head.

"Roxanne!" Kilkenny shouted.

"No," Moug replied icily. "At least not yet, anyway."

"They killed Joan," Tao said, her words slurred by a badly swollen lip.

"You son of a bitch," Kilkenny cursed.

"When I need to be. Good-bye, Kilkenny."

Moug yanked out the power cables feeding the HS5000's electronics gear; the readouts and displays went blank.

Static.

Not wanting whoever had taken *Sea Lion* to know what he was doing, Kilkenny switched off the video and digital uplink. Then he doused the suit's external lights and switched back to AD mode. Against the gray haze of the surface, he saw two tiny black silhouettes—*Sea Lion* and her attackers. He tilted the left foot control and began his ascent.

Kilkenny had to treat both ships as hostile and had no idea what he was going to do once he got there. For the moment, he was stealthy and bulletproof and had a mile to come up with some kind of plan.

* * *

"Mayday, Mayday," Moug called out over the ship's radio. "This is the research vessel *Sea Lion.* We are in need of emergency assistance. Does any one copy? Over."

"Sea Lion, this is the freighter *Soga Maru.* What is your position? Over."

"This is *Sea Lion.* We are at zero-three-three-point-two south latitude, seven-eight-point-six west longitude," Moug lied. "We've suffered an explosion and are taking on water. Many injuries. Can you assist, *Soga Maru?*"

"We are moving to your position, *Sea Lion.* We are four hours out at best speed. We will relay your distress call to Chilean authorities."

"Thank you, *Soga Maru.* Please hurry."

Moug switched off the radio.

"Scuttling charges are set and the men are assembled on the stern deck," Unger reported.

"Then it's time to leave."

At twelve hundred feet, the dark shapes on the surface had grown more distinct but were still a long way off. Unlike the AD system he and Grin were testing on the *Virginia,* the one he was using now didn't have a zoom capability.

A small black shape broke off from one of the larger ones and headed toward the other. It sped quickly across the surface, a vee-shaped wake expanding behind it. The small boat pulled alongside the second ship, then the two silhouettes merged, and Kilkenny lost sight of it.

The second vessel pulled away, leaving the other behind, motionless in the water. Kilkenny felt an anxious knot tightening in his gut.

The silhouette of the stationary ship fractured into a

thousand tiny black triangles. The broken bits furiously repositioned themselves as the AD system struggled to reassemble the image. When the acoustic disruption cleared, Kilkenny realized that in place of the gray keel, he now saw the entire ship.

Sea Lion had slipped beneath the surface and was picking up speed as she headed toward the bottom. Inside, her crew was either dead or dying, the last trapped pockets of air escaping in a stream of turbulent bubbles. She was falling at a sharp angle, bow first.

"Damn bastards!" Kilkenny railed. "You murdering sons of bitches!"

38

Halting his ascent at two hundred feet, Kilkenny watched *Sea Lion* slip downward, unable to turn his eyes away. His thoughts were of Roxanne Tao, trapped with the men and women of the research vessel, entombed at the bottom of the Pacific.

He struggled with a tremendous sense of loss. Tao was in many ways more than a friend to him. Where Kelsey was his complement, Tao was more a kindred spirit—a partner of the mind rather than the heart. Theirs was an intimacy of dark secrets, of incidents that few people would ever know, but ones from which they bore the scars.

Wall it off, he could hear Tao saying. *You'll have time to mourn later.*

The attacker's ship was barely visible in the gray noise of the ocean's surface. The HS5000 was equipped with a radio beacon and a Xenon strobe—all designed to get someone's attention should he need to surface in an emergency. At the moment, the only attention he'd draw on the surface was decidedly the kind he did not want.

"They left me for dead. The least I can do is return the favor," Kilkenny vowed.

He knew that reaching land was his only shot at survival, and the closest landfall, Isla Robinson Crusoe, was just under thirty miles south of his current position. While not equipped with a GPS, the Hardsuit did possess an AD system and a compass. As a master diver, Kilkenny was very comfortable navigating underwater. He checked current location against known GPS coordinates for the *Mir* wreckage and Cumberland Bay, then set his course and hit the thrusters.

To successfully reach the island, he needed two things: breathable air and power. He checked the life support display. Cabin pressure was good. Temperature a bit chilly but survivable. O^2 and CO^2 levels were both in the nominal range, which meant the scrubber was still functioning, keeping the air around him healthy. The port and starboard oxygen bottles were both in good shape.

Well, at least I won't suffocate, he thought, *for a while.*

The HS5000 was designed for a normal dive time of eight to ten hours, of which Kilkenny had already spent nearly four. In an emergency, he knew the suit had enough oxygen to last forty-eight hours, but that estimate was based on the assumption that the ADS had lost power and the diver was running life support manually while awaiting rescue. Kilkenny's situation was entirely different.

He switched the display to the power system. This latest evolution of the Hardsuit design replaced the umbilical power feed with an internal fuel cell, which generated electricity through a chemical reaction between hydrogen and oxygen. The suit's ability to generate power was limited to its supply of the two gaseous fuels.

At the time of launch, the power system had a full supply of hydrogen and oxygen. The readouts now showed two-tenths depleted from each of the tanks.

At the present rate of consumption, I can go another twelve hours before I run out of power. And if the island is thirty miles away, and, against the current, I'm doing about one knot, Kilkenny calculated, *I won't make it unless I cut back.*

To extend his power supply, Kilkenny shut down everything he didn't absolutely need to survive. He put all the onboard computers into an energy-saving sleep mode, so he could call them up quickly if needed. With the communications system, video, and external lights already shut down, the only power draw remaining other than the thrusters was life support.

Kilkenny switched off the recirculation fan that pumped air inside the suit through the CO^2 scrubber—in this situation it had become a luxury. In place of the fan, he slipped the emergency breathing mask over his mouth and nose so that his own lungs would force used air through the scrubber.

Except for the Traser lights illuminating the features of his dive watch, Kilkenny stood in complete darkness. He folded his arms across his chest and focused on the rhythm of his breathing.

It would be a long, slow trek back to the island.

39

Pearl Harbor, Hawaii
August 18

Since Kilkenny's departure, Grin had basically taken up residence in their office at the naval base, emerging only when his food deliveries arrived at the main gate. Work on the acoustic daylighting system for the navy had stalled, with Grin's energies focused solely on locating a weapon in space.

Over the past four days, he had painstakingly documented every rocket launch conducted during the past decade, versed himself in launch sites, payloads, and the minutiae of shroudology. So intense was this course of self-education that he could now, with a casual glance, tell the difference between a French Ariane and a Russian Proton M.

His first pass through all the data had yielded nothing. Based on the information provided—some from sources Barnett had assured him he didn't want to know—Grin had accounted for every rocket launched and every payload put into orbit. But he knew the answer was in the data somewhere, and the fact he hadn't found it yet was really starting to piss him off.

Grin poured a fresh cup of coffee and cued up Gustav Holst's orchestral suite *The Planets* on his iPod. As he became more frustrated, his musical needs turned to instrumental jazz and classical—he could not stand the distraction of a human voice in the room. Drink in hand, he returned to his workstation and stared at the multiple screens arrayed there.

I'm the only guy in the world who'll come back from Hawaii paler than he arrived, Grin thought.

He looked at the sleek Cinema Display and the anodized aluminum alloy case of the Power Mac G5, then compared it to the beige-and-black PCs. The machines provided by the navy for the acoustic daylighting project were cutting edge—one of the PCs was a custom-built computational hot rod. But for years, it seemed, Apple's product designs had oozed a sexy cool that the PC makers could not touch.

The reason, Grin mused, following the tangent of his thoughts, was that Apple controlled its products from soup to nuts. They could produce cases shaped like cubes or hemispheres because they designed everything that went inside. PC makers were little more than assemblers of parts built by other companies. In most cases, either type of machine could do the job, but with a Mac you did it in style.

Soup to nuts, Grin thought, returning to satellites and launchers. *If you're going to put a weapon in space, and you don't want anyone to know about it, you have to control everything from soup to nuts.*

Grin brought up the Enth datamining engine and defined a search to locate any soup to nuts satellite launches that had occurred before the *Mir* deorbit—ones in which a single company controlled everything. Then he sat back and let Enth go to work. He didn't wait long, and the list was a short one.

DATE: 1-10-2001
COMPANY: SKYE AEROSPACE
LAUNCHER: SKYE-4 GR
PAYLOAD: TEST SATELLITE
SITE: AEQUATUS

"Test satellite?" Grin mused.

He brought up the payload details for the launch and learned the payload was a five-ton dummy satellite—an object with just enough equipment aboard for ground controllers to move it around and communicate with it. Puzzled, Grin checked the records for all the *Aequatus* launches and learned that this was the first one.

As a player in the commercial satellite industry, Skye Aerospace stood out from the competition because of its launch site—it was the only one sending up rockets from the middle of the ocean. Grin discovered that Skye Aerospace had launched a dummy satellite to prove to its potential customers that they could put a heavy payload into orbit.

"So, what became of the dummy?" Grin asked himself.

According to company press releases, the dummy satellite was temporarily placed in geosynchronous orbit, then moved into a parking orbit and shut down. Grin tapped into the terabytes of orbital data provided by U.S. Space Command and, in the hologram chamber, displayed a three-dimensional model of the Earth and all the objects in orbit around it on the day of the test launch.

Eliminating everything but the dummy satellite, he reconstructed the *Aequatus* launch—which had been captured by the western edge of the Fence—and followed the satellite through the various stages of its ascent into high orbit. Speeding quickly through several weeks of data, he finally saw the satellite move into its final, useless orbit.

During one of the laps, Grin caught a flicker in the projected image. He stopped the simulation and rewound it slowly. The tiny yellow dot flew backward, orbiting the Earth east to west. Then he saw it. He froze the image and enlarged it. The flicker was two yellow dots so close together, the computer had trouble discriminating between them.

Thinking it was a glitch, he rechecked the data and discovered that Space Command had indeed spotted two objects in such close proximity. Based on Space Command's consecutive numbering, Grin knew the second object had been detected in orbit after the *Aequatus* test launch.

He reset the simulation to display both objects, starting the day before the dummy satellite was placed in orbit. At first, the space above the Earth was empty. Then the dummy satellite lifted off and began orbiting the Earth. There was no sign of the other object.

Grin kept an eye on the time index and slowed the animation as it neared the date when he first saw the second object. The dummy satellite slowly continued lapping the Earth, and then there were two objects. He enlarged the image, centering it on the orbiting pair—the fragment of the Earth still visible in the chamber spun below. The second object was much smaller than the first. The second object then moved away from the dummy satellite and descended into a lower orbit, where it finally disappeared.

Grin couldn't believe what he was seeing. He reset the animation to display a projected orbit for the second object based on its trajectory. An arc drawn in a solid yellow line defining the object's known orbit stretched over the Earth. The line became dashed red at the point where it disappeared and continued around the globe, extrapolating where the object should have been, but apparently wasn't. And the elliptical orbit was too high for the object to have simply fallen to Earth.

Grin combed through the raw data from Space Command and found that this was the only instance of this object in their records. Its purposeful movement in orbit precluded it from being a meteorite or a piece of space debris, but there was no record of where it came from or, after its brief appearance, where it went.

"It's as if the dummy satellite birthed the thing in space," Grin mused aloud, "which might explain how it got there."

On a hunch, Grin redefined the animation to show any objects with short durations in orbit, and to display them in order of appearance. The first was the object he was looking at. Others appeared at odd intervals, usually with a few months between them.

Starting with *Mir,* he then compared the anomalous appearances with the presumed attacks in space. In each case, Space Command not only detected a new object in orbit, but at the time of the attack, the new object had a clear line of sight with the damaged satellite. The pattern held not only for *Oculus* and *Liberty,* but for *Shenzhou-7* as well.

Grin then checked the projected orbits for each of the anomalous objects. All were following a highly elliptical path over the Earth's poles. It was the type of orbit favored by spy satellites because it allowed them to pass over every part of the globe twice each day.

"I'll be damned."

He picked up the phone and two minutes later had a secure connection with Jackson Barnett in Langley.

"It's Skye Aerospace," Grin blurted out, "They did it."

"Care to clarify that remark, Mr. Grinelli?"

"I found the weapon—well, not exactly found, because it comes and goes, and I haven't figured quite how they pulled that off, but it's Skye. They're the ones who blasted *Liberty* and a bunch of other stuff, including that Chinese rocket back in June."

"Slow down, Grin. Are you certain Skye Aerospace is responsible?"

"Absolutely. Everything fits. They have control over the entire process—rockets, satellites, launchpad—everything. I even found the rocket they put this thing up on. They hid it inside a dummy payload."

"Is this all theory, or can you actually prove it?"

"If you're asking if I have a picture of a killer satellite with the Skye logo on it blasting *Liberty,* the answer is no. But the data all point to them."

Grin ran Barnett through a synopsis of his investigation and the chain of logic that had led to his conclusion.

"Circumstantial as it is, I detect no fault with your reasoning," Barnett admitted. "The real trick is finding the smoking gun and placing it in the hands of Skye Aerospace. Are you familiar with NMD—Nuclear Missile Defense?"

"The latest version of Star Wars? Yeah, a little."

"Skye has a piece of the research, as does every other major aerospace company in the U.S. As I recall, their expertise is in energy weapons, space-based lasers."

"Are we actually building this stuff?"

"Some ground-based elements. No decisions have been made on anything that could be placed in orbit, largely due to the international political ramifications of such a deployment. The president rattles the saber well, and I applaud his efforts to continue the research on all fronts, but I don't think even he is ready to weaponize space just yet."

"So, if Skye put one in orbit, they did it on their own?"

"Exactly. I'm going to look into their research program, see what I can find. Nicely done."

"Thanks. Any word from Nolan and Roxanne?"

Barnett paused. "I have received a report, unconfirmed at the moment, that the ship they were on has sunk with all hands."

"Oh no."

"The Chilean authorities are conducting a search of the area where the ship was last reported, but so far they've turned up nothing."

40

August 19

Eyes fluttering, Kilkenny's head slowly began to droop. His body slackened, joints relaxing. Then he jerked up rigid, eyes wide open, panicked—his startle reflex kicking in again.

He had been experiencing mircrosleep for hours. The constant whirring drone of the thrusters and the darkness conspired like a nocturnal lullaby. His neck ached and he'd hit his forehead against the frame around the vision dome more than once. If it weren't so cold, he'd stuff his fleece jersey up there to soften the blow. Standing inside the suit made sleep difficult, which was good because he needed to stay alert if he was to stay alive. A long nap might be welcome, but he might drift far enough off course during his slumber to put him permanently out to sea.

Kilkenny checked his watch—he was five minutes late for a visual check. The marathon run to shore had stretched past the twenty-four-hour mark and he'd been in the Hardsuit for nearly twenty-eight. The sandwich he'd brought from the ship's galley was long gone, leaving him just a tin of cinnamon Altoids to subsist on.

Life support was still in good shape, enough oxygen to last another day, but the fuel cell was heading toward empty. He switched on the AD system and the darkness was replaced by the computer-generated landscape. He'd held his depth at two hundred feet—deep enough to avoid surface turbulence, but not so deep that denser water became a hindrance.

Below him, the ocean floor was rising steeply like the rocky foothills around a mountain—a welcome sign that he was nearing land. Ahead, he saw the jagged outline that had become his current reference point and he estimated it was under a half-mile away.

At this distance, the shape was more distinct and certain features became recognizable. He struggled against a welling excitement, but there it was. Smokestacks. Forward guns. It was the landmark Kilkenny had hoped to find.

Cumberland Bay was the only decent anchorage off Robinson Crusoe Island. Jagged rocks and sheer cliffs dominated the rest of the coastline. When *Sea Lion* headed out a few days ago, Peretti had pointed to a spot less than a half-mile from shore where the World War I German cruiser *Dresden* had come to rest. Out of fuel, she'd been cornered in the bay by three pursuing British warships and scuttled by her captain.

Kilkenny switched off the AD system, trying to squeeze the last few electrons from the fuel cell for the home stretch. He switched on the flashlight around his neck and left it on—it was time to do or die.

His eyes darted from his watch to the suit's compass. The current was changing, turning west as it rounded the eastern half of the boomerang-shaped island. Kilkenny adjusted the thrusters to compensate.

Fifteen minutes—site check.

AD system back on, the *Dresden* was closer now, a massive hulk that filled the width of his field of view. He tipped the left thruster, pushing himself higher to clear the wreck. Slowly, the cruiser passed beneath him, her forward guns long silent. Ahead, he saw the floor of the bay rising up toward shore.

The image staggered like a movie jumping frames, and details started dropping out. Kilkenny switched the AD off. The pitch of the whirring sound made by the thrusters had dropped. The blades were slowing, losing power.

"Don't you give up on me, baby! Not this close!"

The blades sputtered, hesitating.

Then they stopped.

"Damn it!"

Without the thrusters, Kilkenny could feel the current pulling on the Hardsuit. He clenched the dim flashlight in his teeth and began searching the waist of the suit. The emergency crank was folded flush into the HS5000's forged aluminum skin. He extended the crank and tried to turn it. It wouldn't budge.

As he pressed his weight onto the crank, the flashlight popped out of his mouth and bounced against his chest. Finally, the handle turned. Just a few degrees at first, then a few more. He was fighting against the six atmospheres of pressure surrounding him.

The crank turned slowly and Kilkenny's arms burned, providing torque to the mechanism. Straining, he held his breath, his temples throbbing with his racing heartbeat.

It started with a low groan, then all at once—*pffffft!*

The seal broke and a rush of seawater burst in. Kilkenny was standing in the middle of a circular waterfall. The crank turned freely now and Kilkenny spun it for all he was worth. The gap in the waist widened and more water poured in, flooding the legs. Then the lower torso dropped free.

Kilkenny let go of the crank and braced himself inside the upper half of the suit, fighting to keep it level and protect the precious bubble of air trapped inside. Icy water surrounded him from midchest down—the cold sucked the breath from his lungs.

Relieved of more than half its weight, the buoyant upper torso shot toward the surface like a cork. The dark water turned deep blue, then green. Light filtered down, adding color.

As he broke the surface, the upper torso lunged up, then toppled backward. Kilkenny stripped off the breathing mask and swam free. Low waves rippled the surface, breaking close to shore. Only the Hardsuit's chest and vision dome were visible now, the last bubbles of Kilkenny's air escaping. It was the middle of the afternoon and he was just over a quarter-mile from shore.

Fighting the numbing cold, Kilkenny willed his body to move, each stroke a struggle. When he finally tumbled ashore, his eyes burned from the salt water and his mouth felt raw and briny. He pulled himself up and took a long look around.

Exhausted and shivering, Kilkenny staggered along a gravel path. His joints were stiff from hours of standing and the cold, difficult swim ashore. Ahead he saw a small, weathered home and, under the covered patio, an old man tinkering with a fishing reel. The man looked up as Kilkenny walked toward him.

"Buenos tardes, Salvador," Kilkenny rasped. Then he lifted his fingers to his mouth, pantomiming a drink. "Rum?"

41

154° W Latitude 0° Longitude
August 19

"Captain, *Argo* reports they are in position and ballasting operation has commenced."

"Thank you, Mr. Perez," Captain Bob Werner replied.

Werner was a thickset man, standing five-ten with a barrel-shaped body gradually going soft. His naturally blond beard and hair were bleached white from a lifetime at sea, his skin tan and leathery. From his chair on the bridge of *Aequatus,* Werner enjoyed a panoramic view of the sea around his ship. The ocean was calm, the sky blue, and the sun high overhead.

Off the port side, the launch platform *Argo* straddled the equator—the combined effort her DGPS and thrust control system kept her within ten meters of that imaginary line.

As the two vessels neared the equatorial launch site, the seventy-two-hour countdown clock was started. Technicians on both ships were now busy making final preparations for a launch in less than three days—at noon on Saturday. One of those preparations was the pumping of millions of gallons of seawater into the *Argo*'s pontoons and legs, lowering her stance in the water sixty-five feet to stabilize the platform during the launch.

In his twenty-year career in the navy, Werner had fired missiles from the ships under his command, but none had ever made it to space. The sheer scale of this operation impressed the hell out of him and was the main reason he had signed on for duty. In three days, he'd have one of the best seats on the world to watch a space launch.

42

The Sikorsky S-76C+ glided over the sparkling blue ocean, her twin Turbomeca Arriel 2S1 engines powering the helicopter along at a comfortable speed of 139 knots. The aerodynamically refined exterior of the craft glistened brilliant white in the late-afternoon sun. Emblazoned on each side in navy-blue letters was the name *SKYE Aerospace*.

Based at Kiritimati, the former British colony discovered by Captain Cook in 1775 and centuries earlier by Polynesians, the helicopter's primary function was the transport of VIPs to and from the company's equatorial launch site without subjecting them to a weeklong voyage at sea. C. J. Skye recognized that most of her guests viewed rocket launches like a New Year's Eve party—they wanted to be there for the countdown, but not the days of preparation that preceded it.

Tao sat limply in her seat, her head resting against the window. She didn't have the strength to lift it, or any other part of her body. Without the seatbelt, she would have slipped down to the floor. The lids of her eyes drooped low, and through the narrow slits her dilated pupils were unable to focus on anything.

How long . . . ? She thought, trying to reestablish a timeline. *How long . . . since I was captured?*

More than a day had passed since the sinking of *Sea Lion*, and the careful application of drugs had kept her in this nightmarish state for much of that time. She remembered a boat. Then a plane—the jet engines whistled like teakettles. Now, she heard a dull thumping and a loud rush of air.

Still moving me . . . where?

Unger sat beside her, reading a book to pass the time. He'd been her constant companion, seeing to her needs, injecting the chemical cocktail that so disconnected her mind and body. He had not taken advantage of her in her present state, nor allowed the security men who accompanied Moug to Chile to do so either. It simply wasn't sporting, and he had his orders. For now, Tao was baggage—something to be transported from one place to another as efficiently as possible.

Moug gazed out the window as the helicopter approached the launch site. *Argo* sat low in the water, the added weight of her ballast dampening out all motion from the light seas. *Aequatus* had taken up position alongside the launch platform and a rigid steel-truss bridge had been cantilevered over her side, spanning the gap between the two. From the air, the bridge looked like something only a Flying Wallenda would hazard.

The pilot circled the mated vessels, then approached the large octagonal pad on the bow of *Aequatus*. As soon as they landed and the engines began winding down, a pair of crouched crewmen ran out to meet the new arrivals.

"How is she?" Moug asked.

"Stable," Unger replied. "Just on the edge of consciousness."

"Good. Let's get her aboard."

Moug and Unger each took a side and maneuvered Tao out onto the helipad—between them, her feet rarely touched the deck. Entering the superstructure, they were met by Captain Werner.

"Do you need a doctor?" the captain asked.

"No," Moug replied. "She just had a bit too much to drink in Kiritimati and it caught up with her on the ride out. You there."

Moug motioned one of the security men over.

"Help Mr. Unger get our guest to a VIP stateroom."

"Yes, sir," the man replied as he took Tao's arm.

Werner watched the pair carry the listless form down the passageway, his expression wavering between pity and disgust. As a young sailor, he'd come back to the ship from shore leave in a sorry state on more than one occasion, but it was something he quickly outgrew. A man was entitled to only so much libation during his life, and he'd drunk his personal quota by the age of thirty.

"Who is she? I wasn't aware we were having any visitors during this launch."

"A last-minute addition," Moug replied. "A guest of Miss Skye. You remember those environmentalists, the ones always complaining about how we're sonically polluting the ocean with our launches and damaging the hearing of whales?"

"She's one of *them?*"

Moug nodded. "Miss Skye thought having one aboard to see what it is we really do might calm them down. From the looks of this woman, I have my doubts."

43

Los Angeles

Barnett and Grin greeted Kilkenny as he stepped off the Air Force Learjet that had retrieved him from Chile. He was dressed in whatever clothes Delmar and his neighbors could find to replace the sodden fleece he swam ashore in. It was a mismatched lot, but Kilkenny was glad to be warm and dry and thankful for the islanders' generosity.

"Jesus, Nolan," Grin said as he threw his arms around Kilkenny. "You look like roadkill, but it's good to see you again."

"Thanks."

Grin eased back. "I'm sorry about Roxanne, man. I know you two were tight."

"Yeah. And somebody's going to pay for that."

"Indeed," Barnett said, extending his hand. "Welcome back, Nolan."

Kilkenny nodded and shook Barnett's hand. "When we last spoke, you said something about a lead."

"Grin has forwarded a very interesting theory, one in which, tonight, I hope to find some substance."

They left the airport in a black Ford Expedition—both the vehicle and the driver were government issue. A thin coil of wired descended from the man's right ear into the starched white collar of his shirt.

The sun was just slipping below the horizon as they headed north along the Pacific Coast Highway toward Santa Monica. During the drive, Grin quickly outlined the results of his research. Traffic moved steadily for a Friday night in Los Angeles and, thirty minutes later, the SUV pulled up in front of a small house with redwood siding in the steep hills overlooking the lights of the city.

A tan Saab was parked in the carport. Behind it, Kilkenny saw a second SUV identical to one he'd just arrived in. It, too, bore government plates.

"I got three coming in," the driver said into a microphone concealed in a shirt cuff.

A man in a dark suit opened the front door as they approached. Inside stood another, keeping watch over a nervous-looking man seated on the denim couch.

The man was in his late thirties, Kilkenny guessed, dressed in a golf shirt and khaki shorts. Except for a slight paunch growing around his midsection, the man was thin. He wore glasses with gold wire frames and his graying Afro showed signs it was in full retreat.

"Thank you, gentlemen," Barnett said to the two agents. "I don't believe Mr. Rainey will give us any trouble. If you'll wait outside."

The senior of the pair nodded and the two agents exited the home.

"Are you guys Secret Service or something?" Rainey's voice quivered slightly as he spoke.

"Or something," Barnett replied in a friendly tone as he showed Rainey his credentials. He then introduced Kilkenny and Grin.

Rainey eyed Kilkenny's and Grin's less-than-conventional wardrobe. "They CIA, too?"

"Let's just say they have an informal relationship with the agency."

"I haven't done nothing," Rainey protested.

"And no accusations have been made. For the moment, all we want to do is ask you some questions."

"Shouldn't I have a lawyer?"

"That is your privilege, but the presence of someone lacking the appropriate security clearance for the information that we wish to discuss could pose something of a problem."

As Barnett spoke, Kilkenny looked around the room. His mother would have said the place lacked a woman's touch, which was a polite way of saying Rainey was a man who lived alone and his environs reflected it. Much of the furniture was the kind you bought in a box and assembled yourself. A set of golf clubs stood in the corner of the living room, along with a pair of soft spikes. The toppled stack of magazines beside a leather recliner dealt primarily with electronics, science, and aerospace engineering—not a *Redbook* or *People* in the bunch.

There wasn't much in the way of family photos on the walls. On the mantle stood an old portrait of a man proudly wearing the uniform of a marine gunnery sergeant with his wife and toddler son. Beside the portrait was a framed wooden box that contained a folded American flag.

"If, at any time during this interview," Barnett continued, "you feel it is in your best interest to have counsel present, we will discontinue until proper arrangements can be made. You will have to be placed in protective custody until we can reconvene."

"I'd be under arrest?"

"You misunderstand me. We're investigating a rather dangerous situation. When I say protective custody, I mean we wish to protect you."

Barnett spoke with a calm, reassuring voice, the kind that made you want to believe him. As a prosecutor, Kilkenny thought, the man must have been a devastating opponent.

"Do you wish to have counsel present?"

Rainey shook his head.

"To begin with, you are Anson Rainey?"

"Yes."

"And you are employed by Skye Aerospace?"

"Yes, for the past twelve years."

"What is the nature of your work there?"

"Research and development. I design satellites."

"Are you familiar with work done by Skye Aerospace for the U.S. government, specifically Nuclear Missile Defense?"

"I lead that design team."

"Where, specifically, do you work?"

"At the company's Palmdale campus. My group has a separate facility there because of our work."

"And your particular field of expertise is space-based laser systems, is that correct?"

Rainey nodded. "Our proposal utilized a constellation of space-based weapons platforms to intercept ICBMs during their boost phase."

"Could such a weapon be used offensively, say against another object in orbit?"

Rainey nodded. "ASAT is an integral part of our overall concept."

"How about murdering astronauts?" Kilkenny asked icily.

Rainey looked at him, confused. "Excuse me?"

"Please pardon my associate," Barnett said, his annoyance barely concealed. "The past few days have been rather difficult for him. Prior to leaving Washington, I met with several high-ranking officials in the Department of Defense. Those familiar with you and your work spoke very highly of both. They also informed me that at this time no space-based NMD testing has been authorized or conducted. Is that correct?"

"Y-y-yeah," Rainey stuttered. "That's right."

"So, Sky Aerospace has not placed a laser weapon in space, because if they had, you would know because you would have designed it? Is that correct, Mr. Rainey?"

Rainey's eyes darted between the three men staring at him, but he offered no reply to the questions.

"Mr. Rainey, is that correct?" Barnett asked again.

Rainey sagged into the couch. "Look, I work on black projects. You're CIA, so you understand black, right? I talk about any of my work and I go to jail."

"I assure you, we are both cleared for anything you have to say."

"How do I know that?" Rainey pleaded.

"Fair enough. If you'll give me a moment, I think I can address your concerns."

As Barnett went out the front door, he pulled a cell phone from his pocket.

"How'd your father die?" Kilkenny asked.

"My father?" Rainey was thrown completely off-guard by the change of topic.

"I see the uniform and the decorations and the flag. He must have been quite a soldier."

"He was. Spent his whole adult life in the marines. He died in the attack on the barracks in Beirut. He served in Vietnam as well."

"That why you work in the defense industry?"

Rainey nodded. "Couldn't enlist, funky heart rhythm. My father died for this country, so I do what I can to honor his memory."

Barnett returned with a thick Haliburton briefcase. He set it on the coffee table and popped open the latches. An LCD screen filled the upper half of the case; a keyboard and other equipment filled the lower. He pulled a small, square antenna out of the case, then pointed at the front window.

"Is that south?" Barnett asked, pointing at the window.

"Yes," Rainey replied.

Barnett set up the antenna by the window, then sat beside Rainey on the couch, switched the unit on, and typed a long string of digits into the numerical keypad. A brief chatter of electronic tones, like fax machines shaking hands, squawked from the built-in speakers, then disappeared.

The White House Seal appeared on the screen, then Darcy Oates appeared in what looked like a study. The president's national security advisor was dressed formally.

"Director Barnett, are things ready on your end?"

"Yes, and thank you for pulling this together so quickly."

"We'll talk about that later."

Oates stepped off-camera and was replaced by the president. Rainey's mouth dropped open.

"Mr. President," Barnett began, "I'm here with Anson Rainey."

"I see that," the president replied in a West Texas drawl. He was dressed in a tuxedo. "Mr. Rainey, do you recognize me?"

"Yes, sir, I do."

"Wonderful. Most folks don't when I dress up like this. I think it's the bow tie that throws 'em. I'm told y'all are having a little trouble deciding whether or not you should talk with Jackson here about your work for the guvment."

"Uh huh."

"Then let me make this real easy for you. The United States does not have any weapons in space, nor have we told anyone to put one in space for us. Congress and the Department of Defense have not authorized the spending of any money, black or otherwise, on the deployment of a space-based weapons system. If you are acting in the belief that you are protecting your nation's security by *not* answering Mr. Barnett's questions truthfully, then you are gravely *mistaken.* Director Barnett and his associates have my full faith and confidence, and I hope you will grant them yours."

Barnett watched Rainey as the president spoke to him—the man seemed transformed.

"I think that'll do it, Mr. President. Thank you, sir."

The president nodded, and then the screen went blank.

"I-I-I just spoke with the president," Rainey stammered.

"That puts you one up on me," Grin said.

"Same here," Kilkenny chipped in. "But now that you know we're with the good guys, answer the question. Has Skye Aerospace put a weapon in orbit?"

"Yes."

"Did it go up in January of '01 with a dummy satellite?" Grin asked, his curiosity transparent.

"How did you know?"

Grin stretched his arm out and pumped it back in with the fist curled. "Yes! I am *good.*"

"There will be time to celebrate later," Barnett said. "Mr. Rainey, exactly what type of weapon are we talking about?"

"Chemical laser—deuterium, hydrogen fluoride, and helium. It's in our Nuclear Missile Defense design proposal—the one the DOD funded, or at least I thought they did."

"Who else knows about your work?"

"Outside the design team, just C. J. Skye and Owen Moug—he's the head of Defense Systems. Like I said, we're kept separate from the rest of the company." Rainey turned to Grin. "How'd you find it?"

"Wasn't easy," Grin replied. "That thing stealth?"

"Yeah, we designed *Zeus-1* with a very small radar cross-section. Should've only been visible at all when the solar panels were deployed."

Grin nodded knowingly. "That explains it blipping in and out of view."

"But why were you even looking for it?"

"Because it was used to murder six astronauts aboard *Liberty*," Kilkenny replied.

"Sweet Jesus," Rainey said, horrified.

"That wasn't the first time, either," Kilkenny continued. "We believe it has destroyed dozens of spacecraft."

"I don't understand. Why would anyone do this? It's insane."

"Money," Kilkenny replied. "This is all about gaining market share. I'll bet every time a satellite went out, Skye Aerospace was waiting with one of theirs, ready to take up the slack. If you just lost part of your global paging network, are you going to wait months to get a replacement up when your customers are howling, or worse, bolting? No, you sign with Skye and thank your lucky stars that they had the bandwidth when you needed it. This is damn near the perfect crime. Hard to detect and harder still to investigate. And in the end, the victims pay you to help them out and the rest is covered by insurance. It's brilliant."

"Can you help us find *Zeus-1?*" Barnett asked.

"No, we designed the system so that all command and control information is protected by some very serious encryption. Once we turned the bird over, my access was reduced to monitoring onboard systems, which I can do from here."

"Show us," Kilkenny demanded.

Rainey led them into his home office, a technological inner sanctum that impressed even Grin. To help him with his work, Skye Aerospace had provided Rainey with a dedicated high-speed fiber line into the company's network.

"*Zeus-1* is a prototype," Rainey explained as he navigated through the Skye computer network, "a chance to try out a few things before building a full production model. For diagnostic purposes, it was programmed to transmit a daily status report. I usually compile the data at the end of the month, see how the systems are performing. I'm going to pull in the most recent report."

"Would these reports tell you what *Zeus* had been doing?" Kilkenny asked.

"Nothing specific. I could tell that the spacecraft had been moved and fired, I just didn't know when or where, or at what. I'd see things like a drop in propellant or laser fuel—performance statistics." Rainey paused as the information he was looking for came up. "This bird is getting close to the end of its service life."

"What do you mean?"

"Look at this," Rainey said, pointing at a column of chemical symbols—He, He32, and NF3—followed by a column of numbers.

"That the fuel for your laser?" Kilkenny asked.

"Yeah, and it's getting pretty low. Same with propellant. I'd say it's got one decent shot left, then game over."

"One shot is probably more than enough to scuttle the ISS and murder its crew," Kilkenny offered bitterly.

Rainey paled at the reminder of how his work had been used. "Sorry if I sounded a little glib. I'm just used to thinking about this project like a big computer game, just shooting down the other guy's missiles before they hit my cities. I never thought . . ."

"Never thought what?" Grin asked.

Rainey locked eyes with Kilkenny. "You said *Zeus-1*

had been used to kill six astronauts, but all the news reports said there were seven onboard *Liberty.*"

"I misspoke," Kilkenny backpedaled.

"I don't think so. If you're worried about *Zeus* attacking the space station, there's got to be a reason."

Kilkenny looked over at Barnett with an expression that wordlessly asked the question: *Do I tell him?* Barnett sighed and nodded his assent.

"One of *Liberty*'s astronauts survived the attack. He saw everything, recorded it all, and somehow managed to get to the ISS before his air ran out."

Rainey's eyes grew wide. "Jesus, Mary, and Joseph."

"Mr. Rainey, based on what happened with *Liberty,* we have very strong reason to fear your employer's reaction should she learn of the existence of a witness to her crimes," Barnett said, his drawl steely with authority. "That piece of information is not to be repeated, and now that you've heard it, steps will have be taken to ensure your compliance."

"We have to stop Skye before she can use that thing again," Kilkenny added. "Even if she only has one shot left."

"Oh shit," Rainey blurted, "she doesn't."

"Doesn't what?" Grin asked.

"She doesn't have just one shot left—she has hundreds."

"I thought you said your satellite was almost out of fuel."

"It is, but my team delivered *Zeus*-2 a week ago, and it's going up in a couple of days."

"From where?" Kilkenny asked.

"Out in the Pacific."

Kilkenny looked at Rainey as if the man had made a bad joke.

"He's not kidding," Grin said. "Skye Aerospace really does launch rockets from the middle of the Pacific, about fourteen hundred miles south of Hawaii. They shoot 'em up from the equator off a modified oil rig."

"*Aequatus* and the launch platform are there right now," Rainey added. "Skye, too—she never misses a launch and we're inside the seventy-two-hour countdown."

"We cannot allow a second weapon to be placed in orbit," Barnett said.

Kilkenny turned to CIA director. "Then let's get a plane out there and bomb the fucker."

"You can't," Rainey pleaded. "*Aequatus* is tied alongside the launch platform until just before the launch. There could be as many as three hundred people onboard."

"Then we'll hit it after the ship pulls back," Kilkenny countered. "We only need a few seconds."

"But blowing the rocket up is also *not* an option. *Zeus*-2 isn't just another *Zeus-1*—it's a lot more powerful."

"All the more reason to hit it before it gets in space."

"I'm not just talking about the laser," Rainey explained. "This spacecraft is powered by a nuclear reactor. Blow it up, and you'll contaminate a huge chunk of ocean and probably kill everyone on *Aequatus.*"

"I think he's right, Nolan," Grin said, mulling over the scenario. "Bombing that rocket would be like setting off a dirty bomb with enough explosives to push a cloud of radioactive shit way up into the atmosphere."

"Gentlemen, we have two clear and ordered objectives," Barnett said decisively. "The first is to apprehend C. J. Skye before she can again make use of her weapon.

The second is to prevent the impending launch of another weapon."

"But Skye's out in the middle of the ocean right now," Rainey argued. "How are you going to stop her?"

Kilkenny smiled. "There's only one way."

44

Pearl Harbor, Hawaii
August 20

"Man, that's a big ship," Rainey said as he followed Kilkenny and Grin down to the submarine pens.

Virginia stood high in the water, her jet-black sail and upper hull exposed in the Hawaiian morning sun.

"Submarines are boats, not ships," Grin corrected.

Kilkenny shot a glance at his friend, but said nothing. They presented their credentials at the gangway and were permitted to board.

Inside the submarine, the crew was busy making preparations to put out to sea. Kilkenny's first stop was the captain's cabin.

"Three civilian guests reporting aboard, sir," Kilkenny announced. Johnston was running through some paperwork when Kilkenny appeared in his doorway.

"So you're the guys responsible for canceling our shore leave," Johnston growled. "Crew's not going to be too happy with you."

"We'll keep our heads down," Kilkenny promised.

"Good. I hope my men didn't jostle your equipment too

much. We had to reconfigure the torpedo room to accommodate the SEALs and their gear."

"Understood. Captain, this is Anson Rainey. He's familiar with the two vessels we're going after."

Johnson stood and extended his hand. "Welcome aboard, Rainey."

Kilkenny led the way down to the torpedo room. As Johnston had warned, the largely empty center section was now stacked with berths for nineteen men and every available bit of space was filled with SEALs and their equipment.

"Where's the lieutenant?" Kilkenny asked a SEAL checking over a Heckler-Koch MP5.

"Yo, LT!" the young man boomed out. "The man wants a word with you."

A lean, well-built young man with close-cropped dirty blond hair turned from the empty imaging chamber and navigated through the mass of men and material toward the hatch. He eyed the three men standing there, looking for soft targets.

"I'm Lieutenant Ralph. What can I do for you?"

"We're your bunkmates for this trip. I'm Kilkenny. This here's Grin and Rainey."

"Good to meet you. We saved you three bunks up front by your gear."

"Cool." Grin turned to Kilkenny. "I'm gonna see if there's anything I need to fix."

"I'll join you in a minute," Kilkenny replied.

"You led a platoon with Two, right?" Ralph asked, referring to SEAL Team 2, based in Little Creek.

"Yeah. Did my six."

"Miss it?"

"Nah, I manage to find enough trouble all by myself."

Ralph laughed. "Ain't that the truth. What's all that equipment up front?"

"Research project. Admiral Dawson cleared it, so if we have time, I'll walk you through it. I think the first order of business will be reviewing your OP. Rainey here is the *Encyclopedia Britannica* of Skye Aerospace, complete with the full schematics on both ships."

Ralph clapped a strong hand on Rainey's shoulder. "You, sir, are my new best friend. Let's go have a chat."

At noon, *Virginia* sailed out of Pearl Harbor and slipped beneath the Pacific on a southerly course.

45

Aequatus

After arriving onboard, Tao had been allowed to regain consciousness. Though her chemical restraints had been replaced with physical ones, she preferred the latter as they were less invasive. She lay on her left side atop a queen-sized bed, wrists tied behind her back and her ankles bound.

She had carefully eaten the first meal she was given after coming to—a broth soup, crackers, and ginger ale—only to regurgitate it halfway through. The lingering effects of Unger's injections had left her weak and nauseated.

Opening her eyes, she saw her guard seated in a chair by the door, his interest more on a DVD of *The Ugly One* than his listless prisoner. The sound of bare knuckles impacting on flesh in one of the film's fight sequences caused him to snort approvingly.

Tao rolled over, her left arm numb and tingling. Through the window, she saw that the sky outside was dark, but the glow of the ship's lights obliterated all but the brightest stars. She detected only the faintest roll, but was unsure if it was the ship or her degraded sense of balance.

She flexed her arm as best she could, felt the blood coursing through it and the feeling return. Then she tilted her head up off the pillow and held it. The room didn't spin around on her. She sighed and rolled back over.

"Excuse me," she said, her voice hoarse and dry.

The guard ignored her.

"I said excuse me." This time loud enough to be heard over the movie's pulsing soundtrack.

"What do you want?" the man answered.

"I need to use the bathroom."

"Why? You haven't had anything to drink since yesterday!" the guard snapped, annoyed at the interruption.

"Just the same, nature is calling and I'd like to answer. Could you please untie me."

"All right." The guard picked a two-way radio off his belt. "Yeah, Bobby, it's Jim down in the stateroom. She wants to use the can."

"I'll send somebody down," a voice crackled over the radio in response.

"Thanks."

A minute later, the guard let another man into the room. This one stood by the door with pistol in hand, watching as the guard approached the bed.

"Sit up," he ordered.

Tao slid her legs over the edge of the bed and struggled upright.

"Whoa," she said weakly.

"You gonna puke?"

"No, just a head rush."

The guard bent on one knee and clipped the zip-ties around her ankles. The plastic straps left a deep groove in her skin.

"Stand up," the guard demanded.

Tao rose and turned her back toward him. He grabbed her joined wrists and cut the ties. Her hands tingled with the increased blood flow.

"Do your business, then get back out here."

Tao stepped into the bathroom and closed the door. The windowless room had been stripped of towel rods, toilet paper roll holders—anything that could easily be torn out and used as a weapon. She turned on the water faucet and sat down, massaging her wrists and ankles. Starting with her neck, she carefully stretched and rotated her limbs and back, warming the muscles.

The door rumbled as the guard pounded the meaty side of his fist against the flush surface.

"You 'bout done in there?" he demanded.

"Just finishing up."

Tao ran her hands through the water, then turned off the faucet. Hands dripping, she opened the door.

"There are no towels in here."

The guard rolled his eyes, grabbed a hand towel off the stack on the bureau, and handed it to her.

As she reached for the towel, Tao balled her hand into a fist and rammed the first two knuckles into the guard's throat. Driving forward, she pressing her fist deep in the soft neck tissues, collapsing his airway.

Shocked at the sudden loss of breath, the guard staggered backward. Tao grabbed his crotch and pushed—he was going wherever she aimed him.

The man at the door had just raised his pistol when the bulk of Tao's guard rammed into him. His arm twisted back against his chest, and the impact caused his weapon to discharge. Most of pistol's report was muffled by the bodies that surrounded it. The bullet caught the man under the chin, fragmenting into shards inside his skull.

Both men went wide-eyed, their stares glassy and distant. Slowly, their legs gave way and Tao let them slide to the floor. She collected pistols from both men and her guard's two-way radio. Checking the window, she saw nothing but dark water reflecting the lights of the ship.

Unless shore is on the other side, Tao realized, *I'm somewhere out at sea.*

Tao slipped one of the pistols into her coat pocket and hid the other beneath a towel draped over her forearm. Beside the stateroom door, she noticed a sign depicting emergency egress from her room. From it, she learned that she was on one of the upper levels of a very large vessel called *Aequatus,* and that exit stairways were located at both ends of the passageway out side her door.

The radio was quiet and she heard no sound of approaching footsteps. Slowly, Tao opened the door. The wide passageway was empty, the lights dimmed for the night.

She stepped out and eased the door closed behind her. The electronic lock made a dull metallic click. Framed photographs mounted to the walls depicted the ship from a variety of angles—some in port and others at sea. Most were of the ship paired with a large floating platform and a rocket with the word *SKYE* in bold letters up the side. A few of the pictures were artists' renderings of satellites in orbit—all with the same name on their outer skin.

She descended a few floors before encountering a couple of women in the stairwell. They were dressed in running shorts and T-shirts with towels draped around their necks and each glistened with a sheen of sweat from a vigorous workout. Tao made sure her pistol was still concealed before they turned at the landing.

"Excuse me?" Tao said. "I seem to be a bit lost."

"Oh, where are you headed?" one of the women asked.

"I'm looking for a place where I can send a message."

"E-mail room, level two. Go down another flight, then take a right. First time aboard?"

"Yes." Tao smiled meekly.

"Don't be embarrassed. I've been out a half-dozen times now and didn't really get my bearings until my third launch."

"Thanks."

Tao descended to level two and stepped out into the passageway. It was empty, but she heard voices down the way. Following the woman's directions, she found the e-mail room. It was unoccupied. She went in and locked the door behind her.

The computer displayed a blank e-mail screen, ready to go. Her fingers flew as fast as she could form the words in her mind, tersely describing the sinking of the *Sea Lion,* Kilkenny's murder, her abduction, and what she knew of her present situation.

The radio by her side squawked—the bodies of her guards had been discovered. Tao continued typing, racing to report as much as she could.

Orders were barked. Men were now combing the ship, searching for her. Some were moving to level two.

In midsentence, she hit SEND, then fled the room, locking the door behind her. As she descended the forward stair, she heard pounding footsteps on the treads above her.

"There she is," a voice called—she'd been spotted from an upper landing.

Tao rushed out onto the main deck, the white superstructure towering over her. Just off *Aequatus*'s port side floated a man-made island illuminated in the harsh white glow of metal halide work lights. At the stern of the launch platform, a tall, slender rocket was slowly being raised to the vertical. A number of people were on the platform, watching the procedure.

She darted for the steel truss bridge that spanned the broad gap between the two vessels. The pair from the stairway was right behind her, one with a radio pressed against his face.

"She's heading for the bridge," the man reported.

Tao stepped onto the cantilevered truss and began moving across. The man who had interrogated her aboard *Sea Lion* stepped onto the far end and began walking toward her, his eyes fixed on her. He approached with both hands visible. As far as she could tell, he was unarmed. Tao stopped at midspan and removed the towel from her forearm, revealing the pistol.

"You can't get off the ship," Moug said. "There's nowhere to go."

"I know."

"And shooting me won't change that."

"But it would make me feel *so* much better."

Moug took a step closer. Tao raised the pistol to eye level, aiming at his head. She then pulled out the second pistol, which she pointed toward the men on the opposite side of the span. Moug stopped and motioned for the men from *Aequatus* to halt as well.

Tao pointed the two weapons just long enough to see a glint of uncertainty in Moug's eyes. Then she tossed them over the side and surrendered. Whatever sound the pistols made when they struck the water was lost in the din of activity aboard *Argo*.

46

August 21

Upon her surrender, Tao offered no resistance and returned quietly to the stateroom where she'd been held. She'd done what she needed to; anything else would have been counterproductive. Her objective now was simply to stay alive.

The bodies of the two she'd killed were gone and a foul-smelling chemical agent had been applied to the stains on the carpet. Both Unger and Moug watched as she was bound once again and placed on the bed. Two guards were left to watch over her with orders that her restraints, now including a gag over her mouth, were not to be removed unless a weapon was trained on her. She was not to be fed or catered to, simply watched.

In the hours since her brief escape, Tao had done her best to sleep, conserving her strength and resting her mind. She heard a helicopter circle the ship, then approach to land. Thirty minutes later, she was taken by Moug, Unger, and the two guards from her room to a large suite atop the ship's superstructure.

She was escorted through an elegant salon with commanding views off both sides of the ship into a private office. The room was painted in subtle grays and whites, sculpted more than equipped, with fixtures and furnishings that could only have been designed with this space in mind. It struck Tao as the kind of space where she would find a modern-day Captain Nemo: stylish, high-tech, and nautical.

In the black leather chair behind the desk sat a woman in her mid to late forties with a long mane of brown hair flecked with gray.

"I'm C. J. Skye. Please, have a seat."

Tao remained standing. The two guards who accompanied her forced the issue, unceremoniously depositing her in the one chair positioned directly in front of Skye's desk.

"I'd like to know why someone running a small venture capital firm would be interested in a collection of failed satellites," Skye began. "The fact that your firm's primary financial backer is the Central Intelligence Agency further spurs my curiosity. And your search for that old Russian space station has made this mystery quite irresistible, which is why I asked my associate to bring you here so we can talk. Unfortunately, I'm on a tight schedule right now and I don't have the time to do this politely."

Unger nodded and the two guards each took a side and held Tao down. He then rolled up her sleeve and wiped Tao's arm with an alcohol swab. Tao tensed as he tightened a rubber tube just above her elbow and tapped the skin lightly to raise a vein. The guards held her arm steady.

Tao felt the needle slip beneath her skin. The prick was followed by a hot sensation, like liquid fire burning inside her arm. The warmth crept into her shoulder, her neck, and then blanketed her brain. She sagged in the chair, head lolling against the back. Unger checked her eyes; both were dilated. Her pulse was up—a combination of adrenaline and the narcotic.

"She's ready," Unger said.

Skye rose and moved around to the front of her desk, sitting back against the edge while looking down on Tao's slackened form.

"Can you hear me?" Skye asked.

"Uhhh . . . huhh," Tao answered softly.

"What are you looking for?"

"Weapon."

"What kind of weapon?"

"Sspace . . . lasser," Tao hissed.

"Why do you think there's a laser in space?"

"Liberty."

"The space shuttle *Liberty?*"

"Uh huh."

"But *Liberty* was hit by a meteoroid."

"No," Tao's head lolled from side to side. "Lassser."

"Why do you think *Liberty* was attacked by a laser?"

"Oculusss."

Skye looked to Moug, who shrugged his shoulders. Tao's answer meant nothing to him.

"What is *Oculus?*"

"Ssspy sssatellite. Hit by lassser. *Liberty* ssent . . . retrieve."

"Liberty went after a ZetaComm satellite," Skye protested.

Oculusss."

"How do you know a laser hit *Liberty?*"

"Asstronaut . . . saw."

Skye stared at the drugged woman. "The astronauts are dead."

"One . . . still . . . alive."

"Can't be," Moug said. Turning to Unger, "You sure that stuff is working?"

"It's not like a lie detector," Unger replied. "She can't fake out the drugs."

"Enough," Skye said, silencing the two men. "Roxanne, is one of *Liberty*'s astronauts is alive?

"Yesss."

"Where is this astronaut now?"

"Sstation."

"The International Space Station?"

"Uh huh."

Skye stood and backed away from Tao, her face paler than before.

"Take her back to her room. Now!"

The two guards scooped Tao out of the chair and quickly retreated from the office.

"There's no way she could be lying?" Skye demanded.

"None," Unger replied. "The drug strips away all inhibition, all initiative for that matter. In that state, all she could do was answer your questions."

"How could an astronaut get from *Liberty* to the space station?" Moug raged. "It's incredible!"

"Evidently not," Skye countered. "And this astronaut saw enough to convince some powerful people in Washington to investigate. I thought something wasn't right when ZetaComm announced they'd hired NASA to retrieve that satellite—it would've been more cost effective to launch a replacement. A new-generation spy satellite, on the other hand, is a billion-dollar investment."

"What was all that about a spy satellite?" Moug asked.

"The government did exactly what we did—switched

payloads." Skye glowered at Moug. "And *your* people missed it. All this trouble was for nothing."

"What are we going to do?" Moug asked. "This surviving astronaut poses a huge threat to us."

"I'm well aware of what this astronaut represents, and I'll deal with that problem just as soon as the new satellite is in orbit."

"We still have *Zeus-1*," Moug reminded her.

"Too little fuel left to attack something like the ISS—the crew could easily seal off any breached areas, and a survey of the damage would eliminate a natural collision as the cause. The measures we've taken to compartmentalize the *Zeus* project will keep any hard evidence out the government's hands. Without that, statements made by any of our employees are just hearsay that's easily deflected."

Skye's tone grew icy. "To kill any case the government may try to launch against us, the ISS must be destroyed and its wreckage scattered so widely that the pieces can never be reassembled."

47

USS Virginia

"Sir, we got a signal on the ELF," the executive officer reported.

"Bring her up to communications depth," Johnston commanded.

"Communications depth, aye, sir," the XO replied. "Make five degrees up angle on the bow planes."

"Five degrees up, aye," the pilot confirmed.

Activated by the boat's digital fly-by-wire controls, *Virginia's* bow planes silently rotated, pointing the submarine on an upward path toward the surface. Soon, the column of water atop the vessel diminished to sixty feet.

"Level the bow planes," the XO called out.

"Zero degrees on the bow planes," the pilot replied.

"Message coming in, sir."

Johnston leaned over the comm station. The short-burst transmission was received, decrypted, and displayed as scrolling lines of text in seconds.

"That it?" Johnston asked as he finished the text.

"Aye, sir."

Johnston straightened up. "XO, take her back down to two hundred and continue on previous heading at flank speed. I'm heading down to the forward torpedo room. You have the conn."

The sixteen SEALs aboard *Virginia* seemed to be everywhere, from running checks on the lockout trunk to exercising in any available space to, in the words of the cook, going through the galley like a plague of locusts. Johnston found himself reminding those under his command that *Virginia* had been designed with these merry marauders in mind and it was their job to take the SEALs wherever ordered and to unleash them on any poor dumb sonsofbitches who had gone and riled old Uncle Sam.

In the torpedo room, Johnston found Kilkenny and the two SEAL lieutenants huddled around a flat-screen monitor reviewing schematic drawings of the launch platform.

"Officer on deck," a SEAL announced on sighting Johnston.

"Carry on," Johnston said quickly, stifling the hardwired response to snap to attention at the sight of polished brass on a man's shirt collar. "Kilkenny, you got a minute?"

"Sure, Cap'n."

Kilkenny joined Johnston by the hatchway.

"We just got a message off the bird. Seems a friend of yours has sent an e-mail from a most unlikely place."

"Kelsey?"

"No, Roxanne Tao. Message I got says she's onboard *Aequatus*."

Kilkenny shook his head and smiled.

"Good news, I take it?"

"The best."

48

Aequatus
August 22

Aequatus was holding station three miles upwind from *Argo*. The unmanned launch platform was now being run remotely by her crew from a virtual control room aboard *Aequatus* that was identical to the real one.

From her suite atop the ship's superstructure, Skye studied the projected orbit for the satellite poised atop the 4GR rocket. Little more than an hour after launch, the spacecraft would separate from the upper stage of the rocket and move into high Earth orbit. At that point, the satellite would link in with the rest of the Skye constellation and control would be transferred from the launch crew aboard *Aequatus* to the satellite operations group back in the States.

In the moments following that exchange, the satellite would run through a postinsertion diagnostic and report a series of cascading failures in the transponder and other electronics. Unable to maintain stable communications with the satellite, and with other systems reporting failure, Skye engineers would make the painful decision to deorbit the useless craft and at least salvage the position in space for a replacement. As the spacecraft dipped into perigee, it would disappear from view of ground-based tracking stations and be presumed destroyed.

Skye smiled at the thought of her insurer paying for the lost satellite, allowing her to recover some of the cost of *Zeus-2*.

The moment Skye Aerospace lost contact with the dying communications satellite, *Zeus-2* would shed its metallic skin and slip undetected into an orbit around the Earth's poles. From there, only C. J. Skye would know where it was, and only she could direct its actions.

And in those first hours in space, *Zeus-2* would stalk its first target.

49

Sanya

Commander Shi Yucheng, executive officer onboard the Chinese destroyer *Sanya*, peered over the radar operator's shoulder at the electronic display. A line of pale-green light swept the display in a clockwise fashion—like the second hand on the chronometer Shi had purchased while on liberty on Honolulu—refreshing the image with new data gathered in by the array spinning atop the ship's superstructure. Aft and off the port side sailed *Sanya*'s sister ship, *Hangzhou*. Both vessels were Russian-built Sovremenny Class destroyers, two of five to be commissioned by mid-decade and the pride of the People's Liberation Army Navy. *Hangzhou*'s radar return was strong and well defined.

After departing the final stop on their goodwill tour to Mexico and the United States, the destroyers and their fuel tenders had sailed out into the Pacific toward home. Two hundred miles west of the Hawaiian Islands, they changed course, heading due south. Both ships then switched off their three-palm frond I-band surface search radars and *Sanya* activated a Raytheon system favored by commercial vessels. It was an old trick, playing the part of a wolf in sheep's clothes, but one that worked well.

Shi and the radar operator were in the Command Information Center, a windowless room protected deep within the armor of the ship. Captain Yao Shouye, a twenty-five-year career naval officer, sat in his chair near the center of the room, reading through a sheaf of messages. Around him, dozens of other men on the current watch monitored all the ship's systems—they were the mind of this lethal dragon.

Peeking up over the edge of the horizon, *Sanya's* radar painted two strong returns—large vessels parked squarely on the equator.

"Captain," Shi called out, "radar contact with target vessels. Thirty-two kilometers out. Both are holding position at 154 west by zero north."

Captain Yao ran the numbers in his head; they were less than forty minutes from *Aequatus*.

"Inform *Hangzhou* we have contact with target vessels. She is to move into position off the command ship's port side. Increase speed to thirty knots. XO, you have the conn. I'll be on the bridge."

50

Aft of *Virginia's* sail, Kilkenny and the SEAL platoon stood outside the lockout trunk, waiting for the submarine to reach the target area. The men were clad head to toe in black Neotex wetsuits and over their chests wore Draeger LAR-VI closed-circuit rebreathers. Each man's body bristled with the weapons and equipment needed for his particular task. Fins dangled from waist clips and most of their masks were pulled down around their necks.

The premission excitement as they suited up had transitioned, as it always did, into a stoic silence. The game faces were on; it was almost time to do the job.

For this mission, the platoon had divided into two elements—a four-man unit to attack the unmanned launch platform and a twelve-man group to seize *Aequatus*. Kilkenny was to accompany the larger element.

Ralph and Stivers, the platoon's junior officer, were initially resistant to the idea of a civilian traveling with them, even one who'd once been part of the teams. Years outside the insular community of SEALs could dull the razor's-edge conditioning—both of mind and body—required for special warfare. But the order stood, and for his part,

Kilkenny had proven over the past two days that he could still think like a meat-eater. Kilkenny also understood that he was an outsider to the platoon and, as such, accepted a peripheral role in the assault.

Rainey remained with Grin in the torpedo room along with an off-duty sonar man named O'Roark who would assist in relaying targeting information to the control room.

The undersides of both Skye vessels were painted clearly in the imaging chamber—white solid shapes surrounded by the hazy, rippling surface of the ocean. *Virginia,* in the center of the chamber, was on a line that passed directly beneath the launch platform.

"Can you tighten up on the first target?" O'Roark asked.

"You bet."

Grin trapped the keyboard and the holographic image zoomed in on a smaller cylinder of ocean. The dual pontoons and the eight partially submerged legs of *Argo* were now easily discernible. Eight small whirling vortices sprang from equidistant points on the pontoons—thrust controllers holding the structure in position over the equator. Grin placed a projection line stretching from the top of *Virginia*'s sail to the nearest of *Argo*'s pontoons—a numerical display beside the line measured off the angle and distance in feet.

They were approaching the first target from the northeast. Johnston's plan was to pass beneath the launch platform and drop off the first unit of SEALs, then transit a shallow arc, sweeping behind the stern of *Aequatus*.

"Control Room, Torpedo Room," O'Roark called out

over the mike. "Target bearing two-six-five, distance four hundred yards."

"Roger, Torpedo Room. Target bearing two-six-five, distance four hundred yards."

Inside the imaging chamber, the multibladed prop on *Virginia's* tail slowed as the boat neared *Argo*. The submarine was reducing its relative speed of three knots—barely a crawl, but enough to maintain control of the vessel in the ocean current.

"Alpha, into the trunk!" Stivers announced.

Three SEALs followed him up the ladder into the arched chamber built into the boat's upper hull. *Virginia* was the first submarine built with an internal lockout trunk, allowing her to deploy and recover nine SEALs at a time.

The last man into the trunk closed the watertight hatch. As soon as the hatch sealed, seawater began flowing in. The men set their masks and respirators and waited for the compartment to flood. When the water reached chest level, the men slipped on their fins. A complex assembly of valves controlled the flow of water into the trunk, filling it at a quick but even pace. In less than three minutes, the chamber was filled and pressure equalized with the ocean outside.

Stivers opened the hatch at the top of the vaulted ceiling and pushed it out. The flush-fit door on the top of the submarine rotated open and, one by one, the SEALs exited. When the last man was out, Stivers closed the hatch and the four divers swam out of the submarine's slipstream. Less than a hundred feet above them was the dark silhouetted shape of *Argo*.

* * *

"Damn, that's slick," Rainey declared as four human figures emerged from the back of *Virginia* and began swimming toward the surface.

"Control, Torpedo Room," O'Roark said. "Alpha is clear."

"Roger, Torpedo Room. Proceeding to second insertion point."

During *Virginia's* transit toward *Aequatus*, the nine men of Bravo climbed into the lockout trunk and opened it to the sea. As soon as the submarine slowed, 120 feet below the surface and just astern of the target, the men exited and the evolution was repeated for the three remaining SEALs and Kilkenny.

Grin watched as the thirteen divers swam toward the large white shape on the surface. At the current resolution, *Aequatus's* tapered bow extended beyond the confines of the imaging chamber. With nearly three hundred feet more length in the keel and triple the breadth of beam, the surface ship dwarfed *Virginia*.

"I'd hate to be on that ship when those SEALs climb aboard," O'Roark said. "If they're smart, the folks up there'll just give up."

"Oh, C. J. Skye is smart, all right," Rainey offered. "Genius-level smart."

Grin kept his eyes on the ascending figures in the chamber, hoping all thirteen would return safely. "I think you two are confusing intelligence with wisdom. Given what's happened so far, I just hope Skye's wise enough to know when the jig is up."

"Torpedo Room, Control," the voice of *Virginia*'s XO crackled over the intercom.

"Roger, Control," O'Roark answered.

"Sonar reports surface contact bearing three-three-five, range seventeen thousand yards and coming in hot. Can you give an idea what's going on up there?"

Grin keyed in the information as quickly as Paulson spoke. The view inside the imaging chamber shrank until it described a twelve-mile-wide cylinder of ocean.

"Roger that, Control." O'Roark's eyes fixed on the holographic image. "We have two hulls—"

The two ships quickly grew in size until the image of each vessel was nearly a foot long. Like knives, the bows of the speeding ships cleaved the surface of the ocean, wakes spreading behind them in narrow pointed vees.

"—both hulls dual screw."

"Here you go," Grin said as his fingers pounded out a flourish of keystrokes.

Wire frame representations of both hulls, complete with dimensions, appeared in the imaging chamber beneath the acoustic daylight images.

"Length five-one-one-point-eight feet," the sonar man read off. "Beam five-six-point-eight feet. Draft two-one-point-three feet."

"Running it through the naval database," Grin said, "and we have an ID."

"Control, inbound surface contact appears to be a pair of Sovremenny Class destroyers."

"Sovremenny?" Johnston spat. "What the hell are the Russians doing here?"

"Could be Chinese, sir," Paulson offered. "And a pair

of their destroyers pulled out of Pearl just ahead of us."

"All I know is those aren't U.S. Navy, so make sure we have targeting solutions on both of 'em in case this little party turns into a cluster-fuck."

51

As Alpha approached *Argo's* submerged pontoons, the element split into pairs. Each of the pontoons was equipped with two thrust controllers—essentially small directional propellers mounted strategically along the sides of the vessel below the water line. When linked with a computer and DGPS, the four controllers could hold the platform in position in all but the worst seas.

Stivers and his buddy went after the thrusters on the port side; the other pair of SEALs took the starboard. At the pivoting joint on each thruster, they placed a timed explosive charge. The amount of explosive in the charges wasn't large—just enough to destroy the controllers without scuttling the platform.

The SEALs worked their way from stern to bow, up the keels of the pontoons. When the last charges were set, they swam up along the inside of the bow columns, took a short decompression stop at thirty-three feet, then proceeded to the surface. Four black heads bobbed out of the water into the shadow of the platform.

Stivers checked his dive watch.

Three . . . two . . . one . . .

* * *

On the *Virginia*, the four simultaneous detonations created a fuzzy ball of jittery fractals beneath the holographic pontoons in the imaging chamber. The four SEALs were headless forms, their upper torsos lost in the undulating surface layer. Then, one by one, the SEALs slipped out of the water and disappeared from view.

"Control, Torpedo Room," O'Roark reported. "Alpha has taken out *Argo* thrust controllers and are moving topside."

Argo's captain stood at the virtual bridge of his vessel, checking over displays of the ship's status. Minute changes in the launch platform's latitude and longitude from the DGPS caught his eye.

"We're drifting off position. What's the situation with the thrust controllers?"

"They're not responding," his first officer replied. "I'm not getting a signal from any of them."

The captain glanced up at the countdown clock. T minus seven minutes and counting.

"Damn. This is going to rile a lot a people." He picked up the phone and punched in three digits. "Launch director, this is *Argo*. Be advised. Thrust controllers are not responding. LP is starting to drift off position."

"How bad is the drift?" Skye asked the launch director.

"Negligible. The seas are calm. In the time remaining until launch, I estimate no more than twenty feet off the line"

"Then continue the countdown."

52

Peng stood with Captain Jin Goujun on the bridge as the *Hangzhou* moved into position off the port side of *Aequatus*.

"Slow to five knots," the captain ordered.

The steady low-frequency drone that accompanied their thirty-knot run to the equator ebbed away. To Peng, the sudden silence was a relief. He stared at the long white form just a few hundred meters away.

"So, now we catch this woman who murdered our *yuhangyuans*, eh?" the captain said with a confident leer.

"Yes," Peng agreed. "Justice will be served."

Peng kept to himself the nagging fear that a woman who could destroy a spacecraft in orbit was not to be underestimated.

"Cap'n," Perez said, his voice slightly shaken. "You know those ships we picked up on radar a half-hour ago?"

"The sightseers? Yeah."

"They pulling up alongside and I don't think they're here to watch the launch."

Werner got up from his chair and grabbed a pair of binoculars on his way to the bridge windows. He didn't need them. The long gray ship was less than a mile away, the entire length of its main deck bristling with weaponry. It was a sight that projected awe and fear. Werner raised the binoculars to his eyes and scanned the warship. Fluttering in the breeze he saw the flag of the People's Republic of China.

"There's another one just like it off the other side," Perez said.

"Cap'n," the radio operator called out. "We're being hailed."

"Pipe it through."

Werner returned to his station and picked up the handset.

"This is Captain Werner of the *Aequatus*."

"*Aequatus*, this is the Chinese destroyer *Sanya*," Captain Yao announced. "Prepare to be boarded."

"Negative, *Sanya*," Werner said defiantly. "This is a United States flagged vessel. You have no right to board us."

"You are harboring a criminal wanted for murder by the People's Republic of China," Yao snapped back.

"The hell we are," Werner muttered off mike. "*Sanya*, we haven't been anywhere near China. We are a commercial ship engaged in the peaceful launch of a communications satellite and your presence is interfering with our work."

"Your work is irrelevant. Prepare to be boarded."

"Cap'n, they're lowering boats into the water."

"CIC to Bridge," Commander Shi called out over the intercom. "Radar control is locked on target."

"Mr. Lin, how much do you think that rocket standing out there costs," Captain Yao asked the bridge watch officer.

The lieutenant commander considered the question for

a moment, fully aware that *Sanya's* commanding officer was enjoying every moment as the instrument of his nation's revenge. It was an assignment that guaranteed his promotion to flag rank.

"Possibly as much as a billion yuan, sir."

"A suitable down payment for this woman's crimes, don't you think? Commence firing."

Signals from the Kite Screech H/I/K-band radar poured into *Sanya's* computer control system, where they were used to continuously update the firing solution on the *Argo* launch platform. As the ship's forward turret swiveled into position, the dual 130-millimeter guns angled upward slightly, preparing to unleash a hellish barrage on the target three miles distant.

53

Atop the launch platform, the erector arm pulled away from the upright rocket, folding back down to horizontal. Communications tests between the rocket and *Aequatus* continued with all systems reporting nominal status.

Stivers and his SEALs removed their fins and clambered up the steel framework supporting the transfer hoist. It was a difficult climb equipped as they were. A SEAL nicknamed Spider-Man led the way up, pointing out the best handholds to his teammates. Arms aching, they swung themselves onto *Argo*'s lower deck.

Stivers again checked his watch. "Bravo's in the water. Let's move it!"

The two-hundred-foot Skye-4GR towered over *Argo*'s stern, a tall, slender column topped with a smooth-domed cap. White clouds of evaporating gases billowed around the rocket and the air was filled with the low rumble of the boiling cryogenic fuels.

"LT," Spider-Man called out, "it don't look like they hit the off switch."

Stivers led the team in a sprint to the control room. The door was unlocked and the room eerily empty. An LED display on the wall counted down the final seconds to launch.

"Shit! It's still going up! Everybody off, now!" Stivers ordered.

The four men ran with all they had toward the starboard rail. A deafening shock wave, accompanied by a roiling cloud of superheated steam, scalded the SEALs as they leaped toward the water just a few hundred feet from the rocket. Their wetsuits liquefied, sticking to the men like hot tar. The blast struck them with such force that it crushed their chests and threw them over eighty feet away from the platform.

They were dead before the first rounds from *Sanya*'s forward guns hammered into *Argo*'s deck. In a minute of continuous fire, forty rounds of high-explosive, armor-piercing ordnance shattered the rigid structural framework of the main deck. Under the sagging weight of the weakened superstructure, *Argo*'s massive pontoons splayed outward and the ship folded in on itself.

The imaging chamber flashed solid white, the acoustic shockwave blasting through the water, swamping the AD supercomputer with an overwhelming surge of data.

"What the heck was that?" O'Roark asked.

"They must've launched," Rainey answered.

"That can't be good for our guys," Grin said.

As the data buffers cleared from the sonic overload and the holographic image resolved once more, Grin zeroed in on *Argo*. Debris littered the water and the submerged portions of the launch platform were separating. Rainey moved closer to the chamber, almost pressing his face against the acrylic enclosure.

"*Argo*'s breaking up," Rainey said, "and there's something in the water, off the starboard side. I think it's the SEALs."

"I see 'em."

Zooming in closer, four human forms were clearly visible. The sonar man hit the talk button on the mike.

"Control, Torpedo Room. We have four, repeat, four injured men in the water off the starboard side of *Argo*. Be advised, *Argo* is breaking up."

Grin zoomed out and traced a guideline between *Virginia* and the fallen men.

"Bearing zero-nine-six," O'Roark continued, reading the data off the display. "Distance five thousand yards."

"All right, we got men in the water. Bring us around to zero-nine-six," Johnston ordered. "Put us on the top. XO, I want the divers ready to hit the water as soon as we break the surface. Have the med team standing by and have 'em check for radiation in case that rocket blew."

54

The thirteen men of Bravo were still underwater when the rocket leaped off the platform, but they heard and felt the deep rumbling of the launch and *Sanya*'s barrage clearly. They swam up between the huge vessel's twin screw propellers—both were idle, the ship being held in place by thrust controllers running down the keel. Above them, the ship's stern ramp was folded up in place, covering the watertight door that sealed the hold. The metal hull was smooth and seamless, impossible to scale unaided.

Two of the SEALs took aim and fired grappling lines into the upper face of the watertight door, just below the stern rail. The hardened composite tips punctured the thin steel plating of the upper hull and found solid purchase. Lines set, the men removed their fins and began climbing.

The two point men quickly reached the rail, then carefully surveyed the stern deck. It was empty. One after the other, the SEALs hauled themselves over the side. As they hit the deck, they drew out their MP5 submachine guns and covered the port and starboard approaches. Silently, they moved forward, leaving room for the rest of the element to climb aboard.

Kilkenny was last over the rail, and that's when he saw

the destroyer holding position off the starboard side. A cloud of gray smoke hovered ominously around the forward gun turret.

"Shit! Did they blast the—" before Kilkenny could finish the question, he saw the smoke trail rising in the sky.

"They must've missed," Lieutenant Ralph said wryly, his SEALs now in control of the stern deck. "Thing is, they got boats in the water heading this way, and there's another one of those on the other side."

"Then we'd better get to it."

Bravo broke into two groups. Ralph led five men up the port side of the superstructure, while a master chief took point with the seven-man group that included Kilkenny on the starboard. Rounding the corner, Kilkenny saw the white arcing trail of smoke set against the clear blue sky.

They had just reached the lifeboat davits when a small group of people stepped out onto the deck, their laughter arrested by the menacing sight of the Chinese destroyer.

"On the deck! Now!" the chief ordered, rushing toward them.

A woman screamed, startled by the command. Several of the people dropped immediately, the startling approach of a threatening figure in black more than enough reason to comply. The SEALs behind Kilkenny followed his lead and secured the frightened civilians.

Just inside the door, a man fled, rushing back into the launch control room. Most of the technicians were still inside, monitoring the rocket's progress through first-stage separation and second-stage ignition.

"We're being boarded!" the man shouted hysterically. "There's a bunch of armed men out there!"

"What?" the launch director said.

"They're coming this way!" The man was in a full panic.

Moug rushed to the observation platform forward of the superstructure and found Skye standing by the rail, watching the smoke trail extend upward.

"They've destroyed *Argo,*" Moug announced.

"I expected that as soon as they announced their intention to board us. That's why I moved up the launch." Skye's voice was flat, eerily devoid of emotion. "They're out for blood—yours and mine."

"I've no intention of letting them have it."

Skye checked her watch. "Neither have I."

55

Zeus-1 crossed over the Tropic of Cancer five hundred miles east of the big island of Hawaii, exhausting the last remaining propellant to shift its orbit. The target was close now, less than five minutes away. The inertial gyros spun up, turning the spacecraft's stiletto form around, aiming down at the deep blue of the Pacific. Inside, the chemical fires began to burn.

Directly over the equator, *Zeus-1* fired for the last time. The long burst flew straight down, just over two hundred miles, hurtling through a cloudless sky.

Where the laser struck the ocean, seawater instantly flashed into superheated steam, the vapor lost in the drifting smoke from the barrage. It crossed *Sanya*'s main deck, slicing through men and metal with equal ease, igniting small fires in its wake with droplets of molten steel.

On the bridge, sparks flew as equipment shorted out, bundles of wires fused into circuits never imagined by the ship's engineers. The scent of burning flesh and liquid steel mingled with electrified ozone.

Captain Yao died almost instantly when the beam sliced through his left shoulder, carving him open and bisecting his heart and lung—his moment of glory evaporating in less than five minutes.

The beam crossed *Sanya* diagonally, back to front, through the forward island. Exiting the bridge, it struck the destroyer's most potent antiship weapon—a cluster of four Raduga 3M-80E Moskit surface-to-surface missiles. Though equipped with a solid-rocket booster, used to quicken its acceleration to Mach 3, the Moskit's primary source of propulsion is a liquid-fuel ramjet engine. The laser burned through the first of the upper tubes on the quad-launcher and cut into a Moskit.

Flames erupted from the missile tube, the kerosene fuel exploding, triggering a second concussive blast from the Moskit's three-hundred-kilogram warhead. Fire and shrapnel from the first missile set off the other three, a quartet of explosive power that easily broke the structurally weakened *Sanya* in half. A fireball nearly eighty feet in diameter rose from the doomed ship as *Zeus 1* exhausted its last joule of energy.

Sanya's Commands Information Center shuddered violently and those standing were thrown against bulkheads or onto the deck. The room plunged into darkness and to Commander Shi, who struggled to capture his breath after colliding with the fixed seat at the weapons console, it seemed an eternity before the emergency lights flickered on and the alarms sounded.

Shi grabbed the sound-powered phone. "Damage Control Central, CIC. Report!"

"'We've lost contact with the bridge. Reports indicate an explosion in port side quad launcher. No contact with forward damage-control party, we've sent another team forward to investigate. Electrical systems isolating forward section of the ship and we've also lost pneumatic lines and pressure in fire main forward. We have no contact with the forward section and we're taking on water in all the lower decks."

On deck, damage control teams dressed in heavy fireproof suits raced toward a scene of total destruction.

The SEALs moving along *Aequatus*'s starboard main deck stopped when the massive fireball erupted from the Chinese destroyer. Flames roared from the gaping wound in the hull and a roiling cloud of oily black smoke billowed upward. Seawater flooded the open deck, turning to thick steam where it touched the inferno.

As the nearly severed bow filled with water, the ship folded and *Sanya*'s stern rose into the air, exposing her rudder and screws. Fuel for the twin turbine engines poured from the keel tanks, spreading in a thin layer across the calm water.

"My God," Kilkenny said softly.

"Still got a job to do," the master chief shouted. "Let's move."

In seconds, the sea was aflame.

"Investigators report the entire port quad launcher is gone along with half the bridge," the officer in charge of Damage Control Central reported.

Commander Shi felt the same sickening knot in his stomach last shared by the officers and crew of the *Kursk*. A hit by just two Moskit missiles was more than enough to send a ship the size of *Sanya* to the bottom. A low, sickening groan filled the CIC, the howl of steel plates and beams twisting, stressed and deformed beyond their strength toward failure. The room pitched forward steeply and Shi knew the weight of the incoming water had lifted *Sanya's* stern out of the sea. There was no hope now.

"Damage Control Central, sound alarm to abandon ship."

56

Moug grabbed Skye's arm and marched her back inside.

"What are you doing?" she demanded, struggling against his bruising grip.

"My job." Moug checked the passageway—other than a few of his men it was still clear. "The ship's been boarded. My men are moving into defensive positions, but we have to get to the helicopter now."

"What about that other ship?"

"C.J., I'll admit it's a crapshoot, but staying here will get us killed, either now or sometime after our trial in Beijing. Your pilot's a hell of a flier, spent a dozen years in Apache gunships before I hired him. He'll get us to Kiritimati."

Skye detected a tone in Moug's voice she didn't often find—fear. "All right, but what about Tao?"

"I've sent Unger to get her."

The two groups of SEALs quickly swept through the main level of the superstructure, encountering no opposition, only bewildered crewmen. Covering the fore and aft stairways, they moved up to the next level.

"Cut her ankles loose and get her on her feet," Unger ordered as he burst into Tao's stateroom.

When Tao was standing, Unger grabbed her by the arm and wheeled her toward the door.

"You," he barked to the first guard, "go to the forward stair and take up position with the others."

The guard nodded and ran down the passageway. The remaining guard stood ready, awaiting Unger's orders.

"Cover my back."

Uzi in one hand and Tao in the other, Unger headed toward the forward stair.

Moug and Skye descended the stairwell. On the landing below, they saw members of his handpicked security force crouched with weapons at the ready. He nodded to the men, then escorted Skye onto the third level.

The passageway in front of them was empty and spanned almost the full length of the ship. From here, it was a straight run to the helipad on the bow. They moved quickly, Moug leading with a pistol in his hand.

"Oh, God!" Skye exclaimed. "My laptop."

"Forget about it."

"But that laptop has *everything* on it. If they crack the encryption—"

Realizing that the information stored in Skye's computer would be enough for even the most inexperienced federal prosecutor to land a death sentence against them, Moug stopped. "Where is it?"

"In my suite."

"I'll deal with it. You just get off this ship. And once *Zeus-2* is operational, cut a deal."

As soon as Kilkenny and the SEALs reached the second floor, the men posted in the aft stairwell opened up with a burst of submachinegun fire. Bullets ricocheted wildly off the stair framing and the tubular steel handrails.

The chief on point caught two fragmented rounds in the neck and shoulder. Kilkenny fired several rounds of cover fire back up the stairwell as a pair of SEALs pulled their wounded leader back to safety. Fire from above ceased.

As the platoon medic went to work on the wounded man, Kilkenny took command of the group. He squeezed off a few timed bursts from his MP5 and signaled for flash-bangs. Two of the men backing him each lobbed one of the nonlethal weapons up the stairs—then the SEALs protected their eyes and ears.

On the upper landing, the grenades exploded amid a group of five defenders, blinding them with a flash of light more intense than the sun while simultaneously assaulting their hearing with a blast of mind-numbing sound.

"Go!" Kilkenny shouted, the stairwell still echoing like the inside of a cathedral bell tower.

The SEALs wasted no time slamming the defenders face-down on the deck and disarming them. The stunned prisoners were bound hand and foot with zip-ties. Kilkenny left one man with the medic and the wounded chief and led the remaining three upstairs.

Unger and Tao reached the third-level landing just as Ralph's group of SEALs mounted their assault on the other group of defenders. A burst of gunfire from below sent a shower of blistering rounds rattling around them like lethal pinballs. Unger pressed himself back against the wall and pulled Tao in front as a human shield.

Two loud metallic clinks preceded a pause in the ferocious gunfire. Unger pushed Tao toward the door, the remaining guard trailing behind them. The two flash-bang grenades exploded, one of them on the landing between the second and third levels.

Unger's backup clenched his burning eyes shut and raised his hands to his ears. Stunned senseless by the grenade, the man was no longer conscious of the Glock in his hand and struck himself with it squarely on the side of the head. Partially shielded by the bulkhead, Unger and Tao caught only a piece of the grenade's sonic assault.

"Drop it!" Kilkenny shouted.

Unger raised his pistol, and the last thing he saw was the muzzle flash from Kilkenny's rapidly approaching MP5. Two short bursts—one to the head, one to the chest—ended Unger's life. Kilkenny was there before the man's body dropped onto the deck. He pulled Tao aside, allowing his men to leapfrog past, slung his weapon back, and removed her bonds.

"Ugh, I can't thank you enough," Tao said, her eyes on Unger's corpse.

"All in a day's work, ma'am."

She looked up at him, surprised by the sound of a familiar voice. Kilkenny removed his dive mask and balaclava.

"Nolan!" She threw her arms around him. "I thought you were dead."

"Naw, just stubborn. I'm glad to see you're still among the living, too."

"Hey, Kilkenny, this isn't the love boat," Ralph said, poking his head out of the stairwell.

Kilkenny flashed him an all-clear and the rest of the SEALs stormed into the passageway, stepping over Unger's body.

"This here's the lady from the message, LT," Kilkenny replied "The chief, damn, I forgot the guy's name . . ."

"Harwell."

"Yeah, Harwell. He took a hit back there. Ricochet. I left him with the medic and another guy. The rest of my men are up ahead having a look-see."

Ralph pointed his men forward, then nodded to Kilkenny. "I'll take it from here."

"All yours."

57

Hangzhou

"Captain, a civilian helicopter has lifted off from *Aequatus*," the bridge watch officer reported. "The tactical weapons officer reports SAM lock on target and awaits your orders."

"Let them go," Jin said without turning away from the dark column of smoke rising from the *Sanya*.

"Sir?"

"Lieutenant, our orders were to secure that ship and capture the leadership of the Skye Aerospace Corporation," Jin said sternly. "Beijing wants them alive and wants no unnecessary civilian deaths—two points on which Admiral Guo was most emphatic. Skye had entertained many world leaders aboard that ship, including our own foreign minister. We do not know who is on that helicopter and destroying it is a poor way to find out."

"Aye, sir. What are your orders?"

"This possibility was considered during the planning of this mission. Instruct the radio room to make contact immediately with our diplomatic mission to Kiribati."

USS Virginia

"That definitely cannot be good," Grin said, zooming in on the destroyer standing off *Aequatus*'s starboard side.

The bow of the ship sank low in the water, her main deck and forward gun turret clearly visible in the underwater image. Like a gaping wound, a massive fissure rent the hull nearly down to the keel a third of the ship's length back from the bow. Connected only by the structure and plating of the lower decks, the rapidly flooding forward section became a millstone around the rest of the vessel's neck, raising her stern out of the water, threatening to drag the proud ship down.

Men and debris were in the water, the image merely an artificial approximation of the hellish nightmare on the surface. The keel twisted at the fissure, steel plates folding like paper, until the destroyer's bow pointed straight down. It was a moment of impossible balance, a tug-of-war between buoyancy and gravity. The tensile forces building within the structure of the keel grew well beyond what the ship's builders had ever imagined. As one piece failed, those remaining picked up the load until they, like fibers in a rapidly fraying rope, could carry no more.

The forward section twisted again, dangling by the most tenuous of bonds until, at last, it broke off and fell away. Relieved of the burden, the rest of the destroyer settled back into the ocean, listing forward and taking on water.

O'Roark keyed the mike. "Control, Torpedo Room."

"Go ahead, Torpedo Room."

"One of the destroyers has taken a hit. There's a lot of

men in the water and a big piece of it just went to the bottom."

"Periscope up!" Johnston ordered.

The photonics mast rose up silently from the sail and quickly broke the surface. Unlike previous generations of submarines, *Virginia's* periscope did not penetrate the boat's cylindrical hull. Instead of optics, the submarine employed the latest in digital imaging cameras and processors.

Johnston watched the periscope's view of the surface world on one of the control room's high-resolution displays, panning a three-sixty sweep with the keyboard controls, stopping briefly on *Hangzhou* and *Aequatus,* until he spotted the rising column of smoke. Zooming in, he saw every sailor's worst fear.

"Captain," should we belay the order to surface?" Paulson asked.

Johnston shook his head. "We don't know what did that, but I don't see anybody shooting up there and we've got men in the water."

"What about the other destroyer?"

"They don't fuck with me and I won't fuck with them. But to be on the safe side, load and flood the tubes."

"Weps, you heard the man," Paulson ordered. "I want four fish in the tubes, locked and loaded, and a solution on that second destroyer."

Hangzhou

"Bridge, CIC. Contact bearing zero-nine-seven, distance four thousand five hundred meters. It's a submarine surfacing near the wreckage of the launch platform."

Captain Jin remained at the port side windows as his ship rounded the bow of *Aequatus* for a clear view of *Sanya.* The sea was on fire and a huge piece of the destroyer had been torn away. Men were leaping from the stricken vessel; where possible, boats were being lowered into the water. The mangled wreck of a KA-28 helicopter covered the landing pad and much of the stern deck, making it impossible to ferry survivors off by air. The ship's complement numbered 296 officers and men, and Jin knew that many of them would not survive the day.

Hangzhou's starboard thirty-millimeter guns remained locked on *Aequatus* as the destroyer circled around to *Sanya.* Jin found the situation baffling. He could find no sign of weaponry on the large white vessel, and something capable of killing a destroyer with a single blow, he imagined, would be difficult to hide. His ship's sonar had detected no mines in the water, but the sudden appearance of an unidentified submarine lessened his confidence in that technical resource. Jin knew that American submarines were very quiet, and at low speed impossible to detect, but he also knew that the sound of a torpedo racing through the water was something even the poorest sonar operator could hear.

Unless, he theorized, *it was lost in the noise of that launch.*

"CIC, this is the captain. Target unidentified submarine with the forward guns."

"Captain, that Chinese destroyer has spotted us and she's painting us real bright with her fire control radar."

"Damn," Johnston cursed. "Sparks, see if you can raise that destroyer before they put a hole in our nice new boat."

"Aye, Captain," a seaman replied from the radio room.

58

Aequatus

"Skye interrogated me," Tao said flatly.

Kilkenny found no sense of shame or embarrassment in Tao's admission, only concern.

"I'm sure you didn't tell her anything."

"They drugged me. I have no idea what I told her, but we have to assume she knows about Washabaugh."

What Tao didn't say, Kilkenny already knew—Skye eliminated anything she perceived as a threat. And outside, the rocket's white smoke trail was slowly dissipating.

"Where did Skye question you?"

"In her suite, top floor."

Kilkenny grabbed Unger's pistol and handed it to Tao. "Just in case we run into anything on the way."

Tao checked her weapon and followed Kilkenny into the stairwell. They ascended to the superstructure's fifth level quickly, encountering no further sign of the ship's security personnel.

"Skye's suite is the double doors at the end," Tao directed, her voice low and even.

At the top landing, Kilkenny stood beside the door with his back flat against the wall and signaled for Tao to pull open the door. As she did, he swung around with the MP5 tight to his shoulder and swept the passageway for targets.

Kilkenny caught the motion peripherally at first, and as he turned, saw one of the brushed aluminum entry doors swinging closed. He bolted down the passageway hoping to catch the door before its electronic locks could reset. Tao was right behind him.

As the opening narrowed, Kilkenny tucked his head and lunged. He struck the door with his shoulder, sending it springing back against the wall, and rolled into the suite.

Moug opened fire as Kilkenny planted his feet and pulled out of the roll. The first shot struck the thick body of Kilkenny's submachine gun, flattened and hammered the weapon back against his chest. The second caught the upper left corner of the Draeger rebreather that covered most of Kilkenny's chest and sent him sprawling backward. His head struck the door with a dull thump.

Before Moug could fire a third time, Tao leaned through the doorway and squeezed off two shots of her own. Both drilled into Moug's torso, one puncturing the lower lobe of his right lung.

Moug staggered back, but instead of returning Tao's fire, aimed off to his side and squeezed the trigger. Tao fired again, placing a bullet in the side of Moug's head to finish the confrontation. Skye's most-trusted confidant collapsed on the plush carpet of her suite, blood pouring from his wounds.

Beside the door, Kilkenny let out a low moan.

"Are you okay?" Tao asked, her pistol still aimed at Moug.

"Better than the alternative," Kilkenny rose slowly, testing his balance. "Still seeing a few stars, but I think I'll live."

"More than I can say for Skye's pit bull over there. That's the bastard who sank *Sea Lion*."

"Then do us both a favor and put a couple more into him, just to make sure."

Tao cautiously approached Moug, but as she drew closer it became clear that he had already expired. She looked to the side where Moug had fired his final shot, expecting to find his last victim. Instead, she saw the desk from which Skye had questioned her. And atop its smooth surface sat a titanium-clad PowerBook with a bullet hole through its TFT display.

"Steve Jobs ain't going to be too happy about that," Kilkenny said as he joined Tao.

"I don't think Moug's preference for personal computers had anything to do with his last shot."

"Even money, he was trying to keep us from getting at what's inside." Kilkenny took a closer look at the damaged computer. "I think we need Grin."

59

In Orbit

Twenty-five minutes after lifting off from *Argo*, the upper stage of the Skye-4GR rocket coasted with its payload high over the eastern coast of South America. The spacecraft was exactly where its owner wanted it to be, even compensating for the minor drift caused by the loss of the launch platform's thrust controllers.

The upper stage fired for the last time, a three-minute burn designed to deliver its payload to a specific point in orbit relative to the rest of the satellites in the Skye constellation.

Five hundred miles above Central Africa, at a speed in excess of seventeen thousand miles per hour, the upper stage released the satellite and began its descent back to Earth. Both objects had just passed through the eastern fringe of Fence, and computers in Dahlgren logged their presence and assigned them consecutive numbers in the Space Command catalog.

Slipping out over the Indian Ocean, *Zeus-2* made contact with the rest of the Skye constellation and its presence was acknowledged by the network. The killer satellite then transmitted a series of false diagnostic messages, warning its controllers of fatal errors in its onboard electronics. It then moved on to the next phase of its program.

Like a knife being loosed from its sheath, the long black faceted craft slipped out of the reflective, metallic enclosure. Short bursts from its maneuvering thrusters allowed it to pull away from the abandoned shell. Gyros spinning, *Zeus-2* reoriented itself, pointing its spear tip due north. Inside, the reactor powered up, feeding electricity to the spacecraft's main engine—a Hall Effect Thruster. As a steady stream of ionized xenon blasted from its propulsion bus, *Zeus-2* moved under its own power into a polar orbit.

60

Aequatus

Kilkenny and Tao found the bridge crew of *Aequatus* under the watchful eye of Lieutenant Ralph and a pair of his SEALs. The battle for the ship was over. Through the panoramic windows, they saw that two destroyers lay off the starboard side, one mortally wounded. Lifeboats dodged pools of burning fuel to pull survivors from the sea.

"What's going on, LT?" Kilkenny asked.

"Mexican standoff. *Virginia*'s over by what's left of *Argo* and the Chinese, as you can see, are just outside the window. Nobody seems to quite know what hit that ship over there, but the Chinese are giving our boat the evil eye. I bet a handful of MK-48s are pointed back this way, just to give the captain of that destroyer something to think about."

"*Virginia* surfaced?"

"Yeah. SAR. The Chinese shelled *Argo*. Between that and the rocket going up," Ralph paused, "I'm pretty sure we lost four men."

Kilkenny nodded. He'd been in Ralph's position before and had written those letters to the families of his men.

"*Hangzhou,* this is the *Virginia,* over," a voice boomed over the radio.

"Our guys are trying to get somebody over there on the horn, but the Chinese are giving them the silent treatment."

Kilkenny studied the Chinese warships and quickly recognized they were of the same class.

"Mind if I borrow those for a minute?" Kilkenny asked Captain Werner, indicating the binoculars hanging from the man's thick leathery neck.

Werner didn't say a word, but slipped the strap over his head and handed the binoculars to Kilkenny. Comparing the two vessels, Kilkenny saw that the destroyer's antiship missile batteries were positioned immediately forward of where the break had occurred on the damaged ship.

"What are you looking at?" Tao asked.

Kilkenny handed her the binoculars. "The ship that's still in one piece."

"Anything in particular?"

"Look of the big tubes, right where the hull curves down from the forward section onto the main deck. There's a cluster of four."

"I see them. What are they?"

"Ship killers. Surface-to-surface missiles. I'll bet that's what took out the other ship. Must've malfunctioned."

"But what set it off?" Ralph asked. "They wanted to board *Aequatus,* not sink her. Nothing in those tubes should have been live."

Tao shifted her gaze to the crippled destroyer. At the break, the main deck was level with the sea. Through the smoky haze, she saw the lines of walls and floors, the interior of a vessel ripped wide open.

"Nolan, did you take a good look at the other ship?" Tao asked.

"Just enough to guesstimate where it broke apart. Why?"

"Check out the break."

Kilkenny saw buckled steel plates and other signs of a devastating explosion along one side of the ship. Scanning across the open wound, the signs of the blast diminished, and what struck him were the neat right angles of the bulkheads and decks and the sharp line of the break. It was like looking at a David Macaulay drawing of a ship—a transverse section.

"It was cut open," Kilkenny realized. "The missiles blew after the act."

"Skye did that?"

"Yeah, which puts us in a good news–bad news situation."

Kilkenny handed Tao the binoculars and picked up the radio handset. "*Virginia*, this is Kilkenny on *Aequatus*."

"We read you, *Aequatus*."

"Patch me through to the torpedo room."

"Go ahead," the radio operator replied.

"Grin, you and Rainey there, buddy?"

"Like where else would we be?" Grin replied. "You find Roxanne?"

"Yeah, and she's fine. Rainey, can your satellite hit a target on the ground?"

"Sure, the beam will lose a little strength on the way down due to the atmosphere, but there'll enough left to do some damage."

"You guys see what happened to that destroyer?"

"Ugly, man," Grin answered, offended by the senseless destruction, "very ugly."

"If Skye did that with *Zeus-1*, would that have drained it?"

"Easily," Rainey replied. "Missiles and satellites are clad in fairly thin materials; to cut through plate steel, she had to use everything on a sustained burst. *Zeus-1* is now space junk."

"Then that's the good news," Kilkenny said. "Bad news is the replacement is on its way up and we're pretty sure Skye knows Washabaugh is on the ISS. Could Skye program the satellite from a laptop?"

"If it had the right software and a link to an antenna for the upload," Rainey replied.

"Then you two catch the next boat over here, because I got a damaged PowerBook and we may be running out of time."

"*Hangzhou* to *Aequatus*, respond," a stern voice cut in.

"We hear you, *Hangzhou*," Kilkenny replied.

"Is this Nolan Kilkenny?" a different voice asked.

"Yes?" Kilkenny replied, puzzled.

"There have been reports of your death off Chile."

"I've heard that. They're wrong."

"Hey, Kilkenny," Johnston's voice boomed out of the speaker. "Now that you got that destroyer on the line, you mind asking them to switch off their fire control radar? It's making us a little nervous."

"How about it?" Kilkenny asked. "We didn't have anything to do with happened to your ship."

"Why are you here?" the stern voice was back.

"I believe for the same reason as you—someone murdered a few of our astronauts. We also had a boarding team on the launch platform."

There was a long pause, and then the calmer voice returned.

"Our forces were unaware of your presence here. Have you captured C. J. Skye?"

"No. She escaped as we boarded this ship. She is heading to Kiritimati."

"The weapon, can she fire on us again?"

"Not for a while yet. That's why I need some help from two of my associates on the submarine. We want to stop her from ever using it again."

There was another pause. Kilkenny stared out at the *Hangzhou,* wondering what kind of men he was dealing with.

"The submarine will no longer be targeted," the stern voice announced.

"Confirmed, *Hangzhou,*" Jonathan said. "We are no longer detecting your fire control radar. *Virginia* is also standing down. We've completed our recovery operation. Do you require assistance with your recovery efforts?"

Classy move, Kilkenny thought, *extending the olive branch.*

"Any assistance you have to offer," the stern voice replied, "would be welcome."

"*Virginia* will be moving into position to assist. Kilkenny, I'll have your two men over, ASAP."

61

"Roxanne, this is Anson Rainey," Kilkenny said as the satellite engineer and Grin came aboard. "The guy who designed the Buck Rogers nightmare Skye just put in orbit."

"Can you shut it down?" Tao asked.

"I'm going to try," Rainey promised.

As they reached the fifth level, they saw two of the ship's medical personnel departing from Skye's suite with a gurney bearing a sheet-covered figure.

"Who is that?" Rainey asked with a shudder.

"Owen Moug," Kilkenny replied.

Upon entering the suite, Grin immediately went to the laptop. Rainey's eyes stopped when he saw the large bloodstain on the carpet.

"Are you all right?" Tao asked.

"Until a few days ago, I thought I worked for two of the best people in the business. Now, to see what they became because of something I created . . ."

"You only built the tool," Kilkenny said. "Skye and Moug were the ones who decided to use it the way they did."

Grin let out a low whistle as he eyed the jagged hole in the PowerBook's screen. "You weren't kidding when you said this puppy took a hit."

"Can you resurrect it?" Kilkenny asked.

"No need," Grin said with a smile. Then he popped out the laptop's hard drive. "When you said you had a damaged PowerBook, I put out the word that I needed a volunteer. I got five offers in under a minute."

From a well-worn denim backpack, Grin pulled out the twin of Skye's damaged computer and transplanted the hard drive. The machine ran through its hardware diagnostics, then stopped and displayed the message: KEY NOT FOUND.

"That's not a standard OS-Ten request," Grin said, puzzled.

Rainey glanced at the screen. "That's our security."

He then removed a thin steel chain from around his neck, at the end of which hung a USB device not much larger than a car key. Rainey slipped the key into a slot on the side of the laptop and almost instantly was granted access to both the machine and the ship's network.

"Have a seat, my man," Grin said, offering Skye's black leather chair. "It's time for hacking and cracking."

Rainey loaded the program he had designed for controlling the Zeus satellites and requested a display of any current targeting commands. The laptop screen filled with a graphic of two tiny objects orbiting the Earth. One of the objects was in a circular low-Earth orbit while the other raced around the poles in a broad ellipse. He ran the mouse pointer over both of the objects, causing small windows of information about them to appear. The one in a circular orbit was the ISS, the other was *Zeus-2*.

"I definitely don't like the looks of this," Grin said.

"Skye's programmed an attack on the station," Rainey said. "Based on the time index, it's going to happen in the next orbit."

"Can you stop it?" Kilkenny asked.

"I'll find out in a second," Rainey replied as he navigated the program graphic interface.

Every attempt Rainey made to access *Zeus-2*'s targeting or operational systems was rebuffed.

"Damn, I'm locked out," Rainey said, frustrated.

"I thought you were already in the program," Tao said.

"Only the outer layer," Rainey explained. "My USB key was enough to pass through the security on that shell. What's protecting all the satellite command functions is something a lot more robust. We don't have the time to crack it before *Zeus-2* fires on the ISS."

"Why don't we just overlay the program?" Grin asked.

"What do you mean?"

"I'm assuming what's on this machine is a compiled program, but you've got the original source code somewhere. We recompile it with the security neutered and put it right over the top of this one. The computer shouldn't know the difference."

"We'd have to be careful with the files containing Skye's instructions," Rainey said, running through the potential for Grin's suggestion. "There's codes in there that we'll need to override the targeting commands."

"But can you do it in time?" Kilkenny asked.

"I think so, but it's going to be close."

Kilkenny picked up the phone on Skye's desk and got the ship's communications officer. "Yeah, it's Kilkenny. I need you to place a call stateside."

With Barnett's help, Kilkenny was able to route a satellite call from *Aequatus* through the Johnson Space Center to the International Space Station. It was the first time he'd spoken with Kelsey Newton in weeks.

"Nolan, the flight director said there's some kind of problem. What's going on?"

"You and your crewmates better get ready to abandon ship," Nolan replied.

"What?"

"The people who attacked *Liberty* know about Washabaugh and have targeted the station. You've got less than ninety minutes before they take a shot at you."

"Can't you stop it?" Kelsey asked.

"We're trying, believe me, but there may not be enough time. I'm sorry to cut short your stay up there."

"I know it's not you."

"Time's wasting. We're going to upload the telemetry data to JSC, so they can keep you updated on how long before this weapon gets in range. If I have any good news, I'll call."

"I love you, Nolan."

"I love you, too, Kelsey. Now get off that station."

62

ISS

"We heard," Molly said.

She and the others floated in Node 1, just outside the Hab module.

"They know I'm here?" Pete asked rhetorically. "So much for the witness protection program."

"That's not funny." Kelsey looked at the anguished faces of Pete and her two crewmates and saw that they, too, had done the math, though none would say it. "We can't all leave."

Though recently finished, the ISS still lacked one major safety component—the crew return vehicle. Prototypes of the X-38 had performed well through several rounds of flight testing and the final production version was scheduled for delivery on the next shuttle mission along with the rest of the sisters of the Most Holy Celestial Convent. All they had for the moment was *Soyuz*, which could seat only three.

"The choice is obvious," Pete said.

"Don't play hero, Pete," Molly replied. "You've got a family back home."

"We all do," Pete shot back. "You want us to draw straws?"

"No. This is our home," Kelsey said. "And I for one plan to defend it."

"How?" Valentina asked.

"We know where this killer satellite is, and we know where it will be when it attacks."

"And if you know where the bugger is," Molly added, "maybe you can do something about it."

"What do you have in mind?" Pete asked skeptically.

"We build our own antisatellite weapon and take out the other guy's first."

Kelsey suited up for EVA and floated out through the airlock. Looking down on the Earth, she tried hard not to think that someone on that beautiful orb was trying to kill them. She worked her way down the length of the station and scaled the side of the Centrifuge Accommodation Module.

High above her, the weblike spherical structure of *Zwicky-Wolff* was backlit by a waxing gibbous moon. Kelsey felt some regret for the years of work that the beautifully engineered experiment represented, years that would be lost whether their desperate attempt succeeded or failed. Using a handheld pistol grip tool, Kelsey began removing the bolts that fastened the array to the top of CAM.

The *Soyuz*, a spacecraft whose initial design almost predated Kelsey, slowly descended from the underside of the ISS. Once clear of the station, Valentina fired a short burst from the maneuvering thrusters. *Soyuz* quietly slipped out from beneath the ISS.

"Hey, Kelsey," Pete called out over her headset.

"Yeah?"

"JSC thinks we're all nuts."

"Do they have a better idea?"

"No, so they sent up the telemetry and wished us good luck. Molly should be uploading it to the *Soyuz* shortly."

"Where is the *Soyuz*? I'm just about ready for it."

"Passing beneath you," Valentina replied.

A short burst from the maneuvering thrusters brought the *Soyuz* up in front of the station's bow.

"That's good, Val," Kelsey said when the top of the spacecraft was level with the end of CAM. "Just tilt the back end out a little, away from the station."

"Da," Valentina replied, then she fine-tuned the spacecraft's alignment.

With one arm pressed against the mast, Kelsey released a short burst of thrust from her SAFER. The base plate of the slender column easily shifted off the top of CAM. The center of gravity for the severed array was somewhere near the middle of the engineered sphere. As Kelsey pushed on the supporting mast, the sphere rotated in place.

Give me a large enough lever and a place to stand and I can move the world, Kelsey thought, the effects of microgravity still magical to her.

She tilted the mast until its base plate touched the mating collar on the top of *Soyuz,* then fired another burst to halt the rotation. Bolt by bolt, Kelsey grafted the experimental array to the Russian craft, transforming two machines of peaceful exploration into an orbital battering ram.

"I'm set, Val," Kelsey announced. "You can pull away."

"Understood. Firing thrusters."

Valentina slowly puled *Soyuz* out in front of the ISS and tilted the array out and away from the station's delicate solar wings,.

"I've finished with the telemetry," Molly announced. "Uploading it now."

"Is coming over good," Valentina reported. "I am setting *Soyuz* for remote operation and preparing to leave capsule."

Valentina opened the hatch on the side of the spacecraft and pulled herself through the opening. She was dressed in a Russian Orlan suit, which was designed for tethered EVAs.

"I must admit," Valentina said, "this part makes me a little nervous."

Kelsey let go of *Soyuz* and held her arms out wide.

"I'll catch you," she promised.

Valentina pushed off toward her and covered the short distance quickly.

"There," Kelsey said as she wrapped her arms around her crewmate. "Now to get back to the station."

"Nervous part still, yes?" Valentina said.

"Not the nervous part, Val. If Pete can do it from the other side of the planet, we can certainly do it from a couple hundred feet."

Kelsey fired the SAFER unit and flew Valentina and herself back to the airlock. With the two spacewalkers clear, Molly and Pete launched *Soyuz*.

63

Aequatus

"Anything?" Kilkenny asked for what seemed like the hundredth time.

Grin was digging deep into his repertoire of programming tricks, trying to aid Rainey in circumventing the encrypted lockouts protecting *Zeus-2*'s operations program.

"This is a weapons-grade hunk of code, Nolan," Grin replied, not taking his eyes from the work.

The answer wasn't an excuse, simply a statement of fact. Grin was the most gifted programmer Kilkenny had ever met, and that included a lot of whiz kids at MIT whose native tongue might have been binary. Given enough time, he knew Grin would eventually solve the intricate mathematical rules governing the encryption and take control of the killer satellite, but the time they were given was growing short.

Soyuz had disappeared from view, the cobbled-together spacecraft shrinking in size until it could no longer be discerned against the star-filled blackness of space. The crew of the ISS had fired their one and only shot against the approaching nemesis and the waiting game had begun.

Since launching *Soyuz*, the four astronauts had sequestered themselves in the Hab module. It was the closest thing to a home for them aboard the orbiting research station—a place where they could draw at least a little comfort. The crew had grown silent, unable to voice their fears. Most of their thoughts were on those they would leave behind if things went badly.

Death would come quickly in the vacuum of space. Once the station's hull was breached and the atmosphere ripped away, the water in their bodies would begin to boil and pockets of water vapor would form in their skin. Within twenty seconds, embolisms would develop in their abdomens and hearts. They would also be unconscious—their brains starved of oxygen. Death would finally take them a few minutes later.

They'd considered donning spacesuits, but in the event of a breach that would only prolong the ordeal. The soonest NASA could get a shuttle up to rescue them would be in two days, and they would still be dead.

"I've got an idea," Valentina announced.

"Let's hear it," Pete replied.

"This satellite knows where we will be, yes?"

"That's right," Kelsey replied. "Our telemetry is pretty easy to follow."

"What if we weren't there? Would it know where to look?"

"That's the dumbest thing I—"

"No, it's not," Kelsey said, cutting Pete off. "It might even be inspired. We don't know how this thing finds its targets, but part of it has to based on telemetry, just to get it into the ballpark."

"Exactly," Valentina agreed. "What if we move the station out of this ballpark? We have Progress Module—why not use its engines to change our orbit?"

"That could work," Pete slowly admitted, the engineering part of his brain starting to wrap itself around the problem. "We'd have to check how our paths are going to cross to see if we need to speed up or slow down."

"Well what are we floating around here for?" Molly asked. "Let's make it happen."

Zeus-2 completed its self-insertion into polar orbit, nine hundred miles above the Earth's surface. All systems were functioning nominally and its weapon was now fully active.

The Eastern Hemisphere of the Earth was in shadow, the terminator between day and night passing just off Europe's Atlantic coast. Soon, *Zeus*-2 would pass over Greenland and the North Pole, and then its target would come into view.

"Ready for Progress burn," Valentina called out, "in three . . . two . . . one . . ."

Attached to the rear of the Zvezda Service Module, Progress-12's S5-80 engine ignited. A tongue of white-hot gases flared from the nozzle, pushing the ISS down into a lower orbit while at the same time accelerating it.

With each passing second of the burn, the ISS picked up speed and lost altitude—a combination designed to shorten the time it took the station to orbit the Earth and place them out of the killer satellite's target area.

"And Progress burn terminates . . . now," Valentina called out.

"Altitude at 186 miles," Molly reported. "Speed thirty-two thousand KPH."

"Not enough to fling us out into space," Kelsey said, "but hopefully enough to keep us one step ahead of the wolf."

As *Zeus-2* rounded the pole, its target acquisition system went active. Projecting the space station's last known orbital track, the killer satellite selected a point ten minutes distant where it would have an optimum firing solution.

It scanned the area of space where the ISS was supposed to be, but found nothing to lock on to. Per its programming, it began systematically searching along the station's projected orbital track, looking for the largest man-made object ever constructed in space.

Passing over the Carolina Islands, *Soyuz-Zwicky-Wolff* was the antithesis of the *Zeus-2*. It lacked the weapon's targeting sensors, supercomputer brain, and nuclear power plant—in almost every way it was an inferior spacecraft. It soared through space silently, emitting no electromagnetic energy. Reduced to the bare essence of what a spacecraft is, the combined object was a projectile moving through space.

Time was running out. Kilkenny had hovered over Grin and Rainey as if his presence could somehow help. It didn't, but neither man would say so because both knew what was at stake for him.

"You mother!" Grin cursed when his latest and most promising attempt ran into a digital brick wall.

It had taken him ten minutes to piece together that last bit of code. With less than a minute left until *Zeus*-2 reached its firing position, the clock was running out.

"I'm sorry, man" Grin said. "We are so friggin' close."

Kilkenny nodded, but he knew it was too late. He left Skye's office and walked out onto a small balcony. Bodies littered the water, many blackened and disfigured by the destruction inflicted on the *Sanya*. The living were the priority of the teams of men in small boats searching the blessedly calm sea, but success seemed a rarity. The only hazard to the rescuers was the burning slick of fuel that spread out from the broken hull like a California wildfire during a drought.

The *Sanya* lay low in the water now, much of her hull hidden beneath the surface. Kilkenny heard a loud gasp from the ship, the sound of air rushing out of the superstructure. Slowly at first, the *Sanya* moved forward, and as she did the weight of her flooded hull pulled her down. As Kilkenny watched, he felt his own hopes sinking into a cold, black abyss.

Kilkenny looked up at the clear afternoon sky. Somewhere, beyond the blue, Kelsey was passing overhead. And while he couldn't see her or the craft on which she sailed, he prayed that Kelsey her crewmates were far enough away from the doomed station. Tao quietly stepped up beside him and placed her arm around his back. She said nothing, because there was nothing that could be said.

Zeus-2 detected a large round object, then quickly dismissed it and moved on. It next found an object passing over the equator, far ahead of where the ISS should have been. It was in a lower orbit, but matched the station's rough physical dimensions. The killer satellite targeted this object and recomputed its plan of attack.

Soyuz-Zwicky-Wolff had no plan of attack, other than the faint hope of being in the right place at the right time. Passing over the Tropic of Cancer, its onboard computer relayed one last instruction to the spacecraft's propulsion system. The lateral thrusters fired a long burst, causing *Soyuz* to spin rapidly about its longitudinal axis. The ninety-foot-diameter sphere of the Dark Matter Array rotated in concert with the Russian spacecraft, the precision-engineered members on the equator of the web-like structure almost a blur.

As the firing point neared, *Zeus-2*'s reactor ramped up to maximum power. Gyros kept the weapon aimed at its target, tracking the ISS like a hunter training his shotgun on a flock of ducks. The orbits of the two spacecraft were closing—the space station was less than two thousand miles away.

Then *Zeus-2* lost its lock on the target. Its sensors were jumping back and forth between the ISS and a much closer, unidentified object. The nearer object was partially obscuring its view of the station. *Zeus-2*'s computer attempted to compensate for the intermittent target lock, trying to time an opening when it could fire. It only needed a second.

When *Zeus-2* reached the optimal position, it fired. A six-megawatt bolt of energy flashed from the conical beam control assembly. The spinning sphere of the *Zwicky-Wolff* array caught the blast. Key structural members were severed and truss work flew apart. Bits of loosened metal debris spun out in every direction and a hail of shrapnel battered the stealthy composite shell of the killer satellite. Stripped of the Dark Matter Array, *Soyuz* passed by *Zeus-2* harmlessly.

The multiple impacts on its hull staggered *Zeus-2* like a boxer caught in a flurry of punches. And by the time its gyros had regained control, the ISS had passed out of range.

64

"Nolan, get in here!" Grin shouted excitedly. "You gotta see this!"

"Did you get in?"

"Just now," Grin replied. "Unfortunately, the thing had already taken its shot at the station, but you have to see this."

Kilkenny sat beside Rainey and looked the animation on the laptop's display.

"Here's *Zeus-2* coming over the pole," Rainey explained, "and this is the ISS. Check this out. *Zeus* is looking for the ISS over here, but it's not where it's supposed to be. *Zeus* takes a few more minutes, and finally reacquires it over there. Then, as *Zeus* moves in for the kill, it loses track of the ISS—something got in the way."

"Whatever it was got right in its face," Grin added, "really messed with the shot."

"It got a shot off?" Tao asked. "Did it hit the ISS?"

"I don't think so," Rainey replied. "Near as I can tell, this other object stood right in the way and took the hit. Then *Zeus* went into a spin and by the time it righted itself, the ISS was gone."

"Do you have control of this thing yet?"

"Yeah," Rainey replied. "And the first thing I did was

purge the targeting memory. Right now, it's just up there waiting for us to tell it what to do."

"What about Skye?" Tao asked. "If she had access to another computer like this one, could she again tell *Zeus*-2 what to do?"

Rainey considered the question. "I guess. Right now, the system thinks we're Skye—she's the only authorized user. But to do this, she'd need to have access to a satellite uplink like we have on the ship or back in California."

"Right now she's heading God knows where," Kilkenny said, "but at least that buys us some time."

The phone on Skye's desk purred and Kilkenny punched the conference button. It was Jackson Barnett.

"Nolan, I just got word from NASA. The ISS came through the last pass unscathed."

"And there won't be another one," Kilkenny said. "Grin and Rainey have control of the satellite for now. Any idea on what you want to do with this thing?"

"Off the top of my head, I'd think the U.S. government should take possession. But, diplomatically, that opens a rather large can of worms. It's one thing to develop a space-based weapon and quite another to actually deploy it."

"And if we have one," Grin offered, "then all the other kids on the block are going to get excited and want one, too."

"Exactly."

"Then how about if we don't have one?" Kilkenny suggested. "How about the five of us decide right now to make this weapon go away?"

"You can't bring it down," Rainey protested. "The reactor."

"I'm not thinking about bringing it down."

* * *

As *Zeus-2* came around the pole and passed over to the sunlit Pacific, it received a stream of new instructions from *Aequatus*. It reviewed the transmission and confirmed accurate receipt of the data.

Then the spacecraft powered up its reactor and activated its main engine. *Zeus-2* gradually built up speed, leaving behind it a wake of ionized xenon. As it rounded the South Pole, it was traveling over five miles a second. And the engine kept burning, accelerating the spacecraft even faster.

In its next orbit, as it passed over northern Russia, *Zeus-2* was moving fast enough to escape the bonds of Earth's gravity. It shot off in a straight line over the top of the world, passing out of the planet's shadow into the bright sunlight, aimed directly at its source.

65

Kiritimati

When word reached *Aequatus* of Skye's detention on Kiritimati, Captain Jin of the *Hangzhou* offered the use of his ship's antisubmarine warfare helicopter to transport a member of the American investigative team to the nearby atoll to witness the formal arrest of the prisoner. Kilkenny accepted and was standing near the helipad when the Russian-built Ka-28 thundered over, beating the air with its dual-triple main rotors, and lightly touched down.

The hour-long flight passed with a minimum of conversation, not that much could be said over the roar of the two TV3-117VK engines aft of the crew cabin. What little Kilkenny did hear was in Chinese, a language with which he had no familiarity.

Kilkenny attempted the engage the man seated beside him in some form of communication, but through hand gestures he learned that the communications link in the man's helmet was on the fritz. The man was dressed in a flight suit with an inflatable vest, which covered his chest and prevented Kilkenny from learning his name or rank. Due to the bright sunlight filling the cabin, everyone onboard had the sun visors in their helmets down, so all

Kilkenny saw of his fellow passenger was the lower half of the man's face.

From above, Kiritimati looked like the letter "Y" with the area between the extended arms dotted with lagoons and a swirl of reefs. Kilkenny wondered what the diving was like here and if he would ever find his way back to this remote speck of land to find out. Employed as a base for nuclear weapons testing in the late fifties and early sixties by Britain and the United States, the world's largest atoll had suffered no measurable radioactive contamination. Unlike the native population of Bikini Atoll, that of Kiritimati never had to be relocated and currently numbered around five thousand.

Three jets and a helicopter sat off to the side of the runway near a single-story building that Kilkenny assumed was the terminal. From the look of the facilities, he guessed it was the most flight traffic experienced at Cassidy Airport since the days of the H-bomb tests. The helicopter and one of the jets bore the logo of Skye Aerospace.

The Ka-28 hovered for a few moments as the pilot received his landing instructions, then at last they touched down. As the rotors slowed, Kilkenny and his fellow passenger unbuckled their harnesses and removed their helmets.

"Mr. Kilkenny," the man said, extending his hand. "I am Peng."

Kilkenny took Peng's hand; the grip was firm but not punishing. Peng smiled at him, and Kilkenny remembered.

"Korolev."

"Yes. I broke cover, but it appeared that you and your associate were in need of assistance."

"I get the feeling your motives weren't purely altruistic."

Peng's smile broadened. "Our interests were compatible."

"Whatever the reason, I owe you my thanks."

"You are welcome. Now, shall we see to our prisoner?"

As they stepped out of the helicopter, Peng and Kilkenny were met by tall, heavyset islander with a thick mane of graying black hair, dressed in a colorful print shirt, loose-fitting white cotton pants, and sandals.

"Welcome to Kiritimati. I'm Eberi Tekinene, the local customs agent."

"I hate to say this," Kilkenny said, "but I don't have a passport on me."

"Me neither," Peng added.

Tekinene grinned broadly. "Too bad, not many folks have our stamp. Fortunately for you, I'm not here in my usual capacity. Instead, I am acting as the official representative of the Republic of Kiribati, at least until someone from Tarawa can get here to sort this mess out. You the guys responsible for me having to arrest Miss Skye?"

"Afraid so," Kilkenny replied.

"Aiee, you guys really know how to stir up trouble."

"If it makes you feel any better, she started it."

Tekinene shrugged. "This way."

The islander led them into the terminal, a long, institutional version of a tropical bungalow with a broad overhanging roof. In a large open room set aside for customs inspections, they found two men engaged in a heated discussion. A handcuffed C. J. Skye sat in a chair beside the wall, a bored distant look on her face, as if what was happening around her was of no importance. She looked at Kilkenny and Peng only long enough to determine they were of no interest to her. Near Skye, a pair of equally bored police officers stood chatting with her pilot, with whom they seemed familiar.

The arguing men stopped as soon as they realized Kilkenny and Peng were in the room. Both men were in their late fifties with spreading midsections and receding hairlines. One of the men was Asian, with the swept-back hair and thick glasses that seemed all the rage with high-ranking communists in China and North Korea, while the other looked like a cross between Danny Glover and Danny DeVito.

"Nolan Kilkenny? Bradley Milford," the Glover-DeVito mix said by way of an introduction. He grabbed Kilkenny's hand and pumped furiously as if he expected water instead of a greeting. "U.S. Consulate, Tarawa."

Next to Kilkenny, Peng was receiving the same sort of greeting from his countryman.

"Nice to meet you," Kilkenny said, extracting his hand before carpal tunnel syndrome set in. "Looks like you and your friend were going at it pretty good when we came in."

"Indeed. My esteemed colleague, Mr. Pu, and I are at odds over custody of the prisoner."

"China has priority," Pu declared. "Our astronauts were her first victims. She should be tried in a Chinese court first."

"Leaving you to interrogate her about this weapon she's built before you execute her," Milford countered. "The United States will not stand for that, and I am certain Russia and France will back our claim 100 percent. We've got seven dead brave souls—"

"Six," Kilkenny offered.

"What?"

"Six dead brave souls, if you're talking about *Liberty*.

And if you two are going to get into a pissing contest," Kilkenny turned to Peng. "How many of *Sanya's* men would you say were lost today?"

"As many as two hundred."

"Body count–wise, China is way ahead," Kilkenny said.

"Excellent point," Pu chimed in.

"Perhaps," Peng said, "but China cannot claim any preferential status as her first victims. I believe her crimes go further back."

Kilkenny nodded. "Probably Russia. Even though nobody died and *Mir* was pretty much junk at the time, there is principle involved. National pride and all that."

The two diplomats looked at Peng and Kilkenny as if they'd come from a different world.

"There is no way in heaven or Earth that Skye is going to Russia!" Milford shouted. "The secretary of state is on his way to Tarawa right now to press our claim for extradition."

Pu shuddered, his face tinged with purple. "This is outrageous! Our foreign minister will file an immediate protest of this action. We will demand an immediate meeting of the U.N. Security Council. This is a matter of international law."

Kilkenny and Peng backed away as the diplomats railed away with such vigor that the likeliest outcome was either a stroke or a full-blown donnybrook. They shared a look of disgust at the men representing their nations.

"You know, in light of this fine example of diplomacy," Kilkenny said, "it's quite possible that Skye will die here in this room of old age."

"In this room, perhaps—"

Peng then unzipped a pocket on the right thigh of his

flight suit, pulled out a pistol, and fired four times. C. J. Skye slumped against the back of the chair; two of the bullets stuck her head in profile, the rest landed in her chest. Aside from the fading echo of the last shot, the room was completely silent. Death came quickly to Skye and her body toppled onto the floor.

"—but not of old age."

"Drop it!" the islander policemen shouted in unison, their weapons clumsily drawn.

Peng flipped the pistol around so that he held it by the barrel, then turned and handed it to Tekinene. "I believe the law of your country requires that all firearms be checked with the customs official upon entry."

Tekinene's jaw dropped open wordlessly as he accepted the pistol. Kilkenny wasn't sure whether it was the violence of Peng's act or its decisiveness that shocked the diplomats more. In any event, both men were caught at a loss for words. Even the police officers seemed unsure how to proceed, murder being a crime of extreme rarity on the atoll. Kilkenny then broke the silence.

"Technically, we haven't entered the country yet."

"How's that?" Tekinene asked.

"Don't you have to pass through customs to officially enter a country?"

"Yes."

"Peng and I haven't done that. We were on our way there, but we got sidetracked. I think the eight of us can agree that what happened here was an unfortunate accident."

"An accident?" Milford shouted, finding his voice again at last. "That man killed her in cold blood."

"No, sir," Kilkenny disagreed. "Peng was in the process

of handing his weapon over to the customs official when it accidentally discharged."

"But that's a lie!"

"More a creative interpretation of the events. But surely, both you and the esteemed Mr. Pu must realize that this unfortunate accident has eliminated the diplomatic impasse and relieved both the United States and China of the expense of a lengthy trial."

"He has a point worth considering," Pu said.

"I'll admit, it has merit," Milford agreed.

"And how does the fair Republic of Kiribati see it?" Kilkenny asked.

"I, um," Tekinene stammered.

"If it helps at all," Kilkenny said reassuringly, "she was directly responsible for the deaths of over two hundred people. And if your country is like mine, there's more paperwork for a murder than an accident."

"The United States government will support a finding of accidental death in this case," Milford offered.

"China as well," Pu added.

Tekinene nodded. "Who gets the body?"

"We'll let the diplomats work that out," Kilkenny replied as he headed toward the door. "Peng, I think that's our cue to go."

66

USS **Virginia**
August 30

Kilkenny stood in the conning tower with Commander Johnston. The sea around *Virginia* extended to the horizon in a flat, glassy sheet—calm and quiet. Two ships lay off the submarine's starboard side—the U.S. Navy rescue-salvage ship *Safeguard* and the Chinese destroyer *Hangzhou*.

On *Safeguard*'s forward deck, navy specialists were performing postdive maintenance on a Deep Drone 7200 ROV that hours earlier had been working on the ocean floor. Following the recovery of the robotic submersible, Kilkenny's attention had remained focused on the cable slowly being reeled in by *Safeguard*'s aft boom.

"So all this trouble was for a bigger piece of the commercial satellite business?" Johnston asked.

"You're talking about a 600-billion-dollar industry, Cap'n. Percentages add up to big money real quick. And Skye had a very good shot at pulling it off, too."

"She got what she deserved."

Dozens of sailors lined the deck of the *Hangzhou*, watching the activity aboard *Safeguard*. Kilkenny studied the sailors through a pair of binoculars, then trained them in the water aft of the rescue-salvage ship.

"Looks like they're getting close to the surface."

The taut cable emerging from the sea gave way to a circular harness from which hung a trio of thick yellow straps. The boom operator stopped the winch so divers stationed in the water could attach guidelines to the harness. With the lines in place on the harness and manned on the ship's aft deck, the last phase of the recovery operation commenced.

It was just a few feet below the water's sunlit surface, an indistinct sphere of blackness buoyed in the water by four large yellow lift balloons. Then, slowly, *Shenzhou-7* emerged. Divers removed the lift bags and readied the capsule to be pulled from the water.

Safeguard held her catch high, seawater raining from its scorched surface. There was no cheering. Everyone observing knew that the artifact raised from the ocean floor was a coffin bearing the bodies of three fallen heroes.

Hangzhou drew alongside *Safeguard* and with the utmost dignity received a solemn gift from the people of the United States. When the transfer was complete and the capsule secured, the destroyer pulled away. It made a slow circle around the two American naval vessels, and as it drew close to *Virginia*, it slowed. Then, as one, the officers and men on deck of the *Hangzhou* snapped to attention and saluted. Johnston and Kilkenny returned the gesture, and the destroyer turned west toward home.

"Wonder if they're the least bit curious about how we found that capsule," Johnston mused.

"After three months of searching, I don't think they really care," Kilkenny replied. "In the aftermath of all this, helping them bring their men home was the decent thing to do, and I don't think they'll forget it."

"I guess it's time we head back to the barn ourselves," Johnston said. "I still owe my crew some deferred shore leave."

"And I have to get back to work."

"Cap'n," the XO called out over the intercom, "we're getting a real-time feed in off the bird. It's personal for Mr. Kilkenny."

"Pipe it through to my cabin," Johnston replied.

Belowdecks, Kilkenny parted company with Johnston, who went to the control room to get the voyage back to Pearl Harbor under way.

The flat-screen monitor mounted to the bulkhead glowed light blue when Kilkenny entered the captain's cabin. Then a voice boomed out from a small speaker.

"Secure air-to-ground loop in five . . . four . . . three . . . two . . . one."

Kelsey appeared floating in the center of the screen, her long blond hair a swirling golden halo around her head.

"You're a heavenly sight," Nolan said, grinning like a teenager.

"Why thank you, though I can't say the same."

"It's been a rough couple of weeks."

"I know. And I have a few new gray hairs because of it," Kelsey admitted, "but nothing my stylist can't handle when I get home."

"How are things up there?"

"We're getting back to normal and looking forward to the next shuttle coming up. We're not worried, but we all feel a little uneasy about not having a lifeboat."

"I heard about the array. Gutsy thinking. Too bad it kind of screwed up your trip."

"Yeah, but they're finding other things to keep me occupied. Molly has me handling all the elementary-school hookups—you know, where we show young students all the cool stuff we can do in microgravity."

"Bet your ratings are through the roof. You're *great* with kids."

Kelsey lowered her eyes and smiled.

"And when you do get home," Nolan added, "maybe we can finally find out just how great."

"Nolan, we're going to find out sooner than you think."

Don't miss these exciting Nolan Kilkenny thrillers by

TOM GRACE!

TWISTED WEB
0-7434-6374-9 / $6.99 / $10.50 Can.

"**A TRULY BELIEVABLE HERO**...Kilkenny is a little Jack Ryan, a little Dirk Pitt."

—*The San Francisco Examiner*

QUANTUM WEB
0-7434-5393-X / $6.99 / $9.99 Can.

"[An] **EXCITING TECHNO-THRILLER**.... Grace has created a moving portrait of America's technological prowess... nicely textured adventure."

—*Publishers Weekly*

POCKET BOOKS
A Division of Simon & Schuster
A VIACOM COMPANY

09714

Visit
❖ Pocket Books ❖
online at

www.SimonSays.com

Keep up on the latest new releases from your favorite authors, as well as author appearances, news, chats, special offers and more.

SIMON & SCHUSTER
A VIACOM COMPANY
www.SimonSays.com

Pocket
Books

2381-01